The Dark Light of Day

T.M. FRAZIER

Dedication

For Logan

Prologue

Jake

THE PAIN IN my head intensified, throbbing in time with the slow beat of my heart. My blurry vision shifted from double to single with each blink of my eyes. I felt the back of my head from where the pain radiated; warm, sticky red coated my fingers. The cold grit of the tile could be felt through my thin t-shirt.

I looked up from where I was splayed on the floor, into the crazed, bloodshot eyes of a man I had known all my life—or at least I *thought* I'd known. I was instantly sober, the fog cleared and my heart raced. He was poised to strike, ready for the kill. Thick veins bulged in his neck; I could see them pulsing with each strained breath he took. I saw past him, to the ax raised above his head. Without hesitation, he brought it down to split my skull down the middle. Just before the blade was able to tear into my forehead, I freed myself of his strong grip and rolled onto my side, avoiding the axe—and infinite blackness—by mere inches.

I stood on wobbly legs, trying to pull air into my lungs as I turned to brace myself for the next attack. I was stunned to see the man who was a monster just moments before crumpled on the floor, face first on the Mexican tile. He opened his hand and let the ax slip from his grip. His shoulders shook.

He was sobbing.

"Dad?" I asked. I'd tried everything I could to take away his pain, and in return he had done his damnedest to make sure I felt the very depths of it.

"Get the fuck out of here!" he roared into the floor between sobs.

"Dad, let me help you," I begged, kicking the ax out of his reach.

"Get out of this house, and *never* fucking come back!" He reared up and sat back onto his knees, slowly lifting his head to face me. Drool leaked from the sides of his mouth. His eyes glistened with moisture. The stench of alcohol stung my nose when he spoke. I'd seen my father in a bad way before, but this was something else entirely. "I don't want to see you in this house ever again."

"Dad, just let me help you," I insisted. I could do just that: get him into rehab, grief counseling—whatever it took to make him stop feeling like his life was over.

I leaned over and grabbed him by the arm to help him up. "Don't fucking touch me!" He jerked out from my grip. "It's you…it should have been you. You're the reason they're gone." His words stung, but it wasn't the first time I heard him say them. It'd been two weeks of cleaning up his vomit and trying to stay out of the path of his drunken rage. "I wish it'd been you," he said, softer this time.

"Dad, you're drunk. You don't mean that."

"Yes, I do. I just tried to fucking kill you, Jake, and in all honesty, I wish I had." He looked me straight in the eye, and in that moment, he appeared completely in control. "It should have been you. You should be dead. Not them. I just wanted to fix it, trade you for them. Make it the way it should've been." His voice turned to a whisper. "You're dead to me now, boy."

Something inside me snapped.

If I had to choose a moment in time when I knew my life would be different going forward—when I knew *I* would be different—this would be it.

It was at this very moment that I knew in my soul I was capable of murder.

I picked up the ax, stood tall and headed straight for him, stepping around the overturned living room furniture. I raise the ax over my head and gripped it with both hands. The look of fear and surprise in my father's eyes was welcome. I savored it. I wanted to remember that fear, to play it over and over in my head. He didn't even try to move out of the way. I swung down hard but stopped the blade less than an inch away from slamming it into his chest.

The sheer look of horror on his face did nothing to unnerve me. I was done fixing him. "*Never* forget that I stopped this time. Because if I ever see you again, I will tear your fucking heart out, old man." I threw down the ax and spat on him, making sure he knew he was as *nothing* to me as I was to him. I left him trembling on the floor and didn't so much as pause to look back at him before I ripped open the front door and stepped out into the night.

I lit a cigarette on the front porch before walking into the shadows of the driveway to mount my bike. I didn't bother to pack a bag.

There was nothing I needed or wanted from that house anymore.

As I started up the bike and let it roar, I could've sworn I heard my father wailing just beyond the noise of my engine. But, it was too late.

I was well past the point of going back.

In more ways than one.

THAT WAS FOUR years ago.

Six days have passed since I last took a life, and now, my bike and I were headed back to the very place I hated most.

It wasn't even the money that fueled my work anymore. If I wasn't the one doing the job, it would've been someone else. Maybe I thought that, in my own way, I was sparing some poor schmuck from a life I was better suited for.

I had no delusions of grandeur. Where other guys seemed to get hard for fast, expensive cars, I preferred the freedom of my bike. Buying a house meant putting down roots, which was the last thing I wanted, so I never lived anywhere longer than it took to complete the job. And I hated being bored, so when I needed to lay low after a high profile kill, I'd sell a little weed or some blow—just enough to keep me from being idle.

Idle hands make the devil's work, Jake, Mom used to say.

Little did she know.

My hands were never idle. If the past few years taught me anything, it's that the devil's work is exactly what they were made for.

I had no plans to ever return to the place I'd once called home, not even when Reggie, the head mechanic at Dad's shop and the only person from my hometown I kept in occasional contact with, called to say Dad's next crawl into the bottle could be his last. Dad made his bed in hell, and I'm pretty sure it was laced with ashes, vomit and empty bottles of Jameson. But when Reggie told me the house I grew up in—the house my mother had loved up until the day she died in it—was in danger of being lost to the tax collector, something in me told me to go save it. Not for him.

For her.

I needed to help the only woman who'd ever loved me. The only thing I'd ever done for her until then was help her into an early grave.

In my hometown of Coral Pines—a tiny island off the Southwest coast of Florida—trucks with lift kits and big tires were worshiped, and their chrome gun racks shone brighter than Sunday morning sunlight through stained glass. If cities like New York and Chicago are called concrete jungles, then Coral Pines could easily be called a beach prison, or a tropical asylum. Or my favorite: a rancid fishtopia hell.

Nothing but tourists, rednecks and ghosts.

I wasn't sure which I hated more.

The drifter lifestyle I'd adapted after I left that shit hole island suited me just fine. I rode from town to town, never stayed longer than a tank of gas would allow, and did the jobs that came to me through temporary post office boxes and untraceable cell phones. I never settled in one place long enough to make relationships that would matter.

That was exactly the way I wanted it.

I rarely told anyone my real name, which was nothing like home. Everyone in Coral Pines knew who I was, because everyone there knew everyone else—their life story, their mama's maiden name, all the gory family details most people try hard to keep buried deep in their closets. Secrets just didn't stay kept in Coral Pines.

Though I now had some worth keeping.

They may have known the Jake Dunn who was a screw-up as a kid, but they had no fucking clue who I was anymore. Not to mention, what I was capable of.

The Matlacha Pass was the two-lane bridge that delivered you either to or from Coral Pines. It was the only way on or off the island, and for the entire twenty-two years I had occupied the Earth, it'd been under construction. This was still the case on the day that I—under protest—crossed over it for the first time in years. The thick heat washed over me as I rode like I was pushing my bike through a wall of water. Every bit of the unease I'd felt blowing off of me the day I left this godforsaken place, rushed back with the familiar salty wind.

Memories of my brother's funeral four years before were waiting there, too. I hadn't expected to find my mother afterward, still wearing the short-sleeved black dress she wore to the church, face-down in the bathtub with a sawed-off at her side and what had been the better part of her head splattered across the pink shower tile. She hadn't wanted to leave a mess. She'd said so in the note she left, but Mom didn't know enough about guns to realize she had chosen the messiest of them all from Dad's rack.

Dad had been a disaster at the funeral for my brother. He was in the psychiatric hospital two towns over for my mother's. He always blamed me—not just for Mason's death, but for Mom's too. He told me more than once I should have been with Mason on the boat that morning, and it was my fault he ended up floating in the Coral Pines River. The real reason Dad hated me is because he thought it never should've been his perfect, straight A-earning, scholarship-winning, baseball captain and expert fisherman son who died that day. It should have been his weed-dealing, girl-chasing, fight-picking, school-skipping degenerate of a son.

It should have been me.

In some ways, I agreed with him. If it'd been me instead of Mason, Mom would still be alive. Dad wouldn't be trying to drown himself in cheap whiskey, and there would be a few more people walking around in the land of the living. I contributed nothing and took everything. But to be fair about it, I also expected nothing from the godless world that ripped me apart at every turn.

I expected nothing, until the night I met a certain redhead with an attitude.

The night I met Abby Ford, my life changed forever.

Chapter One

Abby

I KNEW SOMETHING was wrong when I walked across the stage on graduation day and was met with only the unenthusiastic slow claps from the sparse crowd. It's not like I expected a standing ovation. I haven't exactly played nice with my fellow classmates. I could've counted the number of real friends I had on one hand. Or no hands, actually. It was Nan's usual whooping and hollering I expected to hear but was nowhere to be found.

Where was she?

An alarm went off in my head when our vice-principal, Miss Morgan, barged into the auditorium, letting the heavy metal doors slam shut behind her. Her heels clacked in quick succession across the shiny yellow floor. With a crook of her finger in my direction, she removed me from my seat. Her gaze was focused on the floor as she led me to the principal's office in silence.

When I entered the office, Sheriff Fletcher sat behind the cluttered desk instead of the principal himself.

Oh shit.

I took a quick mental inventory of anything I'd done recently that would warrant the honor of his visit. There was a dime bag in the back pocket of my shorts under my gold graduation gown, but since the sheriff's weed policy was basically *if you have it, pass it,* I wasn't overly concerned. Although having it on school property could result in some off-colored double standard policies or laws the sheriff being applied. There hadn't been a single marijuana arrest in Coral Pines the entire time I lived here. It would be just my luck to be the very first one thrown behind bars for it. I'd also had an unfortunate incident involving the baseball field fence and a four-wheeler I'd borrowed—without the owner's knowledge—but I was pretty sure there was no way for the sheriff to know it was me who caused the damage.

"Sheriff?" I tried to act casual, but my one-word greeting sounded like a question. Even with his lax attitude and loose interpretations of the law, I couldn't stand the man. His family practically owned Coral Pines, so I was pretty sure Sheriff Fletcher had phoned in his police training. The only somewhat-decent member of the Fletcher family was Owen, a nice enough guy, if pretty boy man sluts were your thing.

The sheriff's shirt was opened three buttons too many, as if to make sure that he wouldn't be mistaken for a professional man of the law. A mass of curly black chest hair poked out of his collar and brushed the base of his throat. "Have a seat, Miss Ford." He gestured with a fat, hairy finger to the chairs in front of the desk. Miss Morgan stood at his side with her hands folded in front of her, almost nun-like. Her tall, thin frame and high-wasted pencil skirt made her look like a giraffe next to the sheriff's squatty physique. Her choppy, uneven bangs hung over her lashes and grazed her milky skin. Being a red-head, I was pretty damn pale; not even the death rays of the southern Florida sun could have changed that. Somehow, she managed to be even paler than me.

I took a seat and hoped that whatever this was would be over soon.

It had only been four years earlier, in another state at another school, in what seemed like another life, when the principal called me out from my classroom and into the hallway to deliver the news that my father had overdosed. I'd been in foster care for over two years by then, and I hadn't seen him in four. But the powers that be had thought his death was important enough to pull me from class, so I felt I owed it to them to fake some of the sadness I knew they were expecting from me.

What I really wanted to do was laugh at the satisfaction, at the justice of it all.

Happy couldn't even begin to describe how I'd felt when they informed me of his death.

Nan had always said that God created man in his image. Where my father was concerned, God was either a sick, sadistic fuck or one hell of a lie people convinced themselves was the truth.

I kept that thought to myself when I was around Nan.

Dad had been at work when they found him in one of the bathroom stalls, sitting on the toilet with his pants down around his ankles, a syringe still hanging from his pocked-up arm. I was more surprised to hear he'd actually been at work than I was to hear he'd died. At least when it happened, he was with the only thing in his life he'd ever really loved: his needle.

Dad was a real winner.

The sheriff didn't look me in the eyes. His gaze focused somewhere over my head, prolonging whatever news he'd come to deliver. As time passed, each of his breaths sounded more like strained snores. I grew impatient. "Maybe, you can just tell me why I'm here," I blurted out.

"Sweetheart?" The word fell out of his mouth like he'd never used it before. "Who's your next of kin?" The blood drained from my face. I didn't answer him at first. I couldn't find the words. My vision spun like I was looking at him through a kaleidoscope.

Next of kin? I thought. *My only kin is Nan...*

"Abby!" Miss Morgan snapped her fingers in my face. I hadn't even seen her kneeling in front of me, but there she was. Behind her, the sheriff was sweating profusely and nervously. "Abby," she repeated, softer now. "Nan was in an accident." She enunciated each word as if she was teaching an English class.

"How?" I asked. "Her truck doesn't even run. It's been sitting in a junkyard and hasn't been off blocks since September," I said, as if somehow this fact would change the truth.

"Not a car accident, sweetie." Miss Morgan looked to be in physical pain. "It was...an explosion."

She squeezed my hand, but I flinched at her touch and immediately pulled away from her grip. "What the fuck?" I whispered. My heart pounded in my ears. I felt the blood in my veins turn to acid. My skin was about to burn off of my bones.

"That's enough of that language, young lady." Sheriff Fletcher had the audacity to scold me. He cleared his throat. "I do realize this is a difficult situation for you, and I'm very sorry." Yeah, right. It sure sounded like he was. "I have to ask something: did your Nan tell you she needed money for anything, by chance? Do you know if she was having any sort of financial troubles?"

I shook my head. We didn't live like royalty by any means, but her social security check and the money she made from selling her jams at the Sunday craft market was enough to pay the mortgage and keep me fed and clothed. "No," I answered. "Not that I know of."

Sheriff Fletcher groaned. "We have reason to believe your Nan was involved in some activities of a questionable nature." He scratched at his five o'clock shadow. "She was in a mobile home in the middle of the Preserve when it exploded."

There was no way this could be happening.

They had to be wrong.

The sheriff started to talk again as Ms. Morgan sat down next to me. She reached out in another attempt to put her hands over mine. I pulled away before she could.

"Sheriff Fletcher thinks the mobile home was involved in *cooking drugs*." Her words were as awkward as she was.

"No, that has to be a mistake." I started to rant like my words were being tossed around in a tornado. "Nan doesn't have anything to do with drugs. I'll call her right now… you can see for yourself"

There was no possible way, especially because of my parents' shitty addictions, that Nan would ever be involved in something like that. She wouldn't even take cough syrup when she had a cold.

I reached for the phone on the desk, but before I could get to it the sheriff put his sweaty bear paw on the receiver "Unfortunately, it's no mistake. Your grandmother died this morning in an explosion at a known meth lab." My mouth fell open as I stared at him. He offered nothing further. Instead, he asked me again, "Who's your next of kin, Miss Ford? It's not listed in your file. I know your parents aren't in the picture, but is there an aunt or uncle we can call?"

"No," I said quietly. There was no one.

"An older sibling then, or maybe a cousin?"

I shook my head, losing myself in the slow spin of the room around me.

Why the hell would Nan be at a meth lab?

There was no reason, except...

It hit me like an anvil why Nan needed the money: to pay for college. She talked about sending me all the time. I ignored her every time she brought it up. My plans for the future never reached further than the weekend. I mostly just smiled and nodded. Much of the time, I just changed the subject. I wasn't going to college. End of story.

Apparently, Nan had thought otherwise.

But involving herself in meth just didn't make sense.

"It's just me...and her." My voice cracked. Inside, I was crying, screaming, raging against whatever higher power would be so cruel that it would give me a taste of normalcy then strip it all away. Outside, I was a robot.

"How old are you, Miss Ford?" Sheriff Fletcher asked. He cracked his knuckles impatiently, like he couldn't wait to get this over with and head to Sally's all you can eat Saturday fish fry.

"Seventeen," the robot said.

"When will you turn eighteen, honey?" Miss Morgan cooed, trying to offer me some sort of comfort.

"Not for a while." Ten months, actually. I had graduated a full year early. When I told Nan I wanted to drop out of high school, she'd given me the only other option she would agree to. "If you want out so bad Abby," she'd told me, "just hurry up and graduate early."

Like it was as easy as taking in the afternoon mail.

It was tough work, but I'd done it. Nan had made me feel as if I was graduating from some Ivy League school instead of public high school in Coral Pines.

I caught my reflection on the window behind the sheriff. I was still wearing my cap and gown. It was like the happy me that was supposed to be there was mocking the pitiful me who was in her place—the me who'd just had her world ripped out from underneath her in one short conversation.

Sheriff Fletcher cleared his throat yet again. "Miss Ford, my office is required to take action to have un-emancipated minors placed in child protective services. By the time the paperwork is filed and the case is assigned a social worker, you would only have to be in the system for a few months before you become a legal adult and would no longer require their care." He shifted in his seat, very obviously adjusting his privates under the desk. He continued. "This is a small town. We ain't got those kinds of resources at the ready, so it'll take a while. For now, Miss Morgan has agreed to look in on you from time to time. If you really want we can send you up north to CPS right away, but I have a feeling that's not what you want, now is it?" It was a statement, not a question. He seemed irritated he had actual paper work to do and less concerned I'd just lost the only person who ever gave a shit about me.

He smirked and tilted his head, like he was waiting for me to thank him. Yeah, thanks for barely skimming over the tiny fact that Nan was dead. Thank you so much, sir, for kindly offering me the option of not being sent away with the afternoon mail and back into foster care hell. I would run before they came for me. I would never go back into that fucking system.

Sheriff Fletcher stood and handed me a card with Reverend Thomas' phone number on it. "The Reverend can help make all your arrangements." He said it matter-of-factly, as if he'd just given me a coupon for a buy one get one free at the car wash. "Sorry for your loss, Miss Ford," he called over his shoulder as he headed out the door. The echo of his heavy-booted stomps trailed behind him as he disappeared down the hallway, whistling as he walked away.

Miss Morgan tried to pull me into an embrace. I jumped when she touched me and took a quick step back, knocking my graduation cap off of my head.

No tears, no sobbing. No praying to an imaginary God who'd forgotten about me long ago. I called on the familiar numbness to take over.

I'd been through shit like this before. I didn't need anything but my barriers.

Nan was dead, and it was probably my fault. I knew that.

Case closed. No need to dwell on something I couldn't change.

Right?

Miss Morgan bent down, retrieved my graduation cap from under the desk, and dusted it off with the palm of her hand. She was careful not to make contact with me as she placed it back on my head. She made no attempt at another awkward *Comforting Troubled Teens 101* embrace. Instead, she studied me intently, as if she were searching for answers to questions she didn't dare ask out loud. I imagined it included something along the lines of, *What happened to you, little girl? Where do you go from here?* I didn't need her pity.

I didn't need anything from her or anyone else.

I turned to leave.

"Abby!" Miss Morgan called out. She stopped me before I could rush out of her range. Carefully, she reached for the tassel hanging from my graduation cap and moved it from right to left.

Chapter Two

THE DAYS THAT followed blended together. Day into night. A permanent dusk. A mix of daydreams and nightmares.

They call the figure that takes our loved ones from this world the *angel of death*, when really he's just a corrupt errand boy who hides deep within his hood when he comes to take souls to the other side. It's not a bad gig really. He probably doesn't feel, doesn't mourn.

He was more like me than I'd realized.

I envied him. To take without feeling. To deliver people from one world to the next without the surprise or shock that always seems to come with unexpected death.

Why do we call the ones we've lost our *dearly departed*? They are not *departed*. The word *depart* means "to leave". They didn't leave. They were abducted from this life by some soulless skeleton dressed in his mother's house-coat who dragged them to their ends.

Nan must have left this world kicking and screaming. I know she must have called out to me as he shoved her soul into his pocket.

She needed me to save her, and instead, I may have been the very reason she died.

This was how the nightmares went night after night: Nan, drowning in a purgatory of dark water, trying to fight her way back to me and never getting any closer no matter how hard she tried. I would wake up in the middle of the night, pale-faced and dripping with sweat, a scream tearing heavily from my throat as I cried out for the only person in my life who ever wanted to save me from myself.

The memories of the days after Nan's funeral played in my head on repeat, in blurry slow motion. I didn't eat. I didn't sleep. Random neighbors would come over to bring the customary Someone Died casserole. They wouldn't even knock—probably because they knew I wouldn't answer. Finally, Irma from next door started taking my casserole deliveries and dropping them off at the church. The uneaten food was becoming too much for Nan's old avocado-colored freezer to hold. I started locking the deadbolt on the front door, which was unheard of in our small town. I wasn't necessarily trying to lock people out. I was trying to keep myself locked in. The more removed I was from civilization, the closer I felt to Nan.

I felt the need to punish myself, by surrounding myself in everything that was Nan. I sprayed her perfume in the air. I wore her old full-length fox fur coat, which she'd never worn and had no reason to own in such a tropical place. I napped in her old red corduroy lazy-boy, and I drank her favorite Scotch every night—and sometimes every morning—until the heat in my throat spread through my blood and I slipped into the oblivion I was searching for.

Nan's home—*my* home—was more cottage than house. The faded pink siding was in need of a fresh coat of paint and the light gray shingles were streaked with the evidence of the daily afternoon heavy summer storms. With two bedrooms and only one bathroom, it was small by anyone's standards. The faux wood linoleum floors and off-white cabinets hadn't been updated since Pops built the cottage for Nan over thirty years ago.

The short gravel driveway gave way to a broken shell road, and the cottage itself sat on nothing more than a measly eighth of an acre within arms reach of Lee's Oriental cuisine on one side and Irma's Beauty Salon on the other. Nan never minded that the green space was so small, because she had the waters of the Coral Pines River in her backyard.

With a tumbler of Scotch in hand, I looked around the cottage Nan loved so much. Had it only been three years prior when I'd been so reluctant to call it my home? Just a few short years since I'd burst into Nan's life with a chip on my shoulder and a tongue sharper than a drawer full of knives?

Her words, not mine.

Nan had welcomed me into her life. She was patient with me every excruciating step of the way, and she loved me without question, without exception.

When a social worker in a pantsuit three sizes too large led a thirteen year old me up the walkway to meet the grandmother I'd never known, I was beyond terrified. She was my father's mother. What if she was just like him? What if she made me promises she never intended to keep, just as he had? I didn't mean the promise of toys and birthday parties. I mean the promise of food, of keeping the electricity turned on. The promise that I would be safe. My father's dirt-bag friends had leered at me every time I entered the room—the same friends who asked if I knew what a cock was, and if I knew what to do with one. At six years old, I'd told the laughing bunch to go fuck themselves. They laughed harder, and Dad got angrier.

It was two days before he untied me from the kitchen chair and threw a cold slice of pizza onto the floor at my feet.

Dad may have thought his form of discipline had taught me

some sort of fucked-up lesson. The only thing it really did was make me cold and numb. He and my mother treated dishing up their drugged-out brand of parental justice the same way they took turns entering and exiting the ever-revolving doors of the state prison.

It turned out Nan was nothing like my father. She was actually excited to have me, but I could tell she was just as nervous as I was. She was cautious but loving.

When Nan had come out to greet us on the front porch that first day, she didn't run up and hug me. She made sure not overwhelm me with the love already written all over her face. She showed me to my room, which was entirely white—or better yet, she told me, it was *blank*. It sure was. White walls, white comforter and pillow, and a white writing desk and chair. "I didn't know what you'd like, so I thought I'd let you tell me how you want to decorate your room and what you'd like in it."

"I can have anything?" I'd asked.

"Sure sweetie, anything at all." Nan was always careful to withdraw her outstretched hand before it found my head or my shoulder... or my arm.

My aversion to physical touch must have been in my file.

The only thing I asked Nan for that first day was a deadbolt on my bedroom door. There were no questions, no hesitations. A handyman was at the house and had installed my deadbolt within an hour. She made me a necklace for the key and told me to put it around my neck. I'd stopped using the lock a few weeks after moving in with her, but I'd never taken off the key.

Then, Nan fed me her homemade fried chicken with mashed potatoes. We had peach cobbler for dessert. She only spoke to ask me if I liked the food. I nodded. In truth, it was the best food I'd ever eaten. After that first meal, Tuesday night became

Fried Chicken Night.

Nan didn't want answers from me. She just wanted her grandchild—her short-tempered, razor-tongued, sometimes violent, grandchild. During my entire life, nobody had wanted me on my very best day on my very best behavior.

Nan wanted me at my worst, and sometimes, that was exactly what she got.

I had come such a long way in my four years with Nan. After just a few short weeks without her, it was like she'd never been in my life at all.

Chapter Three

WHEN THE PERSISTENT shit at the door kept ringing the bell over and over, I was inclined to get the shotgun from the hall closet, shoot first, and ask questions later.

"Go away!" I shouted into my pillow as I raised the comforter over my head. I didn't know what time it was, and I didn't care. All I knew was that it was early, and I wasn't ready to end my hibernation just yet.

The doorbell shit changed his style from ringing it twice in increments of thirty seconds to pressing it continuously like someone waiting impatiently for an elevator.

That's it, I thought. *I'm getting the gun.*

I leapt from my bed, tore open the front door, and *almost* felt bad for the poor soul on the other side who'd be facing my wrath.

A linebacker of a woman wearing a navy blue suit took up the majority of the doorway. I had to look up to see her face. She looked like Dan Aykroyd in drag. Her hair was thin and black with silver running through it, pulled in a tight bun at the nape of her neck. She held a file and a clipboard in her hand.

"Abby Ford?" she asked without looking at me, her focus solely on her clipboard. Her voice was deep and vibrated through her chest when she spoke.

"Huh?" I asked. I wiped sleep from my eyes, my rage replaced with a tired sense of confusion.

The woman-man sighed. "You are Abby Ford—am I correct?" She tapped the tip of her pen on her board.

"Yeah?" It came out more like a question.

She huffed, and if I could have seen her eyes all the way up there in the sky where her head was, I'm sure I would have seen that she was rolling them. "Let's try this again. Are you or are you not Abby Ford, the minor child who was in the care of Georgianne Ford before her passing three weeks ago?"

"I'm almost eighteen," I blurted, "so you can go now."

I moved to shut the door, but she blocked it with her foot without missing a beat. "Yes, well, you aren't eighteen yet, and being seventeen makes you a minor. Therefore, you are currently a ward of the state of Florida, and I will be taking you into protective custody today. You'll be placed in foster care until the day you turn eighteen." She flipped a page on her clipboard. "Which I can see here isn't actually for another nine months or so."

I had known foster care was a possibility. I just hadn't expected Sheriff Fletcher to actually file the paperwork, and that they would show up so damn quickly. I'd also hoped that with me being so close to eighteen, no one would really give a shit.

"May I come in, Miss Ford?" The woman-man asked.

"No!" I moved in front of her to block the doorway. I was pretty sure I'd left some arrestable offenses on the coffee table she didn't need to see.

"Excuse me?" she asked, obviously not used to being defied.

"My aunt doesn't like strangers in the house, and you haven't even told me your name." I heard the lie come out of my mouth before I'd even registered what I was saying.

"Miss Thornton," she replied. "My name is Miss Thornton." I wanted to take her tapping pen and stab her in the foot—the one that kept the door from closing.

It was the first time she tore her eyes away from her paperwork and actually gave me a once over. I was still wearing my pajamas, which consisted of a long sleeved high neck t-shirt and shorts. I'm sure I had bed head and dark circles under my eyes. With all the nightmares, sleep had been no easy feet. Miss Thornton was probably wondering why I was sleeping at one o'clock on a Monday afternoon. "We have no record of this aunt you speak of, what's her name?"

I glanced around the living room nervously. My eyes landed on the old quilt my Nan kept draped over the couch. The gaudy patch in the middle depicted Elvis the day he married Priscilla. They were cutting their wedding cake, her black bouffant was almost taller than the cake.

"Priscilla," I said when I turned back to Miss Thornton. "Priscilla... Perkins." The double *P* sound would make it easier for me to remember the lie.

"Where is this Aunt Priscilla?" She lowered her thick black glasses to the tip of her nose as she looked down at me.

"Um...she's on her way back from Atlanta. She had to go get the rest of her stuff so she could move in here with me." I looked past her so we wouldn't make eye contact. Her eyes were like little lie detectors; I could almost see the needles jumping as my heartbeat sped up and slowed down. "She's my mother's sister. I just met her recently actually."

I really needed to stop blurting shit out.

"Okay. So, when is your mother's sister expected?" Miss Thornton was almost huffing. She was also sweating and not just a little. The beads that had started on her forehead raced down her face and pooled on top of her too-tight blouse collar. It drew my attention to the little yellow stain along the white fabric that grew larger with each passing moment she stood on the porch.

"Tomorrow afternoon," I stated with as much confidence as I could. I faked a yawn to appear more nonchalant.

"Does anyone else know this aunt of yours? Anyone I could speak to?" She stuck her finger into her collar and pulled it away from the neck roll that puffed out above it. I swear I saw steam escape. I was sure she had a lot of kids besides me to go kidnap. I didn't know why she was so worried about me.

"Sure. Everyone knows Aunt Priscilla. You can go ask at the corner store or at the motel up the road. They all know her."

"Okay, Miss Ford," Miss Thornton said. "Here's what's going to happen: I'm required to make certain you aren't living alone, so I need to be sure that this 'Aunt Priscilla'," and she quoted the air with her fingers, "exists and is capable of caring for you. I intend to speak to the people you claim know her, by sometime this afternoon. If they do indeed know 'Aunt Priscilla' and can vouch for her existence, I will be back tomorrow afternoon to interview her regarding the process of becoming your legal custodian. In the meantime, here's my card." She handed me a generic white card with the Florida state seal in the corner. "If by chance she arrives earlier, please have her call me."

I reached out and took her card as she turned and started down the steps.

She turned to me again. "And Miss Ford? If for any reason 'Aunt Priscilla' isn't capable of your care, you will have to come with me." For the first time since she'd rung the bell, there was something resembling concern her voice, like maybe she'd cared about her job once, but over time had forgotten how to keep doing so.

The concern went away just as quickly as it had arrived. "Are you certain you don't want to save me some time and trouble in this heat and just pack a bag now?"

I shook my head.

"Okay, then. I will be back, Miss Ford," she assured me. She opened the car door and maneuvered herself behind the steering wheel of her much-too-small-for-her-body-mass silver Prius before pulling off down the road, in the direction of the corner store and motel.

I ran back into the house before the dust kicked up by her tires could settle. I opened my closet and pulled clothes from their hangers, opening drawers, and shoving as much stuff as I could into my backpack. It wouldn't take her long to verify that no one knew this fictional Aunt Priscilla. I had to get the hell out of there before she came back and dragged me to yet another foster home.

Paid child care, without the care. To me, that was what foster care really was. It funded drug habits and paid rents.

There was no way in hell I was going back in.

My experiences in the system varied between sharing a room with a boy who skinned cats—who I was convinced would suffocate me in my sleep—to listening to Greg, the older boy who slept in the bottom bunk of our four bunk room, angrily masturbating every night and cursing his parents when he came.

Then there was Sophie, the only friend I had ever made in foster care. She was small and quiet with dark hair and large brown eyes. Her skin always looked naturally tanned. She looked like a doll, from what I heard about them, anyway. I'd never actually owned one myself. Sophie shared the same vacant, hopeless look as I had. Her family history and her upbringing weren't all that different from my own.

I recognized a kindred spirit in her.

One morning I'd found her naked on the couch, her eyes

lifeless and unfocused. Bruises marred every inch of her little twelve-year-old body. Her once-olive skin was transparent. I could see all of her blue veins beneath the surface. Her wrists were bound behind her back with a long dirty sock, a needle sat in an ashtray beside her. Blood dripped from the tip and pooled in the bottom of the clear glass. Dick and Denise, our foster parents, used her as their entertainment for the previous evening. They'd doped her with drugs bought with the money given to them by the state for her care before using her as a toy for their sadistic sex games.

They probably didn't even know she was dead until later that day.

By that time, I was long gone.

That was the first time I ran away from a foster home. It certainly wasn't the last.

After throwing my feet into my old scuffed cowboy boots and checking for the knife I kept clipped on the inside of the right one. I secured the straps of my backpack onto my shoulders and ran into Nan's room to grab her charm bracelet off her nightstand. I nabbed my weed from the coffee table and slipped out the back sliding glass doors.

I made a run for the beach.

IT WOULD PROBABLY be a while before Miss Thornton gave up on me and moved her attention to other, more worthy degenerates. Until then, I figured it would be best if I stayed away from home for at least a few days. My plan was simple: keep a low profile, and become invisible. I had a few bucks, but I knew it wouldn't last long. I had planned on selling some of Nan's lesser-beloved items, but that would have to wait until the coast was clear.

I decided to drop by Bubba's Bar just before closing to see if they'd consider hiring me to sweep floors or wait tables. I highly doubted that Miss Thornton would look for me at a bar on a Monday night.

After Bubba's my focus would have to be trying to find a spot to crash for a few nights. A hotel was out of the question. It was the peak of summer, and all the rooms in town were sure to be booked by the flock of tourists. Aside from that, one night in any of them would have cost more than ten times the twenty bucks in my pocket. The beach wasn't safe either. The tides were unpredictable and could sneak up when you least expected it. More than once, a tourist taking a beer nap had been pulled out into the Gulf.

I plopped down in the hot sand among the blankets of tourists and used my backpack as a pillow. I was hiding in plain sight. For a while, I watched people stalling out their rented jet skis and trying to maneuver their wind surfers without falling on their asses. Moms and dads cheered for their teenagers, watching as they finally got the hang of it and caught some wind, which took them just a few feet before they lost control and ended up back in the water. The moms and dads kept cheering, even when the kids gave up on their new sport and dragged their weary, defeated and worn-out bodies to shore. It was just windsurfing. Why were they so proud? Why all the cheering? Besides graduating high school and seeing the look on Nan's face that morning as I dressed in my cap and gown, I'd never had anyone be proud of me.

If I wanted to learn something, I taught myself. There was no one there to cheer for the significant things, let alone the small ones.

I stayed on the beach until sunset, watching the tourists' skin change from pasty white to lobster red by the time the sun and moon swapped places. I took the back roads to Bubba's and lit a joint on the way. Headlights appeared on the dark road behind me. I moved to the side to allow the vehicle to pass so I didn't end up like the possum I just had to step over. Instead of driving by, a superman blue lifted truck slowed and pulled up beside me. It was so tall that my head was aligned with the tops of the tires.

"Alone on a dark road?" I couldn't see Owen Fletcher way up there, but I recognized his voice. "You gotta either be wanting to get attacked by coyotes, or you're getting lit."

He hung his head out of the truck window. His black baseball cap was on backwards, dark unruly hair peeking out from beneath the rim, the sleeves of his white t-shirt were rolled up with a pack of Marlboro Reds—the logo visible through the thin fabric—folded into one of them.

Owen had always been friendly, and he'd always made a point of making small talk with me when we found ourselves in the same place at the same time. But then, he did that with everyone. I suspected it was partly because of who his family was. Maybe, they were grooming him for a career in politics. When you have relatives embedded in every position of power to be had in a county, it's not common to just go off and become the school janitor.

I raised my joint into the air so he could see that it was the getting lit part and not the wanting to be attacked by coyotes that I was up to. I breathed out the smoke I was holding deep inside my lungs. It burned, but I didn't cough. Owen laughed. "I was hoping it was that one." He put the truck in park, leaned over and opened the passenger door. "Get on in, girl, and pass that shit."

I wouldn't exactly call Owen my friend, but I could've put him on the short list of people who didn't make me cringe with either fear or anger when they spoke. At least not too much. I made up my mind to get into his truck when the hundredth mosquito of the night started making a meal of my arm through my sleeves. At the rate they were biting, it wouldn't be long before I had no blood left.

Owen reached down and offered his hand to help me up. I shook my head, refusing his assistance, and leapt up into the truck like I was mounting a horse. I put one foot on the bottom lip of the tire, and I swung my other foot over the top of it before I shifted sideways and slid my ass into the bucket seat.

"Impressive," Owen said, acknowledging my useless skill. I was more impressed by my ability to yet again avoid human contact. "Even Billy Rae still needs my help to get up in here. Then again, that fat-ass has an extra seventy-five pounds on him that gravity doesn't like to give up on so easily."

I passed him the joint and he took a long hit, blowing the smoke out of his nose and mouth.

Owen put the truck in drive and started back down the dark road. The humming of the huge tires on the sketchy pavement echoed inside the cabin of the truck. The dashboard vibrated and the blue light of the clock became blurrier as Owen increased speed.

"Uncle Cole told me what happened to your granny. I'm sorry," Owen said, as he passed the joint back to me. The sudden change in conversation caught me off guard. Owen's apology sounded genuine, but the mention of Nan's name brought back a sinking feeling in the pit of my stomach. I pushed it out and shrugged my shoulders.

"Thanks," I said before I changed the subject. "What are you doing out here anyway? Don't you got some girls to be chasing?"

Owen laughed. "Abby, Abby." He put his hand over his heart and feigned being hurt. "You know the ladies come to me, not the other way around. The only skirt I ever chased was yours, sophomore year, and I do recall you telling me—and I'm quoting now—'You're not my type, Owen, and you never will be'!" He spoke my part in a high-pitched feminine voice, but his attempt at mimicking me sounded more like Julia Child's voice than it did mine.

"I said that?" I asked, even though I knew damn well I had. I also remembered telling him to fuck off, and all he did was stand there and laugh like he'd never been told off before, like my refusal was amusing to him.

"Oh yes, you did. You broke my poor little hillbilly heart that day." He stuck out his bottom lip in a phony pout.

"Okay. I may have said that, but I sure as hell don't *sound* like that."

"That's true. Your voice is much lower and much, much angrier." This time he used a voice closer to Cookie Monster when he recited my rejection.

"Well see, that worked out for the best, 'cause here we are, still...friends?" I used the term 'friends' for lack of a word describing "a person who didn't disgust me as much as others."

"Of course, we're friends, Abby." Owen flashed his big, brilliant, straight-toothed white smile. I could see how girls fell at his feet. Girls who were interested in boys, anyway. I certainly was not one of them—not that I was into girls or anything. Sometimes, I'd think I just wasn't put together like everyone else was. Other times I'd think that I was put together the same way they were, only they'd been left whole while I'd been torn down and put back together over and over again.

Most kids in my high school were into cheerleading and football, trucks and fishing, and the rodeo. Most of all, they were into each other.

The only thing I was into was self-preservation.

But if you were a *normal* teenage girl, you definitely would've thought Owen was a good-looking guy. His emerald green eyes were so brilliant they looked like colored contacts. His skin was tanned from spending most of his days out on his fishing boat. Casting fishing nets all day was no doubt the reason for his well-developed biceps and forearms that flexed as he turned the wheel.

The roads were so dark even the headlights didn't seem like they did much to light up the night. Owen had grown up in Coral Pines and probably knew those roads like the back of his hand. He probably could've driven them without any lights on at all.

We each took a few more hits. I snuffed out the cherry in between my thumb and forefinger and then placed the joint back into the front zip pocket of my backpack.

"So, where you heading?" Owen asked.

"Bubba's. Gonna see about a job." Also, Bubba's was the only place open late, and I didn't want to tell him I didn't have anywhere to go just yet.

"You gonna sleep over there, too?" He laughed and pointed at the backpack at my feet.

"I was at the beach for a while... you know towels, sunscreen and such," I lied. Owen eyed me skeptically, but accepted my answer and didn't press for more.

"You want me to take you over there?" he asked. "It's not far."

"Sure." It was still early, but I figured I could get something to eat before finding a place to crash for the night.

I looked over at Owen as he watched the road, his face illuminated by the blue dashboard lights. I guess he could feel my stare. "What?" he asked with a smile.

"Nothing," I responded, still unable to take my gaze away from him. There was something about him that was intriguing, different than other boys I knew. I couldn't put my finger on it, but he seemed almost familiar to me.

"Nuh uh. You have to tell me why you're looking at me like that." He turned into the broken shell parking lot of Bubba's and put the truck in park.

"It's nothing," I said. Owen made another face, and I found myself muffling a laugh.

"Tell me, Abby!" He locked the truck from the automatic lock button on his door. "I'm not letting you out if you don't tell me *right now* what you were thinking."

"Fine," I said, giving in. "Unlock the doors first, and *then* I'll tell you."

He looked at me thoughtfully for a moment. "Ok, there." He clicked the button. "Now, tell me."

Before the words were out of his mouth, I jumped out the door and ran from the truck. When I was almost to the entrance, I looked back and saw Owen's bright, open smile. He put the truck in reverse and shook his head and laughed as he backed onto the road and drove away into the night.

Maybe, I did have a friend after all.

Maybe.

Chapter Four

B UBBA'S WAS ALWAYS busy, but during the months when the tourists were occupying all the motel rooms and vacation rentals on the island, it was a total madhouse. It mostly happened during the winter, when the snowbirds migrated south, or during a few weeks in summer when families took vacations together.

I knew nothing about either of those.

Vacations or families.

I grabbed a spot at the end of the bar and ordered a burger and fries. I took my time eating, observing all the colorful characters that came out for the night—locals and tourists alike. An older woman with curly maroon hair sat on the lap of a man wearing sweatpants, her use of blue eye shadow was epic, reaching all the way to her eyebrows. A crowd of college kids turned the pool table into a beer pong station. The small dance floor was packed with people who were either rhythmically-challenged or three sheets to the wind. Either way, they all looked like they were having a good time. For a just a moment, I found myself warring with feelings of jealousy. Until I saw a couple of kids my age making out in the corner booth.

The jealousy faded as quickly as it came.

When I finished eating, I ordered another Coke to extend my stay. I was exhausted and certain that I smelled as if my entire body had been beer-battered, deep-fried, and rolled in an ashtray. Still, I stayed until the last person shuffled out of the bar.

"Everything okay, Abby?" Bubba asked. "I was so sorry to hear about Georgie, she was a great woman." Bubba was older, in his late-sixties with salt and pepper hair. He and Nan would always chat whenever she brought me in for Sunday brunch. I'd once asked her if she'd ever thought about going out on a date with him, but she'd always shrugged it off, as if the idea was as ludicrous as wings on a dog. I always suspected there could've been something more between them than just Sunday morning chats.

"Oh, yeah, I'm fine," I lied. "Just not tired yet. Figured I'd hang out late."

Bubba nodded and took out his keys to lock up after me. "Yeah, busy nights like this used to get me all wound up. I wouldn't be able to get to bed until the sun came up." He yawned again. "Obviously, those days are behind me."

"Hey, Bubba, any chance I can trouble you for a job?" I cringed inwardly at having to ask. I knew I wasn't exactly qualified. For anything. I could easily have told him my sob story about being alone and having no money in an attempt to persuade him, but I didn't want his pity. More than that, I couldn't allow myself to sob at my own sob story, so I definitely didn't want others to.

Bubba looked me over. "How old are you now, Abby?"

"Almost eighteen." It was sort of a lie, and sort of the truth. Depending on your definition of 'almost.'

"You ever serve before?"

I shook my head. "No, but I think I'd be really good at it. Nan always talked 'bout how she used to run her café back in the day, and I always listened to how she would handle the customers. I can do it. I promise." I didn't know if that was a lie, too. I had no idea if I could be a good server or not. Now was not the time for honesty.

"Abby, I can't risk my liquor license by putting you behind the bar. And I can't let you be a server, 'cause we're in the height of season and slammed with people and I got no time to train anyone new. But I tell you what, you come back and see me when you're eighteen, and we are less busy, and I promise I'll try and find something for you."

"Yeah, no problem," I said, trying to keep a positive tone.

Bubba ushered me to the front door. "Georgie did right by you, darlin'. She was a good woman. Come see me if you need anything. God's people need to stick together." I didn't know if he was talking about me or just Nan when he said 'God's people'. And hadn't I just asked him for help? I nodded and smiled.

I left the bar feeling defeated.

I still desperately needed money. Once the coast was clear of Miss Thornton, and I was back living in Nan's, I'd need to be able to feed myself—and hopefully keep the lights on. If I couldn't get a job, I would have to resort to stealing.

Bubba's words stuck with me as I walked down the main road between the shadows of our town's few light posts. *God's people stick together.* It actually started to make sense to me as I thought about it. If God's people stuck together, and I was all alone, then I certainly wasn't one of his people. As much as Nan took me to church and prayed for me, I'd never felt like I was being watched over or taken care of by some higher power. I knew then that this was because I wasn't one of God's people.

I probably never had been.

I walked with no destination in mind, with the new

knowledge that if there actually was a God, he'd likely forgotten about me from the beginning. It wasn't even a second after this thought crossed my mind when the ground beneath my feet started to shake, and the bulb on the light pole over me rattled out a warning. The night went dark.

What the fuck?

A single round light, brighter than any I'd ever seen on a car appeared before me, breaking through the darkness and casting away the shadows of the night around me. It sped directly toward me. The rumbling of the earth grew more violent the closer it came. The light overhead buzzed as it struggled its way back to life.

Just when I began to believe it was God himself making his presence known to me, to punish me for my blasphemous thoughts, the thunderous hell-machine that carried the light barreled past me in a blinding blur of chrome, black and blonde. The force of its stream sent me flailing into a nearby thicket of prickly bushes. It wasn't God. It was just a fucking motorcycle. A big one for sure, but still, just a fucking motorcycle, going at least three times the speed limit.

Just my luck, I thought. I pulled myself up from the brush and bent over to pick the sand spurs and shell fragments from the skin on my calves.

Just my fucking luck.

THE SOUND OF my own sneezing woke me. I wasn't surprised. It seemed that if I moved at all, I kicked up a dust bowl and the result was several earth-shattering loud sneezes in a row.

I hated dust.

I hated allergies.

And I definitely hated sneaking into the junkyard behind Frank Dunn's Auto Body to sleep in Nan's old truck. She had taken it there in an attempt to get it running again, but since she'd found out it would take over two thousand dollars to make that happen, it had stayed at Frank's, untouched for almost a year.

Past experience had taught me that the child welfare social worker types didn't stake out kids for too long. Once they'd spent a solid twenty-four hours looking for you without any luck, they'd list you as a runaway and move on to the next unfortunate case. So I needed just one night away from Nan's, maybe two, to make sure that meddling bitch Miss Thornton would be long gone before I went home. I checked the time on my watch. It was almost four in the morning. I figured I could get in another couple hours of undisturbed sleep, so I tucked myself in under my hoodie and closed my eyes.

I tried to ignore the dust and pretend I was home in my bed at Nan's. I curled up and had almost drifted back to sleep when I was startled by the same thunderous sound that had knocked me to my ass earlier. Careful not to be seen, I sat up and peeked over the dashboard. The yard motion light clicked on, and I saw two figures walking around in the night. They were too far away for me to see them clearly, but I heard a feminine laugh and the click-clack of heels, so one of them was probably a woman.

I quietly sank down to the floorboard under the steering wheel and tried to make myself as small as possible. The last thing I needed was a breaking and entering charge. I think I had one of those already, anyway, and I knew that Frank Dunn wouldn't be happy with me when he saw the trash can sized hole I'd cut in the fence in order to break into the yard.

A solid five minutes passed before the weight of the truck I was in shifted to the driver's side, and the unmistakable sound of moaning filled the silent night.

Yes, it was definitely moaning, and it was close.

The passenger side window became a wall of black leather. Metal grommets scratched at the glass each time the figure stirred.

The moaning started moving... lower.

I crunched myself up as small as I could, trying to make myself invisible. It was still dark out and my black hoodie covered most of me, so even if whoever it was could see through the dirty window, they would hopefully think I was just a bunch of random crap piled on the floor.

The woman started to make exaggerated porn noises, larger-than-life sucking and groaning.

Flashes of unwanted memories flooded my mind before I could attempt to push them out, images of the endless parades of bruised and naked bodies writhing against anyone and anything they could find. Piles of men and women littering the stained couches and floors, smearing the dripping blood from fresh needle wounds and opening scabs of older ones onto one another as they grunted and groaned like animals. The unconscious ones in the crowd were treated no differently than the conscious. Their wide-open mouths and lifeless eyes staring beyond the popcorn ceiling weren't reason enough to stop fucking them. They were taken turns with, until someone noticed they didn't have a pulse. I had witnessed more than one dead body being discarded from my parent's trailer like an empty pizza box.

Bile rose in my throat.

The last memory that burst into my head was of the night I'd gotten the scars I kept covered. A burning took over my body when I thought of the sharpness of the knife, and the crazed look in my mother's bloodshot eyes. My chest tightened, and I willed the memory to leave, but it was too late. I tried to take a deep breath to steady myself. Instead, I inhaled a dust cloud. I tried to stifle my cough, but instead I ended up choking. The woman outside shrieked at the same time, and I braced myself to be discovered.

But, the woman only coughed and made a choking noise of her own. She cleared her throat and spat onto the pavement. "You were supposed to tell me when you were close, asshole!" she yelled. My pulse started to race. My hands were sweating.

"Oops," A deep unapologetic voice said. He sounded amused with himself, actually. I heard the sound of a zipper closing. I was going to be sick. I felt it coming up and almost couldn't stop it. I held my breath and placed my hand over my mouth. I heard the sound of their retreating footsteps, followed by the squealing of the fence as it slid open.

The second I heard the gate close, I opened the driver's side door of the truck, leaned out from under the steering wheel, and vomited violently onto the pavement. My body convulsed long after there was nothing left in my stomach to expel. I wiped my mouth with the back of my hand.

Fuck my parents, and who I am because of them, I thought.

"Don't move, motherfucker," a deep voice growled, followed by the unmistakable sound of a gun cocking. It sent chills down my spine and the hairs on my neck stood at attention. My heart stopped. I didn't dare breathe.

With my head still down toward the pavement, I could only see black leather boots and dark jeans. I didn't look up. I didn't want this guy to think I could identify him. Those were the moments when shit usually went bad in scenarios like this, I told myself. He pressed the gun to the back of my head. I could feel the cool metal even through my hood.

I closed my eyes and prepared for the end.

For a moment, there was nothing but silence.

Finally, he spoke again. "Who the *fuck* are you?" His voice was menacing.

I didn't know how to respond to him. Nothing I thought of seemed like the right thing to say to a crazed man with a gun.

"Who sent you, motherfucker?" He forcefully nudged my head down with the gun until my forehead almost touched the pavement. I don't think he was used to being ignored. Maybe, this was the way it was supposed to end. My life had always been a fight, a struggle. Maybe, I was supposed to meet my end in a junkyard without anyone left to care where I was. Maybe, I was just fighting the inevitable by even trying to stay alive.

I remained silent and left my fate to chance.

"Okay. You want to play it that way?" He yanked me forward by my hood and sent me crashing to my knees on the pavement. I barely missed the puddle of my own vomit. He stood behind me and ripped the hood off my head, taking a handful of hair with him. The tearing sensation from my scalp caused me to cry out. He stilled for a moment before coming around to kneel in front of me. His gun was still pointed at my head, but he wasn't looking at me, he was staring at the clump of red hair he was clutching in his other hand.

When he looked up from the hair in his hand, his jaw dropped open. Our eyes met, and even in the poor light from the motion sensors, his eyes were the most brilliant shade of blue I'd ever seen.

Something deep inside me, something I thought to have been nonexistent, stirred.

He wasn't much older than me, maybe just a few years. He

was dressed in a tight black t-shirt and dark jeans. The leather jacket he wore during his earlier activities against the truck was gone. His sandy blonde hair lay in contrast to all the darkness, grown just long enough to keep tucked behind his ears. His blonde goatee and eyebrows matched. Black and grey tattoos, designs I couldn't make out, started on top of his right hand and ran upward, covering his entire arm, disappearing under his t-shirt, emerging again out of his collar, stopping at the base of his neck.

When he spoke, the aggression from seconds before was gone. "You?" he asked in a whisper, which quickly turned to a frustrated shout. "What the fuck? I could have killed you!" The gun wasn't pointed at me anymore. It was resting in his hands instead, like it was an accessory, as unthreatening as if he were holding his keys.

"I know," I muttered. Part of me hoped he would have killed me. I stood up and brushed the hair from my eyes. The blonde stranger looked confused. He scratched at his goatee.

"What the fuck are you doing here?" he asked as he tucked the gun into the back waistband of his jeans.

"Nothing. I'm not doing anything," I said. I reached into the truck, grabbed my backpack from the seat, and started walking toward the fence. The blonde stranger kept pace beside me, eyeing the truck and then my bag.

"Are you…are you *living* here?" he asked. Now, he was just getting on my nerves. I didn't know this guy. He had no right to ask about my business, gun or no gun. "Answer me. What are you doing here?" He grabbed my shoulders and turned me to him.

Even with the layer of clothing in between us, my skin started to burn instantly. I shrugged out of his grip *"Let me go!"* I screamed. When he recognized the panic in my eyes, he did just that.

"Just tell me why you're here," he said, in a softer, less demanding tone. He smelled like leather and wind, and he kept rubbing his hand over his facial hair. I wondered if he always did that when he was trying to figure something out.

"Why are *you* here?" I asked, turning the tables on him. The best way to not answer a question was to ask one.

"This is my dad's yard, and I'm in town running the shop out front for a while. I'm staying in the attached apartment, so technically, I *live* here." He tucked his hands in his pockets the way any boy at my high school would do. He couldn't have been more than twenty-three, but when his face was set in that hard expression, with his forehead creased and his lips set in a straight line, he looked much older.

"Shit," I said. I was hoping he was trespassing just like me. Instead, I'd been caught—and by the fucking owner's son no less.

I needed to get the fuck out of there.

I side-stepped him, to the left and then to the right, and he finally let me pass. I ran for the gate and tried to pry it open as fast as possible, but it was at least twelve feet high and extremely heavy. This was the reason I had cut the hole in the fence to begin with. I heaved and heaved until finally it gave way. Then I turned and found the stranger who, just moments ago, held a gun to my temple, was now helping me open the gate.

"You didn't think you were that strong, did you?" A smirk played on his lips.

"Thanks," I muttered as I stepped through the gate and hurried down the road.

"Hey, wait," he called. I froze. I thought he was going to tell me he was calling the cops or his father, or someone who would end up sending me back into the devil's lair of foster care. Instead, he asked, "What's your name?"

"What's yours?"

He hesitated. "Jake," he finally said. He leaned up against the gate on one arm, crossing his legs at the ankles. I barely noticed I was biting my lower lip. I stopped when I realized I was openly gawking at him. He would be one hell of a good looking guy... for anyone who might like the creepy, angry, violent type.

I don't know what compelled me to tell him my name. For all I knew, he'd use it to file the police report. "Abby," I said as I turned again to walk away.

"Hey, Abby?" he called to me. "Next time just come through the gate. Or better yet, knock on the door." He nodded toward the main building, and then gestured to a small garbage can where the hole I made in the fence was hidden behind it. "No more cuttin' holes, okay?"

Holy shit.

Just when I thought I could finally walk away, he had to add one more thing. "If I'd known you were sneaking in for the show, I would have made sure you had a better seat." He raised his eyebrows suggestively and smiled. I felt the redness creep up from my neck to my cheeks. He started to slide the gate shut. I turned and ran before he had it closed, hiding the evidence of my embarrassment.

I'd never been so irritated, disgusted and intrigued by someone in all my life—and I've met a lot of warped motherfuckers. It was the intrigued part that had me worried the most.

Things would have been so much easier if he'd just shot me.

Chapter Five

THE FIRST THING I noticed when I got home was the junk, a huge pile of debris collected up in the center of the small gravel driveway. My heart fell into my stomach when the realization washed over me that it wasn't junk. It was *our* lives.

Mine and Nan's.

Our clothes, our furniture, all of our pictures and memories had been mangled and thrown into a huge heap. I climbed up the pile and knelt down in the center, running my hands over the matted red hair of Nan's favorite collectable doll she called Daphne. Nan used to tell me the doll reminded her of me. I thought it was just because of the red hair, until one day she told me otherwise.

"It's because she's resilient," she had said. "That doll has been through two house fires, one front yard burial by wayward dog, and an accidental toilet bowl drowning." She leaned across the counter on her elbows and whispered, "She was saved. All Daphne needed was a little sprucing up and a good dose of love. Every single time, she would come out okay, sometimes even better than she was before." I may have been only thirteen, but I knew she hadn't been talking about the doll anymore.

In Nan's own way, she was trying to explain to a thirteen year-old kid that even though life hands you a big pile of shit, you don't have to roll around in it and make shit angels.

My version of her logic.

I climbed down the mound, still clutching Daphne in my hands. As I approached the front porch, I spotted a very official-looking bright green paper with bold lettering tacked to the screen door. I couldn't make out the words until I was right on top of it. The paper shouted:

**THIS PREMISES HAS BEEN EVICTED BY THE
CALOOSA COUNTY SHERIFF'S OFFICE UNDER THE
AUTHORITY OF COURT ORDER IN REGARDS TO THE
FORECLOSURE OF
4339 PINEPASS ROAD
Case #4320951212102013
First Bank of Coral Pines vs. Georgianne Margaret Ford
ENTRANCE BY ANYONE WITHOUT EXPRESS
PERMISSION FROM
THE CALOOSA COUNTY SHERIFF OR THE OWNERS:
FIRST BANK OF CORAL PINES
WILL BE REMOVED AND PROSECUTED
BY THE PROPER AUTHORITY
SIGNED: SHERIFF COLE FLETCHER
Special Notes: LOCKS HAVE BEEN CHANGED**

I ripped the eviction notice from the door and sat down on the rickety wooden steps of the porch. They creaked and groaned under my every move, making me feel as unwelcome as the paper I clutched. I turned it over and over, hoping to see a "gotcha", or some other punch line—maybe even a loophole that would make it all go away.

There weren't any.

This one little piece of highlighter green paper just determined everything, and that everything, was that I had nothing.

Why hadn't Nan told me she was losing her house? I could have helped. I would have quit school and gotten a job.

I'd just answered my own fucking question.

Of *course* she didn't tell me. She wanted me to graduate. She said it all the time, every day if she could squeeze it in. It was like the woman had a one-track mind. "Do you want pie—graduate from high school."

"The sun is sure beating down today—graduate from high school."

"I sure miss your Popop—graduate from high school."

I think Nan believed that as long as I had a high school diploma my life would somehow end up okay.

With the letter of doom in one hand and the Daphne doll in the other, Nan's obsession with me graduating from high school was laughable, in a sad, twisted kind of way.

Nan had gotten her wish. I had graduated and received my high school diploma.

I know she couldn't ever have imagined I wouldn't have anywhere to hang it.

I WENT AROUND back and grabbed a blue tarp from the toolbox on the dock and draped it over the mound on the driveway in case of rain. As I finished covering the contents of mine and Nan's life together, Sheriff Fletcher pulled up along the road in his police cruiser. He didn't bother getting out. I'd have sworn if someone were murdered, he'd probably have just snapped a picture of the crime scene with his phone without so much as stopping the car on his way to Bubba's.

Sheriff Fletcher rolled down his window. "Thanks for the heads up," I spat at him. After all, it was his official signature gracing the bottom of the eviction notice.

"Darlin', we don't get no advance notice on these things. They're sent to us from the state with orders to carry out the eviction on the same day. I didn't know until yesterday morning it was your Nan's house we was guttin' up." He paused. "It's not like I could've gotten a hold of you anyway. Seems you up and disappeared on us." Gruff and unapologetic. Same as every other day.

"I assume by that comment that Dan has stopped by to see you?" I asked as I finished tucking the tarp under the bottom of the mound in case the rain decided it wanted to seep through the sides.

"Who?"

"Miss Thornton," I clarified.

"Oh yeah. Told her the truth, that I didn't know where you was. She'll be back soon, though, so you might want to figure out what your plan is." Sheriff Fletcher offered no assistance, but he also didn't haul me back to Miss Thornton. For that, I was grateful.

"I'll have Owen help you move some of that shit." He grumbled, waving to the crap in the driveway. He pulled out his cell phone and mumbled into the receiver before clicking it shut. He put the cruiser in drive, but before the car moved three feet he stopped again and leaned out the window. "You got any green on ya?" he asked, not bothering to look around to see who might hear him.

"Sorry, that whole keeping myself fed and sheltered thing has really been a drag these past few weeks." I may have been grateful, but I sure as shit wasn't sharing the last of my weed with him.

The sheriff rolled his eyes and waved his hand dismissively. "See you 'round, kid," he muttered. Then he was gone.

A half-hour later, I was lying on the small patch of grass you could hardly call a front lawn, my legs crossed at the ankles, dreaming of a time not long ago when Nan had first taken me in. We were sitting in the living room, and she was working on her knitting.

"What are your dreams, Abby?" Nan asked. When she saw how confused I was, she clarified the question. "What do you want to be when you grow up?" I'd never been asked that before, so naturally I'd never thought about the answer. I'd thought a lot about running away, but my dreams for my life had never gone beyond getting away from my parents, then from foster care, then from the memories that plagued me. I never dreamed about what I'd do afterward.

Getting away had become my everything.

My dreams were of being left alone.

When I didn't answer Nan, she said, "Any answer is a good answer, Abby."

I told her the first thing that came to my bitter mind. "Dad always said I wasn't good for nothin' so I guess that's what I'm gonna do: nothin'." Hope had been stripped from me at every minute of every hour of every day for my entire life.

Nan had tried to give it back to me.

She shook her head. "No honey, your Daddy was a sick man. He didn't know what he was sayin'. You're a beautiful young lady, and you can do whatever you want when you grow up. You can be a singer, a dancer, a doctor, a lawyer—even the president." I thought she was lying to me. I got angry. Why would she tell me I could be anything when we both knew it wasn't true?

I was so full of rage. I remember sweeping my arm across the kitchen table, sending the glass vase in the center crashing to the floor in one quick motion. It shattered around my legs, the shards cutting into my feet and toes.

"You don't gotta lie to me!" I screamed, and I continued screaming until my throat was raw. Nan tried to wrap me up in a hug, and I just got louder. Her touch burned my skin. But, Nan didn't know about the burning then.

She didn't know she was hurting me.

I'd struggled against Nan, but I was so much smaller than she was. She wrestled me to the ground while whispering her brand of loving reassurance in my ear. How much she loved me. How much she believed in me. "You can do anything, baby girl. I promise, I will never lie to you. You are bright and beautiful and resilient. You can do *anything*." She repeated those words until my muscles relaxed and I fell asleep in her arms on the kitchen floor. The fire in me hadn't died.

I had just given in to the flames.

It was my first and only hug.

Ever.

It was the first time I'd ever felt loved, or even worthy of love. I was both elated and frightened by the intensity of it all. I had wondered how people with more than one person to love walked around all day without falling over from the weight of their emotions.

That very day I had fallen in love with my grandmother.

"Abby? You dead?" A voice asked, casting a shadow over me, bringing me out of my daydream and back into the present. I kept my eyes closed.

"Yes," I said. "I'm dead." I might as well have been.

"Well, you look awfully cute for a dead girl."

"Thanks, Owen." I sat up, shading my eyes with my hands. The afternoon sun peaked around Owen, framing him in a full-body halo.

"What're you doing down there?" Owen asked.

"Nothing that matters," I answered. "What are *you* doing here?"

Owen stared down at me with the same grin he always had plastered on his face. I swear his cheeks must hurt at the end of the day. "Uncle Cole called and asked if I could come give you a hand with your…" He looked over to the tarp. "Crap?"

"Owen, I would love for you to help me. There's a huge problem, though, one your kind uncle didn't think much of before carrying out the eviction." I was starting to shout. Owen didn't deserve my wrath, but I couldn't help what was coming out.

"And what problem is that?"

"I don't have anywhere to *take it*!" I threw my arms up in defeat before hanging my head between my knees.

Owen sat down next to me. "Well," he said, lighting a cigarette, "as I see it you have two options." He took a drag and turned his head to the side to blow the smoke away from me.

"And what might those be?" I asked, talking from between my knees.

"You could either sit around here and have a first class pity party for yourself *or* you could come and have some drinks tonight at the woods party with me and think about all this—" he motioned to the tarp and the boards on the windows "—tomorrow. Seems like you got it all waterproofed and whatnot, so what's one night? Besides, you look like you could use a little time to forget."

"That's probably not the best idea, Owen." It was an awful idea, actually. I hadn't avoided being social my entire life for the fun of it, or because I *thought* I didn't belong. I avoided them because I *knew* I didn't belong. Not only in the town, not only with the kids from my high school.

I didn't belong anywhere.

"Well, what else you gonna do? Stare at this shit all night until it magically does something different other than be a pile of shit?"

Would it be so bad to pretend for one night I wasn't the punch line in some universal joke being told at my expense?

"Fine," I said, giving in. I could think about all this later. I mean, what were my other options anyway?

Did I even have any?

"Well come on, then!" Owen looked like a kid on Christmas morning as he hustled over to his truck and opened the passenger door for me. I stood and brushed the grass from my legs. This time, Owen didn't offer to help me up. He knew I could do it on my own. And he wasn't looking for an excuse to touch me, which made me feel better about hanging out with him.

I'd use the night out the same way I'd been using Nan's scotch, as a way to forget, a way to slip into a state of numbness, even if it was just for a little while.

Maybe, it wouldn't be so bad after all?

SMOKE ROSE FROM the fire in the center of the clearing, hissing like snakes being charmed. It crackled and popped, growing larger and reaching further into the night sky. A shorter boy wearing a white cowboy hat stood just outside the flames, feeding it dried brush and branches. Trucks of all makes and models formed a wagon-wheel, parked with their tailgates facing inward toward the fire. One of the larger trucks held a keg and a huge bag of red Solo cups, while another had all its windows down and was blaring country music from one of the local stations. Groups of girls or couples with their arms around one another occupied most of the tailgates. A group of guys gathered by the keg, talking loudly about truck tires and challenging each other to a game of 'who can drink more'.

Why on earth did I agree to come here? I thought. I tugged on the long sleeves of my hoodie, pulling them over my wrists. It was a nervous habit. Owen must have been reading my mind, because he stepped away from his man-groupies by the keg and came over to where I sat on the open tailgate of his truck.

"You look like you could use a beer," he said, offering me a cup.

I took it from him and downed most of it in one gulp.

I was going to need much, much more.

"Thanks," I said. I gave him my best fake smile. Careful not to spill his own beer, Owen hopped up onto the tailgate in one fluid motion, taking a seat next to me. "You don't have to be afraid of these folks, you know. Most of them you've gone to school with for a long time." He tried to playfully nudge me with his elbow, but I dodged the contact.

I looked around the fire at the people I had known for years, but really didn't know at all. Each time I made eye contact with a new person it was met with sneers and whispers.

I held my empty cup out to Owen. "Maybe, I'm just not a group person," I offered. Or maybe I had nothing in common with these people besides a zip code—although considering I'd just become homeless, I was without a zip code, too. Technically, we didn't share shit anymore.

I needed more beer.

Being drunk was the only way I wasn't going to scratch the skin off my face from being so damned uncomfortable, surrounded by all of *them*. Owen happily obliged and kept the beer flowing all night.

A few hours later and too many beers to count, couples started pairing off and disappearing into the woods. Trucks, which just hours ago brought in fresh-faced kids ready to party, now left with the disheveled remnants of those same kids. Limp, passed-out bodies tangled together in the cabs and beds.

There were only a few handfuls of party-goers left. I sat on a log swaying to the music being played on a guitar by a younger kid named Will. I'd spent the last couple hours listening to him play while trying to stump him with my requests. Whether I asked him to play Garth Brooks or Offspring, he just laughed and started playing. I think he was as amused as I was.

Owen came over to me frequently, keeping my beer cup full. But, he spent most of his time chatting with his friends on the other side of the fire. None of them had bothered to say a word to me, but every so often, I would catch Owen staring at me through the flames.

When I felt the space on the log next to me shift, I assumed Owen had come back and brought me round number...I lost count. "Thanks," I said, reaching out to take my cup from him without taking my eyes off Will. He was on the second chorus of "Criminal" by Fiona Apple. The kid should've tried out for one of those TV talent shows.

"You're welcome." The voice wasn't Owen's. A shiver of recognition crept up my spine. When I turned around, I came face to face with the beautiful blue-eyed psychopath from the junkyard.

Had I just thought of him as being beautiful?

Yep.

Jake was still dressed in head-to-toe black, in a tight t-shirt and jeans. He wasn't wearing his leather jacket. His tattoos seemed to glisten under the light of the moon. As opposed to the moment when he was threatening my life, he looked much more relaxed this time around. Maybe, it was an illusion resulting from the firelight casting shadows on his face. No, it wasn't the fire, I realized.

He really was beautiful.

He pushed his hair behind his ears and ran a hand down his goatee. "Hi, Abby," he said, like we were old friends.

What was I supposed to say to this guy? He'd caught me sleeping in his dad's junkyard. He'd held a gun to my head. *Hey how 'bout dem Jets*, didn't exactly feel like the way to start the conversation either.

My stomach flip-flopped as if I were falling.

I straightened my shoulders and pushed away the thoughts I was having about his looks and the circumstances under which we met. "You packing tonight?" I asked him. I turned back around and pretended to focus my attentions back on Will, who was just starting on the first notes of Colt Ford's, "Riding Through The Country".

Then, I hiccuped.

I felt the redness of my embarrassment creeping up my cheeks. I couldn't look back at him. I could hear him laughing, and not just a giggle, but very full, very deep laugh. He slid in closer, his lips a breath away from my ear when he whispered, "I'm always packing, Bee." His tone turned very serious. The way he'd said my name caused the hairs on my neck to stand at attention.

Did he just call me Bee?

"Jake! You made it!" A girl wearing tight jeans and a scrap of a tank top ran up to Jake and threw herself into his lap.

"Alissa," he said sternly, "I'm talking with Abby. Go wait with Jessica 'til I'm done." He wasn't angry, but his tone was firm. He made it clear that he was having a conversation with me, and the bimbo wasn't invited.

Alissa looked me up and down and with disapproving eyes. She scrunched up her nose. "Why are you wasting your time with her, Jake? She ain't nothin' but a freak 'round here. Did you know that no one has ever seen her wear nothin' but sweatshirts and long sleeves—even on them hotter than hell days?" She glared at me, and I glared back. "Yeah, she's hiding something under there all right. It might be a hump or something. Stacey says she hides pregnancies and sells the babies on eBay. Personally, I think maybe she's got scales or something under there. Or something even more hideous."

She was getting closer, in both idea and distance.

Alissa reached over and punctuated her comment by lifting up the hem of my hoodie, exaggerating her movements to peer under it. I yanked it back down before she or anyone else could see anything. I grabbed her wrist and squeezed until she released my shirt, ignoring the fire building in my palm as I crushed her in my grasp.

She gasped and stared at me in wide-eyed shock.

"What was that Alissa?" I asked her.

She tried to wriggle out of my grip, but one thing I'd learned in my life was that hatred and adrenaline make people much stronger then they look. She may have been taller than me and outweighed me by at least twenty pounds, but at full boil, I could take her down with just a few blows.

Lucky for her, I was only on a simmer.

"Did you say something about the clothes I wear, bitch? Because honestly, I'd much rather be known as the girl who wears sweatshirts than the vagina most likely to be recognized in a line up." People had gathered around to watch us. I didn't care. "Did you ever stop to think that it might be whores like you who put every nasty bit of their ugly shit out on display for the world to see that disgust me so much I feel the need to cover myself up so I don't wind up single, with seven kids, barhopping every night when I'm well into my sixties?" I gave her a sweet fake smile. "Oh wait, I forgot to ask you: how are your grand-mama and mama doing these days?" Her glare became even more evil. I pulled on her wrist, and when she tugged back, I released her, sending her falling to the dirt floor, flat on her ass. The crowd laughed as she jumped to her feet, looking mortified.

"You're such a fucking freak! Jake!" She held out her hand to him. "Let's fucking go!"

Jake didn't move. He didn't even look at her. His gaze was fixed on me. "I told you I would come find you when I was done talking to Abby," he said calmly.

Alissa stormed off in a huff, muttering under her breath, but I wasn't paying attention. I was focused on Jake and his reaction to what just happened. He'd remained eerily calm and relaxed during my scuffle with Alissa, while I could practically feel that most people in the crowd had instantly tensed. When you don't want to be touched, you learn to read body language. I was pretty good at judging if a look of pity was going to turn into an attempted hug or if an angry conversation was going to turn into flying fists.

"Impressive." Jake pulled a joint from his pocket and lit up. "You want?" he asked, after taking a hit then offering it to me. I took a few slow, deep hits before passing it back. Alissa had set me back to sober, and I was out to correct that immediately.

Movement in the corner of my eye brought my attentions to where Owen stood by his truck. His friend Andy was talking to him excitedly, making wild gestures with his hands, obviously telling Owen a story of some sort, but Owen didn't seem to be paying attention. Instead, he was looking right over Andy's shoulders in my direction. It wasn't me he was looking at this time. It was Jake. And he wasn't just looking at him. He was *glaring* at him. Owen raised his shoulders as if to ask me if I was okay. I figured he hadn't seen what had gone down with Alissa. I nodded to him, and he focused his attention back on Andy.

"You with him?" Jake asked.

"He invited me. You know Owen?"

"Sort of." He took another hit from the joint and slowly released the smoke in little rings.

"Impressive."

He laughed. "So Abby, is not turning into a whore the real reason you wear sweatshirts in the summer?" It was none of his business, but he wasn't asking in a way that was making fun of me. He seemed curious.

"Not really. I'm also deathly afraid of herpes and the clap. Stand too close to some of these girls, and that shit'll just jump off them and on to you," I joked.

Jake flashed a smile that reached all the way to his eyes. "I'll keep that in mind."

"So you with that crazy bitch that just tried to undress me in public?" I asked. Why was I asking? Why did I care?

"Alissa," he said. "Nah. I went to high school with her, is all."

"You guys are *friends*, then?"

"Something like that." Jake smiled.

Bingo.

And gross.

Alissa had probably been the girl on her knees for him in the junkyard. I tried not to think about it: the choking, the spitting.

It was too fucking repulsive. I shivered.

"You're in my seat, Dunn." Owen seethed as he approached us. His forehead was lined, his brows knitted together.

"Free country, Fletcher," Jake said, taking another hit of his joint. "Find your own fucking seat."

"You know him, Abby?" Owen asked me.

"Not really," I said. "We're just sort of chatting."

"You don't want to *chat* with the likes of him," Owen said. "He may be from around here, but he ain't like us."

"That makes two of us," I said quietly, as I downed the last of my beer.

"What was that?" Owen asked.

"Nothing." I stood up. "Nothing at all." I swayed. It took me a second or two to find my footing. Again, I hiccupped.

Oh, great.

Jake stood and turned to me like he was going to help me steady myself. I made sure to put distance between us. Owen held out another red cup.

"I think she had enough, man," Jake said. Their gazes locked. I swore I could see a heat wave of anger rising between them.

Owen put the cup in my hand despite Jake's warning.

The two men stared down each one another like cage fighters preparing for a match. They were both about the same height, but Jake was blonde with light features and dressed like a member of Hell's Angels, while Owen's dark hair and green eyes stood in contrast to his All-American jeans-and-white t-shirt style.

Just as I thought they would pummel each other, another wayward hiccup escaped my mouth. I suddenly felt as if I would be sick. I leaned over the log and almost fell, but I steadied myself before anyone tried to help me. "I see those drinks are working," Owen said.

"Nope. Not working."

"How are they not working?" Owen asked. Jake wasn't touching me, but I could almost feel his presence beside me.

"I still remember how much my life sucks." It was an honest answer, but one I wouldn't have given nine beers or so earlier.

"Then, let's get you some more," Owen offered, gesturing to his truck. The lightness was back in his voice. The tension from a second ago was gone.

"Don't you think you've had enough, Abby?" Jake chimed in. Alissa appeared from behind him and wrapped her arms around his waist. She peeked out past his shoulder. She looked scared, as she should have been. I had half a mind to throw her into the fire. Jake unwrapped her arms, separating himself from her. She looked offended, but he didn't seem to care. He took a step toward me.

Owen started to say something, but I interrupted him. I didn't need him to answer my questions for me. "Nope. Not nearly enough," I answered. I tried not to slur, but I was pretty sure I had.

The look on Jake's face looked a lot like concern. For me? I chalked that one up to the alcohol. There was no way the same man—the *stranger*—who'd pulled a gun on me less than 24 hours ago was in any way concerned for my well-being. "You and *Alissa* have fun, okay?" I may have placed too much emphasis on her name, as if it tasted bitter in my mouth. He paused to look into my eyes for what felt like hours before looking from me to Owen. Finally, he shrugged and started walking away. Alissa trailed behind him like a lost puppy. "And Jake?" I called out. He stopped in his tracks and looked over his shoulder. "Give the girl a warning next time, okay?" I didn't stay for his reaction but laughed myself silly all the way back to Owen's truck.

"What was that all about?" Owen asked. I pretended not to hear him. I decided I'd actually had enough to drink after all, so instead I took my last joint from my back pocket and asked Owen to borrow his lighter. As soon as the smoke filled my lungs, I started to feel better. I held it there good and long before offering Owen a hit. We sat in the cab of the truck for a while with the windows rolled up, letting the high take over, and becoming mesmerized by the lyrics of the Tyler Farr song on the radio. When the joint was spent and the crowd had thinned to only a few people, Owen turned on the engine, and we headed down the trail that led out of the woods.

I was drunk, I was high, and I was pretty sure I couldn't remember my own name.

Mission accomplished.

Chapter Six

I MUST HAVE fallen asleep in the truck because the next thing I knew, we were pulling into the driveway at Owen's house. At first, I was stunned. I'd made it a rule that I'd never fall asleep unless I was alone. It was a little after three in the morning. I was becoming quite the night owl.

"Thanks for tonight, Owen. It was…interesting."

"How do you know Jake?" Owen asked, cutting the engine, his mouth set in a hard line, his eyes accusing and cold. He rolled down the window and lit a cigarette.

"I don't." It was the truth. I had no idea who Jake really was.

"Then, how did he know your name, Abby?" His voice was getting louder. His eyes were red and blood shot. An open bottle of Jameson sat in the cup holder of the center console; his fist was wrapped around the neck. He took a swig and set it back down, wiping his mouth with the back of his hand.

"I don't like your tone, Owen. I don't fucking know him. I saw him ride into town and he almost blew me off the road. That's all. Alissa must have told him my name or called me by it in front of him." I didn't mention sleeping in his junkyard. I don't know why I was lying, but Owen's current state and attitude didn't warrant the truth. "Does it fucking matter?"

"Yes, it fucking matters! I don't want you talking to him!"

I didn't need his shit. I reached for the handle and pulled the door open. I hopped down from the truck and started toward the street.

"Abby! Abby!" Owen yelled. He jumped out of the truck, too, catching up to me in just a few strides. He made a move like he was going to hug me or restrain me somehow, but I stepped back before he could.

"Don't touch me, Owen. I'm fucking serious."

We were standing under the only street light on that side of the bridge, positioned right in front of the Fletchers' house, which goes to show how much pull Owen's family had in Coral Pines. "I am so sorry, Abby. I'm an idiot. I know I shouldn't have told you what to do. Will you please, please forgive me?" His voice sounded strained, like it was difficult for him to apologize. "I just see the way he looks at you, and I don't want other guys looking at you that way."

"What are you talking about, Owen? I don't even know Jake, and you and I are just friends. That's all." If even that, I thought. "So, you shouldn't care who looks at me, because I'm not into that kind of shit—not with you, not with anyone."

"Okay, okay. I get it. I'm sorry. It's just that…he's not a good person, and the way he looked at you was making me crazy."

How was he looking at me?

"You're forgiven, Owen." I turned to leave again. "But, I gotta go."

"Where you gonna go, Abby?"

I opened my mouth to give an answer, but nothing came out.

"Stay here tonight. I have my own part of the house with my own entrance and everything. No one will even know you're here. I'll even sleep on the couch and give you the bed. Please?" Owen made sad eyes and stuck out a pouty lower lip.

I laughed.

What did he want with me anyway? I wasn't from his side of the tracks. I was a girl who couldn't even tell you what city my side of the tracks ran through. The Fletchers' garage alone was bigger than any house I'd ever lived in.

I really didn't want to sleep in Owen's room with him, just feet away from his family. But I had nowhere else to go. Jake had caught me in the junkyard, so sleeping in Nan's old truck was no longer an option.

I sighed, defeated.

"Okay, but just tonight," I said. He grinned like a Cheshire cat.

Owen really did have his own separate entrance. His room was more like a studio apartment, complete with its own mini-kitchen and living area. His house was huge, and it wasn't even the only one on the property. His entire family lived in four separate homes, on ten acres. The one that held his apartment was the main house, and the largest. It was three stories with white siding and red shutters. It was like *Little House on the Prairie* on steroids, more plantation than house. I was curious how it felt to be so close to family all the time, especially since I had none.

I pulled a pair of running shorts from my backpack and a lighter long sleeved t-shirt and changed in Owens bathroom. When I came out Owen was laying on his bed, wearing only his boxers, flipping channels on the TV, a bottle of beer at his lips. "Want one?" He lifted the bottle to me.

I ignored his offer. "I thought I got the bed?"

"I thought we could watch some TV first. I'm not really tired yet and the view from the couch is lousy." The goofy grin on his face made me hesitate for a second before giving in. There was no trace of the anger he displayed in the truck, just good ol' happy Owen. The Owen I had started to like. And I really needed some time to just sit and watch a little mindless TV.

"Fine, but no funny business," I said sternly, "and I get to pick the show."

"Yes ma'am." Owen saluted me. "Scouts honor."

I jumped in his big comfy bed and scooted under the covers. Just as I was about to put my head on the pillow, Owen lifted his elbow and gestured to the crook of his arm. "Snuggling is always nice while watching TV," he said. I looked up at him with a crooked eyebrow and he crossed his eyes at me.

"You really are goofy, you know that?" I said. "I'll take a pass on the snuggling." We were just sort-of friends, after all, and friends watch TV in bed, I figured. I really didn't know what the guideline was when you were friends with a boy, but before I could finish my thoughts—and before Owen had a chance argue with me about what show to watch—I had already fallen asleep.

I AM NINE years old and it's the middle of the night. I am lying on my mattress on the floor of my old room. My window sounds like it's about to shatter under the heavy pounding of the wind and rain. My pillow is smashed against my ear so I can't hear the thunder crashing or see the lightning that lights up my room every few seconds. It must be why I don't hear the squeal of my bedroom door when he enters.

I am holding on tightly to the only toy I've ever had, my stuffed squirrel Ziggy. Ziggy is a dog's chew toy left at our house by one of my many "uncles".

"Are you a virgin?" a voice asks from above me, hot breath in my ear. "If you are, I'll try to go slow at first. But, if you're not, I'm not gonna lie: I don't want to be gentle with you at all." The

mattress dips deep as the weight of someone heavy lays down behind me on the tiny twin bed. I feel his sharp chest hair poking at the skin on my neck and his enormous protruding belly smashing up against my back. I squeeze my eyes shut as hard as I can, hoping he will leave if he thinks I am asleep.

I know he won't.

I clutch the doll in one arm. I feel around under my pillow for the shard of mirror that just hours ago was used by my mother to chop up white powder before she sniffed it into her nose through a rolled-up dollar bill.

This man, the one with the hairy chest and protruding belly, had been introduced to me as "Uncle Sal" earlier in the day. He is the one who had brought my mom the bag of white powder.

Mom had no money. She screamed about it all the time, and my father was in prison. I am nine, not stupid.

I am payment.

The man reaches out and runs his swollen hairy knuckles down my arm from my bare shoulder to my elbow and back again. My stomach just about bubbles over. I resist the urge to purge what little dinner I had managed to find. I have to hold on for just a few more minutes. I have to bide my time.

He moves his hand to my waist and over to my stomach pulling me around to lay flat on my back.

The time is now.

I pull the mirror out from under my pillow, and as he pushes me down flat onto the mattress, and while his attentions are upon my naked body, I aim for his left eye, hard and fast, and don't stop pushing in until my hand meets resistance.

Thunder muffles his screams. He coughs and produces a red spatter on the white wall, choking on the blood spilling into his mouth. He clutches what is left of his eye as he falls over on his knees to the floor.

I run from the room, still holding my squirrel, and then out the front door and into the awaiting storm. Why was I ever afraid of the storm? Out here it is just wind and rain, the real storm is back in that house, a house I vow right then and there I will never see the inside of ever again.

I run until I reach the vacant field at the end of the street. I no longer care that I am naked. I no longer care about anything. I stand in the middle of that field and raise my arms up to the storm, giving myself over to it. The cold rain rinses the blood from my body, and I pray that the blowing winds will take me away.

Now, I am no longer a nine year old girl, but my seventeen-year-old self. Still naked in the middle of the field, still asking to be taken from this life.

The wind responds by carrying me up in its embrace, and in an instant I float out of this life and out of this world.

"Are you a virgin?" a voice asks. "Because I don't want to have to be gentle with you."

Fear assaults me at first, the pounding in my chest so hard it turns painful, but then I realize that although the words are similar, the voice is not. This one is much younger, less weathered, although it sounds strained.

The wind dies down quickly, suddenly dropping me from its embrace. I start to fall, slow at first then faster and faster as I plummet back toward the earth.

Right before I crash into the very field where I was rescued by the storm, I see a face appear.

Jake.

What is he doing here? Just as quickly as his face appears, it disappears.

An eerie calm washes over me.

The hurt is gone, and I feel... good.

Too good.

I DIDN'T WAKE up right away. I let the unfamiliar good feeling take over for a minute or two. But as the pulling sensation intensified in my lower stomach, a familiar burning started to replace it. As the heat grew, I was coaxed further and further out of my dream…and smack dab into a cluster-fuck of a situation.

I was surprised to see Owen—or feel him, rather. He was on top of me, supporting most of his weight on his elbows, which were caging me in, resting on the mattress on either side of my head. My knees were spread apart. Owen's hips were grinding against mine. White-hot anger flashed behind my eyes. A quick mental inventory told me that I was still fully clothed, my shirt still firmly in place, and thankfully Owen still had his boxers on. He ran his mouth up and down my neck from my ear to my collarbone, nipping and sucking at my skin.

The true cause of the new sensations pooling deep in my belly had been the result of Owen rubbing the hardness between his legs against the most sensitive part of my body, just under the thin fabric of my shorts.

Owen whispered in my ear, "You have no idea how much I want you Abby. I'm going to make you feel real good baby. Gonna make you scream my name real loud when you come." The friction between my legs caused the tension in my stomach to grow.

In the battle between pain and unwelcome pleasure, pain would always win.

Even in sleep, my body had been responding to his touch, while my mind…well, my mind was *pissed*. And my skin was on fire.

I used both of my hands to push hard on Owen's chest. He fell sideways onto the bed. "What the fuck, Owen?" I screamed.

I jumped from the bed and found my boots. I smashed my feet into them, then found my backpack and threw it over my shoulders. I raced for the door. Owen was behind me in an instant. He wrapped his arms around my waist, pulling me against him. I could feel his hardness against my back. My skin felt like it was going to blister off. I struggled to get free from his grip, but he held me tighter, digging his fingers into my shoulders. When he leaned down to press his lips to my neck, I took the opportunity to elbow him in the ribs.

"Fuck!" he yelped, releasing me and gripping his side. "You wanted it, you bitch. You were moaning like a goddamned whore!" Owen stood up straight and looked me in the eye. I carefully backed away, toward the door. The look from earlier was back now. His pupils were small and the whites of his eyes were tinted red, like he was straining for some sort of control. This was the Owen from the truck, the angry, jealous one. All traces of the helpful friend I was stupid enough to think I had were gone. This person was some sort of monster. There was no apology in his tone, no remorse for what he'd almost done.

"I was sleeping! You thought it was a good idea to try to fuck a drunk, high, *sleeping* girl!"

"No! I thought it was a good idea to fuck YOU and give you what I know you want—what we *both* want." He spat between his teeth and lunged for me as I opened the door, he caught me by the legs, and I fell forward, smashing my jaw on the threshold. I kicked my foot out of his grip and managed to right myself as I ran out the door. Owen reached out to me from behind, but I turned and slammed the door as hard as I could, smashing his hand in the process.

The motion lights turned on, illuminating the house and the grounds around it. I ran as fast as my legs would take me into the safety of the darkness.

"*Abby, you bitch!*" Owen wailed in the distance.

I reached down into my boot and grabbed my knife, then kept running down the road. If he decided to chase me, I was going to be ready for him.

I should never have agreed to stay with him. I tried to tell myself that he'd offered it because he wanted to genuinely help me out and be my friend. I should have listened to my instincts to stay away earlier when he was breathing fire because some other raging sociopath knew my name. It was odd that my thoughts even went to Jake, because something occurred to me in the moment after I fled Owen's house. I felt safer staring down the barrel of Jake's gun than I did looking into Owen's eyes.

It's amazing what poor judgment you can have when your options are limited to practically nothing.

Chapter Seven

I SLOWED TO a walk somewhere between the two-and-a-half mile span between the Fletcher family compound and the rest of the town. Clouds shut out the natural light from the moon and stars. Crickets chirped, and the occasional coyote howled. The shell road crunched beneath my boots.

My grand plan was to head back to Nan's, slit the screen on the back porch, and sleep there for the rest of the night. Morning wasn't too far away. I would have to come up with another plan by then. Going back into foster care wasn't an option. I would do something that would send me to prison, before I would allow them to put me back in the system.

I was pretty sure it was about four in the morning, and I estimated it would take at least an hour to get to Nan's, if not longer. It gave me plenty of time to berate myself over and over for making one bad decision after another.

The breeze helped to cool my skin, the fire died down with each step I took. I hated that Owen had touched me. I hated that my body responded without my consent.

I hated that I hadn't been able to reach my fucking knife.

Why was Owen even interested in me anyway? I wore baggy hoodies or long sleeved t-shirts. I never put on makeup. I didn't put myself out there like the other girls in this town. Up until very recently, I was blissfully invisible.

Until Owen.

I wasn't even given a choice in the matter, and what was worse was that my body liked it, wanted it even. "Fucking traitor," I whispered. The thing that really bothered me was that I had been coming around to Owen. He was sweet and nice when he wanted to be, and he wasn't too bad to look at, either. If he would've just given me time, then maybe…

No. Not even with time.

I just wasn't built that way. No amount of time would make me want something I detested so much.

Anyway, it seemed that my desires were apparently very limited to "narrowly being raped" because before that, I'd barely felt even a trickle of desire… except maybe for a certain blonde with a penchant for leather.

Great.

I wondered if there was a box to check for my neurosis on Match.com. I wouldn't know, it's not like I had a computer. Shit, maybe if Owen had really gone for it, I'd have had the time of my life. In my head, I was yelling at myself. If anything, the incident just proved that not only was I one fucked-up cookie, but I needed to build a bigger wall of defense.

One with cannons and guards with big guns.

Of course, it was the moment I was thinking about guns of all things that the floor beneath my feet started to quake, the loose shell rattled around my feet. A single bright light illuminated the night, temporarily blinding me as the motorcycle that was heading right toward me slowed to a stop beside me in the road.

Jake cut the engine and removed clear-lensed goggles from his eyes, but I kept walking. "Little late for a walk of shame, don't you think?"

"You have no idea," I said. I wanted to be offended by what he insinuated, but I wasn't blind to what this looked like: a disheveled mess of a teenaged girl walking home before dawn after attending a party. I would have thought the same thing.

In an instant, he was off his bike and keeping pace beside me. He pulled out a pack of cigarettes and lit one taking a deep drag.

"Why are you out and about? Are you doing the *ride* of shame, or did you have to pop a cap in someone's ass?" He held out the pack of cigarettes toward me. "No, thanks. I don't smoke." He raised a brow at me. "Cigarettes," I added. He opened his pack and pulled out a joint instead. Then, he lit it and handed it over to me.

What did this guy want?

"Why are you being nice to me?" I took the joint from him, careful not to touch his fingers. "If you feel bad about the gun thing, don't. I would have done the same thing if someone broke into my place."

"I'm not nice." Jake took another drag of his cigarette and gave me a small smile. It was the same way I saw him in my dream.

"But, you are being nice to me," I corrected him. He ignored me.

"You need a ride?" he asked. I stopped walking and took another hit from the joint. Jake stopped next to me. I held the smoke in as long as possible. "That kind of night?"

I just shrugged and let my high round off some of the sharp corners of the pain I'd experienced that evening.

"Town is a ways away, and on the off chance you don't get hit by a car you will probably be eaten by either wild boar, coyotes, or at the very least these fucking annoying pterodactyl mosquitoes."

"Well, aren't you the eternal optimist."

"Are you always this sarcastic?" he asked.

"Yes, but usually in my head. Around you, the words just seem to come faster and more…" I was trying to think of the word. "…wise-asser"

I took another hit and passed the joint to him. "Good word," Jake said. He stomped out his cigarette in the dirt and took a hit of the joint. "I guess I bring out the best in you then."

"Why do you carry a gun?"

"Dangerous people out there." He looked down at his feet.

"Like who?" I knew who was dangerous to me. The question was about who was dangerous to him.

"How about we save the twenty questions for another time, and you let me take you home so I am not responsible for your untimely death by rabid raccoon?"

"I thought it was mosquitoes that would be my undoing."

"That, too." His stiffness slowly faded away with the change in conversation.

"All right," I said. "Get me out of here, please." I bent down and scratched my thighs. The mosquitoes had already done some damage.

"This way, then." He gestured with a sweep of his arm, back to where he'd parked his bike.

The moon and the stars had just started to peek out from behind the clouds, finally shedding some much-needed light on the very dark night as we turned around and headed back to his bike.

"You are just going to take me home right?" I asked. After the events of the evening, I felt like I had to ask. Not that this guy would try anything with me, anyway. I was the girl he'd caught sleeping in his junkyard, after all.

When we reached his bike, he took the helmet off the seat

and handed it to me. "If you just want to go home, it's gonna really ruin my plans to dismember you and feed you to the town's people at the county fair," he joked.

"Just thought I'd clarify," I muttered. Jake reached for the strap under my helmet, and I flinched. "I can do it."

His eyes went wide. "Bee," he said slowly, "where the fuck did you get all that?" He pointed to the bruise and the scrapes I had gotten on my chin when Owen had lunged for me at the door.

"Dodgeball." It was none of his damn business. I must have been really tired by that point, because the most important thing about riding the bike seemed to have skipped past my thoughts altogether.

I'd have to hold onto him.

"Abby," Jake said, softly this time. He moved himself in front of me and looked into my eyes. "Who did this?"

"It's nothing. I'm fine," I answered. I tried to sound casual. "That's about as much as I want to tell you, and if you don't want to give me a ride anymore, that's okay." I took the helmet off my head and placed it back on his seat. "I'll take my chances with the mosquitoes." I started walking.

Things had been getting too close for me, anyway.

"Hey, wise-asser," he called out. "Get that wise-ass on the bike, and let's go." It was kind of a joke and kind of a demand, but I got the point. He wasn't going to pry anymore, but that didn't do anything to solve my other situation.

I pulled my sleeves down to cover my wrists and stared at Jake where he sat on the bike. He seemed to sense my hesitation. "You ever been on a bike before?" he asked.

I shook my head.

"Just get on behind me, one leg at a time, be careful not to have your legs touch the metal pipes at the bottom because they can burn." Little did he know I'd prefer the burn from the pipes than the burn of his touch.

"Where do I put my arms and legs?" I asked.

"You wrap them around me," he answered, like it was the simplest thing in the world to do. I suppose for most people, it was.

But, I wasn't most people, and it wasn't simple for me at all.

"Is there an alternative?" I asked.

"To what?" I was hoping he wasn't going to have to make me explain it. I didn't care if he thought I was odd. It was late. I was tired. And if Jake thinking I was a whack-job sped up this process, I really didn't give a shit.

"To putting my arms and legs around you," I answered. Jake looked like he was contemplating my question. He didn't ask me the reason for it. He didn't make fun of me for asking. He just looked like he was thinking, and that was all.

"When you get on, scoot as far back to this chrome piece as possible. He pointed to a chrome semi-circle attached to the back of the seat. Put your feet on the back of these stirrups here and hold your arms behind you, and grab on to the bottom of the seat. It may not be comfortable, but it'll work." Jake got off the bike. "If you get on first, it'll be easier." I did as he instructed, and I noticed that when he got back on he was riding close to the handlebars. There were a solid few inches of space separating us.

I sighed in relief.

"Thank you," I said. He may have been judging me on the inside, but I was grateful he didn't say anything to me about it. I didn't need anything to piss me off further. The night was as over as I wanted it to be.

One good thing did come out of the night after all. It turned out that riding on a motorcycle was my new favorite thing.

Like, ever.

The excitement of the roaring bike beneath me was a thrill I wasn't expecting. The wind ripped through my hoodie like it was no match for its power. It had been so long since I'd found enjoyment in anything that I was shocked when I heard my own voice shouting into the air. All my senses were still humming when the bike stopped just a few minutes later.

"That was amazing!" I shouted, ripping the helmet from my head, forgetting to be careful of the wound on my jaw. "Ouch." I rubbed the spot with my hand and placed the helmet back on the seat.

Jake laughed at my clumsiness, but was still looking at my jaw as though it had offended him in some way. "You've really never been on a bike before?"

I shook my head. It was then I noticed that he never asked me where I lived, and we certainly weren't at Nan's house.

We were at the beach.

"Okay, I know I said I would take you right home, but this is my favorite time of day, and I thought maybe you'd want to take a walk with me. Are you mad?" I was about to tell him that I was too tired for something like that when I realized that I actually was no longer tired at all. The adrenaline from the ride had given me a second wind. I looked out over the water. Sure enough, the sun had started to make its entrance. I'd seen the sunrise many times from Nan's seawall, and it was always beautiful. But, I'd never seen it from the beach.

"No, I'm not mad," I said hesitantly. "We can walk." Jake look pleased with himself and shrugged off his leather jacket. He rested it over the seat and led the way down to the beach. We walked in silence, side by side. The dark light of day flirted with the horizon, peeking out a little at a time. When Jake sat down on the sand, I plopped down next to him, and we watched the sun change from a smear on the horizon to a force to be reckoned with. Its early morning rays were already strong enough to burn the fragile skin of the unprepared tourists.

"I like this," I said, unsure of what I was telling him I liked—the sunset or the company. I supposed I liked both.

He sighed. "Me, too. But, we don't exactly make for the best conversationalists, do we?" He picked up a handful of sand and let it run through his fingers. "I'll sure take a comfortable silence over uncomfortable conversation any day."

"That's an understatement," I said. "I've never been a fan of talking about me anyway."

"Ditto," Jake said. "So, what do two people who don't want to talk about themselves, who obviously have some secrets in their closets, talk about?"

"I never said I had secrets."

"But you do," Jake said. "It's kind of obvious."

"Doesn't everybody? Don't you?"

"More than most."

"Ditto," I mimicked him. He laughed and laid down in the sand, staring up into the newly blue sky. He folded his hands over his chest.

"Maybe, someday you can tell me yours."

"Not likely," I told him. "You going to tell me yours?"

"Probably not." He smiled up at me. "I still want to know why you were in the yard the other night, though."

"It's no big deal, I just needed somewhere to crash."

"So, you picked a truck in a junkyard?"

"It's my Nan's truck. She never could afford to get it fixed.

So, it's just been sitting there."

"You didn't have anywhere else to go?"

I thought about not answering him. It would be easier not to. But he'd given me a ride, and I was tired of running from anyone who asked me anything about myself. "Not really. The foster care gestapo was after me. I was just hiding until she got bored and left."

"Foster care?" Jake asked. "How old are you?"

"Seventeen," I answered. He seemed a bit relieved. "She's probably long gone now." I hoped she was, anyway. I left out the part about the eviction and being homeless. "I live with my Nan... or, at least, I *lived* with my Nan. She died three weeks ago, and since I'm not eighteen they want to throw me in foster care." I volunteered all that. It wasn't even remotely the biggest secret I was keeping.

"And you're running from them because you don't want to go to into foster care?"

"I *won't* go into foster care." It was the best answer I could come up with. It was more than me not wanting to. I wasn't going, and that was it.

"What happens if they force you?" Jake asked.

"I won't go, no matter what," I said. "If they take me by force..." I didn't want to finish my sentence. I knew what I would do. I would either hurt someone and opt for prison over foster care or hurt myself, and simply opt out of life. I didn't consider myself suicidal. Just tired.

"Can't you just get emancipated or something?"

It was a question I actually didn't have to look up the answer for. "No. You have to have parental permission, and you have to prove that you can support yourself. I can't do either. And it takes a long time. I'd be eighteen and an adult before it was granted, anyway."

"Sounds like you've looked into it." I hadn't needed to. I'd been in the foster care system. I didn't look into it. I just knew it.

I changed the subject.

"So, you work at the junkyard?" I asked.

"Yeah," Jake said. "I'm not here long-term or anything. Dad's manager Reggie called me and said he needed some help straightening everything. Their secretary quit, their purchase orders are all wrong, and their ancient computer system crashed and took all their information with it. It's a mess."

"Why doesn't your dad fix it?"

"He's...sick," Jake said. Everyone in town knew that Frank Dunn was a hermit. He rarely came out of his house, and when he did, it was just to buy booze.

"Oh. I'm sorry." I knew what it was like to have a "sick" parent... or parents. Mine were the sickest of them all.

The comfortable silence returned and we sat side by side, watching the pelicans dive into the water for fish. It amazed me how they could see from that far up in the sky. They never seemed to miss and always emerged chomping on their catch, fins flopping between their beaks.

The sun had been up in the sky for way longer than could be called a sunrise, so we walked in silence back to the bike. I told him where Nan's house was. He said he didn't need directions. Of course, he didn't.

I kept forgetting he was from here.

I thought once we got to Nan's, if I didn't acknowledge the giant blue tarp in the driveway then he wouldn't either. "Thanks for the ride," I said. I handed him his helmet.

"What's all that?" he asked, gesturing to the very thing I'd hoped he would ignore.

"Garage sale stuff." He had to go, and go *now*. I needed to come up with a plan. So far, it only consisted of squatting around Nan's house until further notice. I'd forgotten about the boards on the windows. *Shit.* My situation was more obvious than I thought it would be.

I walked up the old steps of the porch, waiting to hear Jake's bike take off. Instead, I heard nothing but the idling engine. I stood facing the door and pretended to rummage through my bag for my keys. Even if I'd had them, they wouldn't have worked. There was a big gold padlock over the board on the door. I hoped he couldn't see it from the road.

"You forget your key?" he called out.

"Yeah," I lied. "I'm just going to go around back where the spare is." I waved again and hoped that when I rounded the side of the house and reached the lanai he would take the hint and leave.

The screen door was locked. I bashed the flimsily latch with my wrist and it popped open instantly. I guess I wasn't going to have to cut the screen after all.

The sliding glass door had another eviction notice taped to it, a duplicate of the one on the front door. I pulled it off and crumpled it in my hands. Then I sank down onto my ass, my back up against the door, and I rested my head in between my knees.

I was fucked.

I had nowhere else to go, and even if I did I had no money to get there. I would have to try to find some tools and break in, but that would only buy me a little bit of time. Nan's house would probably be sold soon and occupied by seasonal renters or blue haired snowbirds in no time.

I pulled my hood over my head. It was ninety degrees out,

but I didn't give a shit. I just wanted to curl up and die.

"Abby?" a voice asked.

I knew exactly who it was without having to lift my head.

It was the foster care devil coming to drag me off to hell.

She was right on time, too. The pattern of my life seemed to be rolling right along on schedule. Something bad happens. Something worse happens. Something really bad happens. The cards I was being dealt were all the Fool.

"Dan," I replied.

"Dan?" She questioned my use of her nickname, which only I knew the meaning of. I looked up at her. She looked down at me like I had three heads, and all three of them saw the pity in her eyes. "What are you doing back here on the lanai?"

"Just waiting for the other shoe to drop."

"I came here looking for you and was alarmed when I saw the stuff in the driveway and that young man out front was holding this in his hands." She handed me the wrinkled notice I had ripped off the front door.

"What young man?" I asked, sitting up and pulling my hood from my face.

She crouched next to me, still sweating from her neck, still holding the same clipboard she'd had the other day. "Your cousin, Jake, of course." She said each word slowly like she was trying to tell me more than what she was really saying.

"My *cousin*? Jake? My *cousin*?" I must have sounded insane. I didn't have any cousins, how would she get the impression that Jake was my…oh shit.

"What did you say to him?" I asked. Suddenly, I cared what he thought of me, though I didn't know why it mattered.

"He just told me that you two stopped here to sort through some of your grandmother's things and that you had come back here to make sure you didn't miss anything," Miss Thornton said.

"He said what?"

She huffed, like she shouldn't be wasting her time on an idiot like me, like there was something I wasn't getting in all this.

I wasn't getting *anything* in any of it.

"I asked him about your Aunt Priscilla, and I was very sorry to hear that she had to leave town so suddenly."

"Me too…" Maybe, I should just agree with everything she said. In the end, it wouldn't matter anyway. She was here to take me away. I was about to tell her to save the paperwork, that I was going to opt-out the first chance I got. "Listen, you can take me if you have to, but it'll be pointless, because if you do I'm just going to…" She was ignoring me. I was starting to get desperate. I was contemplating reaching for my knife in my boot and taking the next ten seconds to turn myself into a felon.

Miss Thornton said something that stopped me, mid-felony.

"I explained to your cousin that I was here to take you to a new foster home…" *Here we go.* "…but he told me it wouldn't be necessary, because you'd be staying with him."

What the fuck?

"I'm doing *what?*"

"I verified with Mr. Dunn that he has a residence, employment, the means to take care of you, and he meets the age qualification of twenty-one and over. It's a shame I didn't know sooner that you had a cousin. This paperwork could have been done days ago. I'd only have to remove you under emergency circumstances, and now that you have a relative here to care for you, there is no need for that."

Residence? I thought. *Employment? He was in town temporarily, wasn't he?*

Jake told her I could live with him?

She flipped a page on the clipboard, placed it on my lap and handed me a pen. "Here, sign this."

"What is this?"

"Since you're over the age of sixteen, you're required to sign an agreement for your non-foster living arrangement." I signed on the line where she was tapping her fat, sweaty finger, but before I handed her back her clipboard, I noticed the line above where I had just signed had another freshly inked signature on it.

Jacob Francis Dunn was signed in bold blue letters over a line that read *Signature of Legal Guardian of Minor Child.*

There was not a lot in this life that confused me. I understood that, aside from myself, people were pretty black and white for the most part. But that paper was definitely the most confusing thing I had ever encountered.

I was pretty sure that the man with the beautiful blue eyes, the temper and the big sexy bike—the very man who I had heard getting sucked off in a junkyard little more than twenty-four hours ago, mere moments before he put a gun to my head—had just adopted me.

Chapter Eight

WHEN I WALKED back to the front yard with Miss Thornton, Jake was leaning against his bike, smoking a cigarette. His eyes followed me, his face completely unreadable.

He nodded to Miss Thornton as she got into her little silver car and started the engine. Then he passed me the helmet and got off the bike so I could get on first, just like we had done earlier. I stood starting at him open-mouthed for what seemed like an eternity before he gave me a *you coming?* look.

I placed the helmet on my head and straddled the bike, grabbing the bar behind the seat. Jake got on after me, and we started down the road. After only a few minutes, we pulled into the parking lot at Dunn's Automotive Repair. Jake parked the bike at the end a small dirt driveway on the side of the building. When I took off my helmet, I discovered that Miss Thornton had followed us and was now parked behind Jake's bike.

What the hell is going on?

Jake said nothing to me as he waited for Miss Thornton to get out of her car. When she met up with us, clipboard in hand, Jake led us down the side of the building on a small concrete sidewalk and to a dark wooden door, almost hidden between two overgrown potted palms. He unclipped a set of keys from his belt loop and unlocked the door, stepping to the side to let us both inside.

Once inside I realized this must have been the apartment

Jake had told me about when we met in the yard last night. It wasn't shop-like at all. It was small and clean and cozy. The floors were a simple beige tile, the walls a creamy yellow. Off to the right was a small galley-style kitchen with plain white cabinets with little plastic dolphins for knobs. The appliances were small and white but looked fairly new. The counter tops were covered in small, dark blue tiles with thick white grout lines. There was an overhang on one side where two wooden barstools were tucked under it, behind it was a small area that looked like it was designated for a dining room table but instead sat a small iron desk and a lap top.

Jake turned on every light switch he passed as he walked Miss Thornton through the apartment, but it did little to brighten the dark space.

There was another door through the kitchen, and Jake opened it for Miss Thornton. She disappeared inside and quickly came back out, scribbling furiously on her clipboard. I was standing in the center of the living room with my backpack still on my shoulders. Jake leaned against the counter and as Miss Thornton ran down a list of questions. "Own or rent?"

"Neither. My father owns the automotive repair company, and I use the apartment while I'm in town."

"How long are you in town for?"

"I'll stay until Abby turns eighteen, but I do travel for my own work, so there will be times when I'm gone for a while here and there." His answers were simple and direct. Miss Thornton nodded as they went along.

"I expect you to take this seriously, Mr. Dunn. Miss Ford is under your care now."

"I take it very seriously, ma'am."

She turned her attention back to me. "Your home seems to

have only one bedroom. Where will Miss Ford be sleeping?"

"In my room," Jake answered. He realized how that sounded when Miss Thornton looked at him suspiciously, and he quickly corrected himself. "Oh, no—not like that. The living room couch pulls out, so that's where I'll be."

She nodded. "I assumed that with you being *cousins* and all that sharing a room is out of the question."

"Of course, ma'am." Jake flashed her a brilliant smile. He really could turn on the charm when he wanted to.

Miss Thornton seemed satisfied with his answers. She tucked her clipboard under her arm and turned to leave, informing us of a follow-up visit in the next few weeks. She smiled, opened the door, and disappeared into the bright light of day, leaving us alone in the dark apartment.

Jake looked much too large for the little kitchen as he leaned against the counter and twiddled his keys in his hands.

"What the fuck just happened?" I asked. "You told Miss Thornton that you were my cousin and that I could stay with you?"

"Yes." He smiled and moved over to the couch where he plopped down and put his feet up on the coffee table. His heavy boots thudded against the wood.

"Why?"

He pushed a stray hair behind his ear, shrugged his shoulders, looked me dead in the eye and said, "I don't know."

At that moment, it didn't really matter why he had helped. All that mattered is that he'd saved me from foster care—or, more likely, he had saved me from prison.

"Thank you." The words were hard for me to say. I hadn't said them much in my life. "I don't know why you did it, but I'm glad you did." I pushed both straps of my bag over my shoulder and started for the door.

"Where are you going?" Jake asked. He stood up from the couch and blocked the door. He towered over me, his presence as intimidating as the bike he rode.

"I'm leaving." I really didn't want to have to remind him that his lie had helped me out of foster care, but it still left me homeless. I had to go back and see if I could salvage some of Nan's stuff, to see if there was anything worth selling.

"Why are you leaving?"

I fidgeted with my hands and looked at the floor. "I gotta go figure some stuff out I guess."

"Like what?"

"Well, what you told Miss Thornton will get her off my ass for a while, but I still have to figure where I'm going to live. I figure I can sell some of Nan's stuff for a bus ticket to a place more inland, where the hotels are less expensive." I hated saying that I had nowhere to go. It made it all even more real. Jake already knew all of it, between sleeping in the junkyard and seeing the state of Nan's, but that didn't make it any less embarrassing.

"Abby." Jake reached out to grab my hand, but stopped himself. He pushed his hands into the front pockets of his jeans instead. "I want you to stay *here*. I meant it when I told her that."

"Why? You don't even know me."

"You need a place to stay, and I have one. Problem solved as far as I'm concerned."

"What do you...want from me?" I braced myself for some sort of perverted answer that would make me reach for my knife again.

"What's going on in that head of yours?" He reached out and

gently pulled my hood off my face, letting my hair fall around my shoulders.

My red face in full view.

"I don't know anymore. It's just that one minute I'm prepared to go to prison, and the next, I'm here in your apartment with you telling me I can stay with you." I just shook my head. "It's a little overwhelming."

"Prison?" Jake asked. "I thought they wanted to take you to foster care?"

"And I told you I wasn't going to go, no matter what."

Jake looked at me with an understanding I'd never seen in anyone before.

"You sure you want me to stay?" I asked. "Knowing that I'm the type of person who was about to hurt someone else just to save herself?"

Jake took a deep breath. "Now more than ever." He smiled. "And I just..." He hesitated. "I like the way you make the silence bearable."

I knew instantly what he was talking about. I felt the same way.

"Okay," I said. "I'll stay. But I'm going to sleep on the couch. I can't let you give up your room for me."

"No, you're sleeping in my room." He pointed to the door off the kitchen. He leaned in toward me, and my heart sped up. I braced myself for his touch. Instead, he leaned past me and flipped the switch behind my head, turning on the lamp next to the couch. "I'm sleeping there."

"You can't sleep on the couch while I take your bed. It's not fair." And it wasn't. He was already doing too much for a girl he didn't know.

"The couch pulls out, Abby, and it's actually where I spend most nights anyway. I'll be gone on a few trips over the next few months, so you'll have the place to yourself for some of the time.

Might as well get used to it being your room, anyway. Besides, I'm not giving you a choice in the matter."

"What about rent?" I asked, "I can pay you—not much, but something, as soon as I can find a job.

"Rent is payable in ass and grass only, baby," Jake answered. His eyes shone as he looked me up and down, biting his bottom lip between his teeth.

My mind told me to run, but my body wouldn't budge.

After what seemed like forever, he laughed. "I'm fucking with you, Bee. The look on your face is fucking priceless, though."

Was I so far gone that I didn't know a joke when I heard one? I really needed to get out more. Or maybe not. "Come on. Let's go get your shit off the driveway, and we can do details later." Jake walked past me and through the front door.

I stood in the middle of the living room, too embarrassed to move. Jake had been teasing me, and I was just a huge moron who just kept embarrassing herself over and over again. It made me question even more why he'd take me in. For the first time in a long time a bit of something I was unfamiliar with crept up inside me.

If I hadn't known better, I'd have thought it was hope.

I wanted this arrangement to work out. I really did. What I *didn't* want was to start acknowledging the very small voice in the back of my mind telling me that I wanted to get to know Jake better. I didn't think it could possibly be worth the risk. I already knew I would have to work extra hard constructing my barriers around him.

What would I do if, for some reason, living there ended up not working out?

Well, I told myself. *There's always prison.*

Chapter Nine

W E DIDN'T GET back on Jake's bike. Instead, he drove us back to Nan's in an old orange pickup truck. It took just under an hour to sort through and load up everything in the yard. That's how little I had.

Jake and I worked in the comfortable silence I was starting to get used to when he was around. I didn't even ask him where he expected to take everything. I wouldn't have been surprised if we'd pulled up to a dumpster to unload.

Jake surprised me once we were back at the shop, by unloading my things into a white shed behind the mechanic bays. When we'd finished, he locked the shed and handed me a key. "All yours," he said. I shaded my eyes with my hands from the brutal sun overhead.

"Now what?" I asked him, tucking the key into my pocket.

"Now, you make me dinner, massage my feet, become my sex slave, and clean the gutters." He winked at me.

"Oh really?" I liked joking around with him.

"Nah. But the receptionist here just quit, so if you want a job, you can help by answering the phones for Reggie. He doesn't exactly have people skills."

"I don't know if my people skills would be much better." I wasn't sure I even *had* people skills.

"Yesterday, Reggie told a woman that if she didn't know how to care for her car than she had no right owning it."

THE DARK LIGHT OF DAY

"Ok, I think I can do better than that," I said. "But only because he's set the bar so low."

"Unless you would rather try to find work somewhere else. That's cool, too. There's a Hooters a few miles away. You'd look great in the uniform." He laughed. He knew exactly what he was doing. He seemed to know the one detail that would get under my skin the most.

"Won't your Dad mind that I work here?" I didn't want to step on anyone's toes.

"Nope. He's locked himself in his house, doesn't come out much. No one's seen him in a while, and I'm not about to pay him a friendly house call."

"That sucks."

"It's better if we don't see each other, anyway. Things didn't end well when I first left town. Shouldn't take me long to sort out the mess of a business he's been ignoring. Then, I'm gone again." He stared off into the sky, his mind obviously on things that places like Coral Pines could not provide.

Back in the apartment, Jake made us both sandwiches while I sat at the counter. I didn't realize how long it had been since I'd last eaten. I could hear my stomach growl when he set my turkey and cheese in front of me on a paper plate. He politely ignored it, although it was loud enough for the neighbors to hear.

"What do you do?" I asked. "Are you a mechanic when you aren't here?"

"Not exactly."

"How can you not exactly be a mechanic?"

"I have mechanic skills, but I only work as a mechanic when I am here." Then, he asked, "Where are you from?" He took a big bite of his sandwich so his mouth was full. Both the question and the face stuffing were avoidance tactics I'd used myself. Maybe, he was embarrassed about his regular job. I didn't push.

"Atlanta area, I think," I answered. I was pretty sure that was almost correct, because my parents had been in and out of the Georgia State Prison system. When anyone asked, I usually said *Atlanta* because it's the only city I remember in Georgia off the top of my head.

"You *think*?"

"I was young when we left, and we moved around a lot."

"And why did you come to Coral Pines?" This was a slippery slope he was heading down.

"To live with my Nan." My ability to give only vague answers impressed me.

"And why was that?"

"Pass."

"Pass?" Jake asked.

"Yes. Whenever you don't want to answer a question, you get to pass. I'm choosing to pass on that one."

"Who came up with these rules?"

"My Nan."

"So you're just gonna take a pass because your Nan invented a game to let you slide on having to tell anyone anything?" He was a perceptive one.

"Pretty much." I took a big bite of my sandwich. The recognition of what I was doing danced in Jake's eyes. He flashed me a smirk.

Once I'd choked my way through more turkey than I should have shoved down my throat in the first place, I laid my out a few questions of my own. "So you're from here?"

"Yes."

"But you left?"

"Yes." That single-word motherfucker.

"Why did you leave?"

"My mother and brother died." I thought I had heard that Frank's wife and son had died, but I didn't put two and two together that it would have been Jake's mother and brother. I avoided apologizing for it. I wasn't sorry. I didn't do anything. I never understood that practice anyway.

"How?" I asked, curious.

My brother drowned in a boating accident, and shortly after my mom couldn't process his death, so she opted out.

"Opted out?" I asked.

"Took matters into her own hands," he said.

"No—I know what it means. I actually use that phrase myself. I've just never heard someone else say it before, is all." I sipped my Coke. "I can see why you left, then."

"Yeah, well… that's not the whole reason."

"Then, what is?" I've never felt the desire to know anything more about anyone before, but Jake intrigued me on a level I was very unfamiliar with. If he had a diary, I would have unapologetically stolen it and read it.

"Pass," he said smiling, using my own game against me.

"You can't pass," I scolded. "It's not your game!"

"It is now." He came around the counter to sit on the barstool next to me. He lifted his sandwich and in one bite had finished off half, laughing with his mouth full.

"You're going to choke," I said. Jake laughed harder and tried to swallow the food in his mouth. His eyes were watering by the time he got it all down. When he pushed away his empty plate, his forearm brushed mine. I jumped. It wasn't just a flinch, either. I jumped high enough to knock over the stool I was sitting on and fall against the computer desk.

"Whoa, there. Are you okay?"

It took me a second to do an inventory. I was okay. It was just a brush of the arm. Nothing inappropriate. No harm done. It didn't even burn all that much. I nodded at him and tried to catch my breath. Jake reached down and righted my stool. He patted the cushion, inviting me to take my seat again. Reluctantly, I did. I naively hoped that he would overlook what had just happened. Of course he didn't.

"What was that about?"

"It's nothing," I answered.

"That didn't seem like nothing. Was it because I touched you?"

"Pass." I didn't want to spend any more time on this subject, and making an excuse for my behavior meant lingering. The pass seemed like my best option.

"This little get-to-know-you lunch is really working out well." Jake laughed. I actually laughed too. "How about this instead: since we're going to be living together for a bit, and we are just so damned forthcoming about our personal lives, what if every day we answer one question and reveal one significant thing about ourselves? We can pass on as many questions as we would like, but at some point we have to answer. And no question can be asked twice in one day." Jake seemed proud of these rules. I was terrified. "Any follow-up questions are allowed."

"Like, I can ask you what is your favorite color?" I asked.

"We can ask those types of little things too, but by the end of the day you have to answer something significant."

"Like, what you do for a living?" I offered. I raised my eyebrow at him.

"Now, you're getting it, Bee," Jake said. "And I'm gonna

pass on that one. How did your Nan die?"

"Meth lab explosion." It sounded downright silly saying it aloud, like it was a TV crime show instead of my life. I didn't like talking about it, but it was public record, and in the vault of my secrets it was a relatively minor one.

"Bullshit! You're making that up."

"Look it up," I told him. "Made the news and everything. Nan didn't do drugs... well, not after the sixties, anyway. And yet somehow she wound up in a meth lab trailer in the middle of the Preserve during the bright light of day when she should have been on her way to my graduation."

Jake threw away our plates and moved to on sit on the couch. Instead of taking the seat next to him, I just swiveled to face him from my place at the counter. "I'm sorry," he said.

"Okay, let's get one thing out of the way: let's not say I'm sorry to one another. I hate that expression. What are you sorry for? You didn't do anything. I'm not sorry because you lost your mother and brother. I didn't do it." The words came out a little rougher than I intended.

"Okay," Jake agreed. "No more I'm sorry's. How about we just tell it like it is?"

"Now we're talking."

"Bee, I am not sorry your Nan died because I didn't do anything to contribute to her untimely demise, but it still sucks."

"Better." I laughed.

"What's your mom like?" Jake asked.

I stopped laughing immediately. "Definite pass on that one." I pointed to his arm. "The tattoo on your forearm: whose initials?" He glanced down at the intricate gray and black design on his left forearm that started somewhere inside his short sleeved shirt and ran down to the top of his hand, creating an interlocking SL.

"Pass," he answered. "How long did you live with your grandmother?"

"A little under four years. How old are you?"

"Twenty-two," he replied.

Jake may have had the hard look of someone who had been through a lot, and people who couldn't recognize what that looks like might have guessed he was a few years older than twenty-two. I knew what that life experience looked like. Twenty-two would have been my guess.

Jake leaned forward, his elbows on his knees. He looked like he was deep in thought until he shook his head and smiled up at me. "Who is your...best friend?" I could tell he was trying to come up with a simple question to lighten some of the heaviness of our previous questions.

"Right now?"

"Yes, who is your best friend right now?" He probably thought that this question would be one I could answer easily and possibly even rant a bit about. Most girls my age had tons of friends. He probably expected an answer about my friend, and her car, and her boyfriend, and the movies we'd seen, and all that shit.

"Pass." I didn't want to have to tell him that right at that very moment, my very best friend, my only friend in the entire world was him.

JAKE TOOK ME next door to the attached garage area and introduced me to Reggie, the head mechanic. Reggie was tall and skeleton-thin, with huge ears and a crooked front tooth. He happily showed me around the building. There were two offices in the front. Jake was using his dad's office since he wasn't around much, and the other was the main office, which is where I was going to be working. It was small—just enough room for two filing cabinets and a little wooden desk with a yellow phone. It had a big window with plastic horizontal blinds that looked over into the three big garage bays that made up Dunns' Auto Repair.

Cars and motorcycles were in all sorts of stages of repair within the bays. Some were in parts on the garage floor with screws, bolts, tires and rims lined up next to them, while other vehicles were on lifts with men in coveralls under them, reaching up into their mechanical guts.

Reggie showed me how to answer the phone and schedule appointments. It seemed easy enough. I thought I was going to work there in exchange for Jake letting me stay with him, but he insisted on paying me exactly what the last receptionist was making before she'd up and quit on them.

After the tour, Jake and I went back to the apartment. He made some room in his closet for my few articles of clothing. It was pretty easy, since neither of us had much. Basically, he just slid some of his stuff down the clothing rod and I hung up my few things on red plastic hangers. He told me I could use any of the drawers in the dresser, since they were all empty anyway.

"Why are you doing all this for me?" I asked. "You don't even know me." Jake stood in the doorway of his room and watched me fold a few t-shirts into one of the drawers.

"I don't know," he answered. I was surprised he didn't take a pass on that one. I didn't know whether to appreciate his honesty or be fearful that as soon as he figured out why, he'd just change his mind, and I would be left nowhere to go. Again.

My plan was now simple. I would save money in the next

several months by working at the shop, so by the time I turned eighteen—or by the time Jake skipped town, whichever came first—I would be able to afford my own place.

"I really can sleep on the couch," I said. "You don't need to give me your bed. Anything is better than the bench seats of a dusty truck. I'll be perfectly comfortable on the couch, I swear,"

"No," he said, without saying anything more. It was one of the things I was beginning to like about him. He didn't feel the need to explain everything all the time. He didn't just talk to fill the silence between us with useless words.

Jake made a grocery store run while I finished unpacking. I offered to make dinner for us as a thank you, even though my skills were more of the heating up variety, but he had told me he loved to cook and never really had a chance or a place to do it while he was on the road.

I sat at the counter and watched him slice and chop vegetables. He finally took pity on my uselessness and let me peel potatoes but not without a thorough tutorial first. He had marinated chicken thighs in different spices and set them under the broiler. "You really know what you're doing, don't you?" I was amazed by his skills in the kitchen. "Who taught you how to cook?"

"My mom. She went to culinary school, but came back here after she graduated. She wanted to open her own restaurant, but then she married my dad and had Mason and me, so she kept putting it off." He dropped some chopped onions into a pan. They sizzled and popped when they hit the oil. "Your mom never taught you how to cook?" he asked.

"I'm not a good cook," I said.

"That didn't answer the question," He answered.

"Why do you want to know about my mother?"

"I just want to know *you*," he said. I know he was serious about getting to know me, but my frustration was growing like it did every time I allowed that woman into my thoughts for more than a minute without dismissing her.

"What do you want me to tell you? Because I honestly can't think of a single thing my mother actually taught me. Oh, wait. She did teach me how to tie off those yellow rubber tubes really good and tight around her arm so she could find part of a vein she hadn't treated like a dart board. That was, of course, until she'd exhausted all those veins and they died in her arms like I wished she would have every time she picked up the goddamned needle or snorted some shit up her fucking nose."

I got up and walked into the bathroom, slamming the door behind me. I was mad, but not at Jake. I was mad that I had let myself get that upset. The woman who gave birth to me wasn't even worth my anger. I'd had a handle on it since the very last day I'd ever seen her, though I don't know if I could really call *avoidance* having a handle on it.

After a several minutes, there was a knock at the door. "Bee?"

"Yeah?" I kind of liked his nickname for me. I'd never had one before.

"I'm sorry I pushed. I said I wasn't going to, but I was curious, and I let it get the better of me. I won't do it again." He was apologizing to me when I was the one who acted like a giant asshat.

I opened the door. "You shouldn't apologize. I'm just screwed up and you're probably thinking that you've bitten off more than you can chew, and I understand, I'm just gonna go and—"

"We're all a little damaged, Bee. Some of us more than others." It was better he knew sooner rather than later how damaged

I really was. He smiled and gestured to the counter where there was more food than any two people could consume in one lifetime. "Besides, you can't go anywhere. Who is going to eat all this? I got a little carried away."

"No shit," I agreed. "Are you feeding an army?"

"I do eat a lot," he said, patting his stomach. I could see the lines of his abs under his shirt.

"Yeah, you should knock out all the eating. It's really making you gross to look at."

"I'm vain enough to know that isn't true, so I'm just gonna let that little insult slide."

We sat at the bar and ate our food. Jake had made some sort of sliced potatoes he fried in butter with baked chicken thighs. The crispy skin was my favorite part. He also prepared roasted corn and a simple salad with dressing he'd made himself.

I was going to be very spoiled by the time I turned eighteen. And very, very fat.

"What do you like to do?" he asked. "Like, as a hobby?"

I had to think about whether or not smoking weed could be considered a hobby. "Not much. I can take pictures—or, at least, *I* think I can take pictures. In school they had loaner cameras for the photography class and I took to it pretty well. Even learned how to use the dark room to develop them. I had a knack for it, but at the end of the semester we had to give the cameras back, so I never got to find out if I was any good."

"My dad might have a camera around you can use," he offered. "I'll see if it's in his office somewhere." He popped a slice of potato into his mouth with his fingers.

"Really? I mean, I don't want to take his camera."

"It's nothing. I know he's never even used it. I think I saw it the other day in his office. I'll grab it for you tomorrow. No big deal."

No big deal? It was a huge deal. I wasn't used to people just handing over expensive possessions for me to use.

When we'd finished and I'd consumed more food than anyone my size should ever attempt to eat, I volunteered to clear our plates and do the dishes since I hadn't contributed anything useful to the delicious meal I'd just devoured.

Jake didn't argue with me. I had just started loading the dishwasher when a phone rang. He pulled a small black flip phone out of his pocket and when he glanced at the screen, his mood changed and his face went hard. The soft Jake from dinner was gone and in his place was a much more serious-looking version of himself. "I gotta take this. Be right back." He stepped out of the back door that led to a small covered patio. From where I stood in the kitchen, I could hear him speaking to someone in hushed tones. He wasn't the only one who was curious. I tiptoed over to the door and pressed my ear against it.

"When?" I heard him ask in a loud whisper. "I can't do it for a couple of weeks. *Why?* Because I'm in the middle of something right now and because it means tracking him halfway across fucking Europe—*that's* why. And as you know, that will take a lot of time *and money*." There was a pause. "Expenses, plus three hundred or I'm out. Yes, that's three hundred thousand." Another pause. "Fuck you, then. I can't do this forever, and I need an out. My prices have gone up." Another pause. "Then, he can get someone else to do it. I don't give a fuck. You need me more than I need you." A longer pause. "I'll text you the address for the drop from a throwaway tomorrow. I won't contact you when it's done. Same as always."

The phone snapped shut.

I ran back to the kitchen and was putting another plate into the dishwasher when he came back inside. "Everything okay?" I asked.

"Yeah. Just some work shit." He rubbed his hand over his eyes and shoved his phone back in his pocket.

"What kind of work shit?" I asked.

"Pass," he said, not even turning to look at me before he plopped down on the couch and put his feet on the coffee table. He grabbed the remote and turned on the TV, raising the volume to a level where having any sort of a conversation would've been impossible. It was like he was using another play out of the Abby Ford Avoidance Hand Book.

I finished the dishes, and by the time I was done wiping the counters, Jake was already asleep in the recliner. I took the throw from the back of the couch and set it over him. I located the linen closet and found what I needed to set up the couch. I had no idea how to pull it out so I decided to make it up as it was. I tucked a fitted sheet around the cushions and used a top sheet and light blanket to lay over it. I took one of the two pillows from the bed and made sure it was there on the couch for him when he woke up in the recliner and realized what painful angle his neck was in. It was all turned down for him, just waiting for him to hop in.

I got myself ready for bed and was brushing my teeth when my thoughts drifted to the conversation he had on the phone outside earlier. Why had he been whispering? What was he hiding? Was he a private detective or a bounty hunter? A million scenarios ran through my head, but not one I came up with seemed right.

The first night I met Jake, just a few days ago, he'd held a gun to my head. The bulge of his gun was always noticeable to me now that I knew that he kept it tucked into the back of his jeans.

There was a reason he wouldn't tell me what he did for a living.

He wasn't embarrassed by what he did. He was simply hiding it. After listening in on his conversation, all signs pointed to the reason for that secrecy being far darker than I originally thought.

Chapter Ten

THE NEXT DAY was my first day working at the shop. When I woke up, I found a note Jake had left for me, telling me he was already working and that I should meet him over there when I was ready. I showered. I pulled my hair back into a simple braid down my back and put on a pair of jeans and a long sleeved t-shirt. I pushed my feet into my boots, but decided against wearing my hoodie in an attempt to look somewhat professional. It was the best I could manage with what I had. I grabbed my hoodie and brought it with me anyway, just in case I felt the need to hide in it.

I reported to the office Reggie had told me was mine the day before. Since the shop didn't officially open for another half an hour, I took the opportunity to organize the clutter and dust off the furniture. I felt like someone was staring at me as I worked, and when I turned around, sure enough, I saw Jake through the blinds, wiping the grease off a wrench with a rag and smiling at me through the window. I didn't take my gaze from him until the phone rang and snapped me out of my fog.

"Good morning. Dunn's Garage," I answered the way Reggie had instructed.

THE ENTIRE DAY flew by so quickly, I barely had time to finish the coffee and donut Jake brought me while I was on the phone making an appointment for a tune-up on Mrs. Grabel's Chevy. Jake had checked in on me a few times, and each time I saw him he had more grease on his face and coveralls. I scheduled all the appointments, answered the phones, placed orders brought to me on tickets the guys scribbled on, and at noon, I ran across the street to get lunch for all four mechanics. They were grateful but ate while they worked. I had a feeling they were used to the craziness and may have eaten a little grease with their sandwiches.

Jake had taken the truck after lunch and didn't come back for a couple of hours. I figured he was out getting parts or running shop-related errands. I reminded myself to tell him I would be more than happy to run his errands so he wouldn't have to.

At the end of the day, Reggie came over and practically yelled at me to leave. The filing I was in the middle of could wait until tomorrow. I was sure it could, but I was enjoying my job. It gave me a small sense of purpose and kept my mind busy. It was like another way for me to stay numb.

Busy equals numb

I'd have to remember that.

I didn't see Jake around the shop, so I headed back to the apartment. I heard the shower running and assumed he'd beaten me home. My attention was captured by what was on the counter. A camera, a state of the art Canon, with three long lenses lined up next to it. Next to that was what looked to be a brand new camera bag.

There was no way this was his dad's *old* camera.

Jake came out of the bathroom, wrapped in a towel and nothing else. Steam billowed out after him. He halted when he saw me standing in the kitchen. His carved abs were on full display, the tattoos I'd only seen portions of before were now in full view, winding up around his shoulder in beautiful vine type lines connecting smaller pictures and letters I couldn't quite make out. I followed them with my eyes up to where they ended at his neck. The stirring in me came back.

"Hey, sorry. I didn't know you were home yet," Jake said.

Home.

I tore my eyes from his bare chest and focused on the floor instead. "Oh, don't worry about me I was just…looking at the camera."

"Yeah, check it out while I put some damned clothes on. Don't want you thinking this is one of those nakey houses." He smirked. "Unless you're into that kind of thing."

"I don't even know what that means," I said. But I had an idea. Something told me it was him who didn't know what a nakey house really was.

He gave me an exaggerated wink and disappeared into the bedroom, emerging just a few seconds later in a pair of black draw string sweat pants and a gray wife-beater.

"He owns something with color in it!" I covered my open mouth in mock surprise.

"Is gray considered a color?"

"I think it is."

"Then, I'm gonna burn it tomorrow!" he shouted. "I wouldn't want to ruin my rep."

"No, you wouldn't want that," I agreed. I looked back at the counter and gestured to the camera and equipment. "What is all this?"

"I told you. It's my dad's old camera. You can have it. He left it here years ago and hasn't ever used it."

"Really?" I asked him. "Your dad's *old* camera?"

"Yeah, why?" he asked nervously.

"What do you mean *why?*" I picked up the camera bag and showed him the price tag still stuck underneath it.

"So dad left the tag on. He does stuff like that." He grabbed a bottle from the fridge and twisted off the cap. "Beer?"

"Yes, but don't change the subject." He grabbed another beer, opened it and handed it to me. "Did your dad also go to Herman's Electronics at two this afternoon and spend two-thousand four-hundred dollars on a brand new Canon, a camera bag, accessories, and two prepaid phones?"

"Shit," he said. He knew he was caught, and his face told me didn't really care. He was smiling from ear to ear.

"Yeah, shit! You left the receipt in the box." I lifted the little white slip of paper up to him and waved it in the air. "You didn't have to buy this for me, Jake. It's too much. I can't accept it."

"Yes, you can. I make good money. I've never bought anything expensive other than my bike. I wanted to get this for you, and I'm not taking it back." He might as well have said the sky is blue, it was that matter-of-fact.

"Yes, you are!" I argued. I'd never owned something that valuable, and I never planned too. In my experience, bad things happened to people with nice things. Besides, Jake had already done too much for me, and I had no way of repaying him.

"Nope. Here's how I see it." He leaned his elbows on the counter and played with the label on his beer. "You can either accept the camera and say 'thank you Jake for my new beautiful camera' or..." He took a sip of his beer, amusement passing through his blue eyes. "...I will throw it off the Matlacha Pass." He took another sip. "Your call, Bee."

"You wouldn't!" I shouted. Something told me he didn't

bluff, and I wasn't about to take that chance with equipment this expensive.

"Oh yes, I would. You have no idea what I'm capable of." I had a feeling he was talking about more than his willingness to toss camera gear from high places.

"Okay fine. But here's how *I* see it." I leaned onto the counter and mimicked his stance. "I am going to use the brand new fancy camera and…I'm going to love it."

"Now we're talking. Case closed."

"No no no—not so fast. I am going to use it and love it, but I am going to pay you back for it. Every penny. As soon as I can save up enough."

"Fuck no," he said. "I'll just burn the money."

"I don't care what you do with it. I'm still paying you."

"Then, I'll just use it to buy you something else."

"Then, I'll just pay you for that, too," I said.

"You're impossible, you know that?" Jake asked.

"Yes, I do know that." I smiled. "Now, make me some food. I'm starving."

"I believe we have some business to get out of the way first?"

"What *business*?"

He smiled back. "Secrets first, then dinner."

"Oh yeah…secrets." I was getting bolder around him, and I liked it. "Go!"

"Why don't you like to be touched?"

"Pass," I answered. "Why did you buy two throw-away cell phones today?"

"Pass," he answered. "What's your middle name?"

"Marie." I already knew his was Francis. I'd seen it on the papers Miss Thornton had showed me. So, I didn't bother asking. "Why do you carry a gun?"

"I've answered this one for you before. Because there are some dangerous people out there."

"Yeah. But you've never said if you were one of them or not."

"What if I am?" he asked. I had the feeling that he was completely serious. "Would it matter?"

Would it matter?

I wasn't sure. "I'll have to think about that one."

Jake grabbed another beer from the fridge. "Now we can eat! What'll it be—steak or pasta?"

"Steak," I said. "The answer to that question is always steak."

"Good answer. I love a girl with an appetite." He went about prepping for dinner, but his words hang heavy in my mind. *I love a girl with an appetite.* Who did he see me as? A girl he was caring for, or a friend he was helping out?

Could I be someone more to him?

Of course, I couldn't be *someone more.* I was barely able to think about that kind of relationship, let alone be in one. Besides, Jake was the kind of guy that girls threw themselves at for a chance to be touched by him.

Why would he ever want one who was only capable of running from that?

While Jake cooked and plated the most beautiful steak and roasted asparagus I'd ever seen, I thought about the game of secrets we were playing.

As much as it was meant for us to learn about each other, it seemed as if the only thing it really did was expose which secrets we fully intended to keep.

Chapter Eleven

A LOUD CRASH woke me. The little blue digital clock on the nightstand read two-fourteen a.m. I sat up straight, my heart racing.

What was that?

My eyes strained as I tried to see through the dark. The door knob slowly screeched as someone turned it from the kitchen side of the door. I pulled the covers up to my chin. I wanted to ask who was there, but when I opened my mouth the words caught in my throat. There was something too familiar about the entire situation. It stopped me in my tracks. The knob began to jiggle violently when whoever it was out there realized it was locked. They weren't too happy about it.

Please be Jake. Please be Jake.

I froze. I felt like I was watching a movie when the bedroom door sprang open, and pieces of wood flew from the hinges. The dark outline of a man appeared in the shadows.

"There you are, you little shit!" The deep voice was slurred and filled with bitterness. "You think you can come back here and hide from me, do you? You think I wouldn't know where you were?"

The smell of whiskey hit my nose right before the man lunged forward and wrapped his massive hand around my arm, squeezing tight enough to cut off circulation to my fingers. My entire arm burned at the sensation of his touch, like he had doused me with gasoline and set fire to it. I tried to pull away, but he was too strong. His powerful grip held me still. I tried to scream, but I couldn't catch my breath. It was so dark I didn't even see his fist flying toward my face. A shattering pain rippled across my right cheek, my jaw bone vibrated from the blow.

Just as quickly as the beating had started, it ended. The man flew off me like he was attached to a rope that had been yanked backward. He crashed into the closet, knocking both doors from their hinges. They snapped in half as he landed inside, a tangle in the clothes and hangers.

Moonlight shone through the window, highlighting the pure rage on Jake's his face as he stood over the man in the closet. His usually-blue eyes were as dark as the surrounding night. He wore only a pair of black draw string sweat pants. His chest and feet were bare.

He knelt next to the man crumpled in the closet, placing his hand behind the man's his neck and forcing him to look in my direction. "Look at her, old man!" Jake commanded. I held the sheets up around my chest, one hand clutching my cheek. It throbbed in time with my racing pulse. "Does that look like me, Frank? Does she look like someone you can get drunk and beat up on, you stupid old man?"

A look of horror crossed the old man's face. His shoulders slumped as he closed his eyes and shook his head. "I thought…" he whispered. "I'm so sorry." He dropped his face in his hands and started to cry.

"Are you sorry for beating on her, or are you just sorry it wasn't me? Cause either way, your apology don't make shit better. What a piece of shit you are, coming here in the middle of the night, tanked off your ass. What part of this seemed like a good idea to you, you stupid fuck? You could have *killed* her!"

Jake pulled his pistol from the back of his sweats and held the barrel to the old man's temple. He leaned down close and looked the old man in the eyes. "I'm here because you have fucked up everything Mom worked for her entire life."

Mom?

"I'm here so the house she loved, the home you spend your time rotting in, doesn't end up with the tax collector, and Reggie and Bo don't end up on the fucking unemployment line. Because you sure as shit don't seem to give a fuck about anything but drinking whiskey and wallowing in your own shit." He cocked the gun.

My breath hitched.

This man was Jake's dad...

The old man kept his eyes closed while Jake continued through gritted teeth. "While I'm in town, you are never to come here again, and if you so much as lay a fucking finger on Abby, I will blow your motherfucking head off." As he spoke the last words, he nudged the gun against the old man's temple, pushing his head against the wall of the closet. "You're lucky I don't just end you now, you sorry bastard."

"Just kill me, then!" The old man cried. "Just fucking kill me, boy!" His face reddened, strings of saliva connected his top and bottom teeth.

Jake yanked the old man up by the back of his shirt. "Not today, old man," he said. Then he shoved him stumbling toward the hall and out of the room. The front door squealed open, then slammed shut.

Once again, there was only silence.

Some people threaten others in the heat of the moment, or as a reaction to an argument. I've heard boys fist-fighting in school threaten to kill each other while they traded blows in the parking lot after class. I know what that sounds like. But there was something different about Jake's threats to his father, and it was more than just the obvious gun pointed at his head. This hadn't sounded like the random anger of someone caught up in the heat of a moment, or the idle ravings of someone who had no intentions of following through on them. Jake's words were solid descriptions of what was to come if the old man didn't stay away. They weren't threats at all.

They were promises.

SLEEP WAS IMPOSSIBLE after that. Not only was my mind racing, but my cheek exploded in pain every time I turned on my side. The pillow might as well have been stuffed with concrete.

The silence was interrupted when Jake came back into the apartment. The front door squeaked. Keys fell onto the coffee table. I could tell he was trying to be quiet, but even the cricket outside the window sounded like he was playing his song on a trombone.

Jake came into the room. As soon as he looked at me he cursed. "Shit." He turned back around, disappearing down the hall, and I heard him fiddling around in the kitchen. Drawers slammed shut, the contents rolling and rattling as he searched for what he needed. Then, he appeared again holding a plastic sandwich bag filled with ice. He sat next to me and reached out to place the ice pack on my cheek. I grabbed it from him before he could make contact.

"I got it," I assured him. "Thanks." I placed the ice pack against my face, cringing at the sting of the cold.

"Bee, I'm so sorry. I didn't think he would ever come here, let alone in the middle of the fucking night. Nobody's seen him

in almost a year. I don't even know how he knew I was here."
He leaned in closer. "Are you okay?" There was hurt and
concern in his voice.

"I'm fine," I said. And I was. I was perfectly fine, because I
was numb. Numb people can't be anything other than fine.

"It's all my fault," he told me. "I couldn't sleep, so I went
out on the patio for a smoke. I didn't even hear him come in."

"Where is he now?" I asked.

"I threw him in the bed of his truck and drove him home.
He was passed out when we got there so I unloaded him in the
front yard. He was lucky I didn't toss him in the canal. I walked
back."

"Is that why you and your dad don't get along? He drinks
and beats up on you?"

"Among other things."

"Like what?"

He took a deep breath. "The night I decided to leave town
he tried to kill me. Told me that it was me who was supposed to
die instead of my brother and he was just righting a wrong. He
was so drunk, but he meant what he said. He took a swing at me
with an ax, and when he missed I came pretty close to killing
him with it myself. Then, I took off, and I haven't seen him
since. Until tonight, that is." He reached out to touch my cheek.
It had started to swell. I flinched, turning away from him. He
frowned and withdrew his hand. "Bee, how come I can't touch
you?"

"Because you can't." It was the truth. My truth.

He couldn't, because I wouldn't let him.

"Are you okay?" he asked, concern in his eyes.

"I'm fine."

"You don't have to be like this! There is no way you can be

fine right now!" Jake smoothed his hand over his goatee. "Someone bursts in here in the middle of the night and attacks you, and you're just fine? Cause I'll tell ya, I'm not fine!"

"Calm the hell down! I'm okay, really. I promise."

"Okay is worse than fine. For fuck's sake, I would rather you scream, and yell, and cry, and blame me!" Suddenly, he was quiet. "I just...I just want to hold, and comfort you." He made a move toward me, but this time I refrained from flinching.

As long as he didn't touch me, he couldn't break me.

"Why do you want those things from me? It doesn't change anything. I'm okay because I choose to be okay."

I'd been saying it my whole life. It was all I knew.

"No!" Jake shouted. He jumped off the bed and started pacing the room. "No, you're not *okay* because *you choose to be*— you just *think* you're okay because you choose to avoid the situation. You're not honest about your feelings, and that's *not okay* at all!"

He reached for me, and I scurried to the other side of the bed as if he were wielding a knife instead of offering comfort.

"No," I screamed. My heart was racing. I didn't want to feel the burn. I didn't want to be pulled down into a place I didn't know if I could ever climb out of.

I didn't want to feel.

"Just let me hold you, Bee."

"No. Fuck you. Leave me alone!"

"Why don't you want me to touch you?" he asked again, this time louder, his voice laced with anger.

"Why do you *want* to touch me? I'm nothing. I'm no one." My voice was shaky. I was on the verge of my first real tears since I was a child, and I was hell bent on not letting them come.

"Why do I want to touch you? Are you fucking kidding me

right now? I want to help you. I want to hold you. I want to make it all okay for you. I want to fucking touch you because you are the most beautiful person I've ever seen, and I can't imagine never being able to hold your hand or kiss you." I thought that was everything, but then he added, "And yes—I want to *fuck* you, too, like I've never wanted anything in my whole life."

Why would he want me?

Sincerity played behind his eyes, the same eyes that had held so much hatred for his father no more than an hour earlier. "You're not *nothing*. Don't ever fucking say that again, because you're *everything*." He said it again, quietly this time, "You're fucking *everything*, Bee."

It was all I ever wanted and didn't want to hear at the same time. We hardly even knew each other. We couldn't have a real relationship. I could never give him what he needed or wanted, and there was no way in hell he was ever going to be able to make things okay for me. He didn't even know what he'd be trying to make okay.

Who the fuck did he think he was?

"How?" I snapped at him. "How the fuck are you going to make it all okay for me? Huh? Are you going to travel back in time and make my parents treat me like I'm worth more than the neighborhood dog? Are you going to tell them to take me to school instead of keeping me home to torture me? Are you going to read to me and teach me how to cook? Are you going to close my bedroom door when they're having a fuck-party in the middle of the goddamned living room? Is that what you're going to do, Jake?"

He stayed silent.

"You think a hug is going to heal me? You can't help me.

Nobody can help me! I help myself. I'm okay, because I fucking want to be okay! I don't want to be touched, because I don't want all the shit that comes with it." Then next part spilled out of me before I could reconsider. "It burns, okay? Is that what you want to hear? It burns down into my bones, and it physically fucking hurts me to be touched!"

I sank from the bed onto the floor so I didn't have to see his reaction to my confession.

"Are you going to make them love me, Jake?" I pulled my knees up to my chest. "You say you want to help me, but how can you when you keep so much from me? You won't even tell me why this 'business' of yours is such a secret."

"You want to know what I do? Do you really want to know? Because once I tell you, I can't just take it back." Jake rounded the bed and crouched on the floor in front of me. "I'm fucking afraid that I'm going to look at your perfect face and you'll see me for the first time as the monster I am. I haven't told you because I can't stand to think of you looking at me like that. I don't want you to judge me for what I've done...for what I do."

He did reach out then, trying to brush a strand of hair out of my eyes.

I jerked my head away. *"Don't fucking touch me!"*

I leapt up and bolted for the door, but Jake's massive frame cut me off. He grabbed me by the shoulders and pulled me into him, wrapping his arms around my back, locking his fingers together. My arms were pinned to my sides. My swollen cheek was pressed against his hard chest. I tried to knee him. I kicked and struggled. I even bit at his chest in hopes of forcing him to release me. The heat of his touch felt like I was lying against the surface of the sun.

"Let me go," I cried out, "it burns. It fucking *burns!*" The tears prickled at the edges of my eyes. I couldn't let them come because once they did, I didn't know if I'd be able to make them stop.

"No, it doesn't. It doesn't burn. It's just me and you here. It doesn't really hurt, I promise. It's all in your head, baby." He kissed the top of my head, but he might as well have lit a fucking match and held it to my scalp.

"*Let me fucking go!*" I wailed.

The intense fiery pain spread down into my feet until I could no longer stand from the torture. My legs gave out from under me, but Jake held me firm against him, keeping me from falling to the floor. I continued to fight and buck in his grip with everything I had left. The sobs I'd kept in for so long burst out from deep within me. Hot tears raced down my face and pooled in the line separating my top and bottom lip. I tasted the salt with each ragged intake of breath. Jake ignored my cries and tightened his grip on me.

"I kill people, Bee," he whispered. For a moment, I wondered if he'd really said it, or if it was in my imagination.

I continued to fight him until the fighting was only in my head, and my body gave out and went limp against him. Jake backed us up until his legs were against the dresser drawers. He slid down to the floor, pulling me into his lap as my head fell against his chest.

"I kill people for money, mostly bad people. But, I work for bad people, too—Mafia types, big corporations." He was quiet and matter-of-fact. "To be honest, I don't check which direction my targets' moral compasses point before taking them out. They could be anyone."

There were too many emotions I didn't want to feel, all of them assaulting me at the same time. I didn't know which feeling was which. The burning in my body had started to die down to a simmer, but my sobbing was so fierce I couldn't find the power to rein it in. I wanted to know so much more. I wanted to ask him a million questions, but I couldn't find a place within me calm enough to form the words.

"I enjoy it," he continued. "I know that sounds sick, but you know what's worse than being a sick son of a bitch?" I didn't even try to answer. My skin and bones had melted into his body, and I was a mute lump of flesh piled on his lap. "Knowing you're a sick son of a bitch." He laughed softly into my hair, relaxed his grip on me and started mindlessly tracing circles on my back with his fingertips. "I know that how I feel inside isn't always right. But, right or wrong, I can't change it. I'm not going to make apologies for it either. I refuse to pretend to be someone I'm not. I allow myself to feel all of the things that I am, the things that make me me, even if they're not what ordinary people would deem right or good. I've learned to feed off of those emotions instead of letting them hold me down by condemning myself for they way I am."

Something inside me started to change during Jake's confession. He had embraced me by force like Nan had, wrangling me into emotional and physical submission. I knew he hadn't done it to hurt me. He'd done it to wake me up, to make me feel, even though it had been against my will. Anger, rage, sadness, hopelessness—so many emotions I hadn't processed for years, if I ever had at all, came crashing together at once within me, all of them occupying the same space inside. After Jake's confession, it felt like all those feelings began moving around, searching for their proper places in my body, and in my life. I could still feel their presence, but they weren't trying to pull me under the surface anymore.

I didn't feel suffocated by them any longer.

Jake talked to me quietly until our exhaustion started to take over. When I could see his eyelids getting heavy, he stood and lifted me onto the bed, setting me under the covers. Just when I thought he was about to leave and go to his regular spot on the couch, he surprised me by sliding under the covers behind me, still fully clothed. He dragged me into his chest and wrapped his arms around me. "I didn't want to tell you this way, Bee. I had another way in mind. I swear was going to try and ease into it. It obviously didn't work out that way." Jake sighed. "You know too much already, but there is so much more you need to know." He pulled me closer, pressing his lips to my forehead. The burn was gone, and for the first time in my life I felt what a kiss was like: warm softness against my newly cooled skin. "There's somewhere I want to take you tomorrow. I want to show you something," he whispered.

It was the last thing he said to me before surrendering to sleep. Shortly after he drifted off, I gave into my own exhaustion.

I fell asleep that night in the arms of a killer.

I'd never slept better.

Chapter Twelve

I F RIDING ON Jake's bike without touching him had been the thrill of a lifetime then riding on his bike with my arms wrapped around him under his leather jacket was fucking extraordinary.

The bright light of day faded into a hazy dusk. The once-enjoyable breeze became frigid as Jake wove his bike down the unfamiliar back roads. They were uneven and most of the time unpaved. There was hardly a stop sign or street light to guide our way as we drove, seemingly headed nowhere.

The last road we turned down was more of a path than a road, just dirt and weeds, barely wide enough for one car. Both sides of it were overgrown with palmettos and weeds. Some of the branches were so long they looked as if they were reaching out to connect with the foliage on the other side.

Jake was quiet, but determined. I had no idea where we were going, but it really didn't matter. All I knew was that he had something to show me, and if it was located at the end of the world, I would gladly follow.

Jake brought the bike to a stop and punched down the kick-stand with his foot. "We have to walk from here," he said. "The ground is too soft for the bike."

We walked hand in hand in silence for about ten minutes, down the path that continued to narrow until there was no longer room for us to walk side by side. Jake let me pass him and rested his hand on the small of my back, guiding me forward.

I smelled the orange blossoms before I saw them. We reached a small clearing surrounded by the fragrant citrus trees arranged in a circle. Purple flowers covered the ground below. Rays from the coming sunset traveled through the branches and lit up the clearing. The only sound was the breeze rustling the leaves, sending a wafting of sweet scent into the air.

"It's beautiful here." I said, admiring how the tops of the trees created a small canopy. When I turned to face Jake, he wasn't there with me. He was on the other end of the clearing, kneeling at the bottom of the largest tree. I approached him slowly and put my hand on his shoulder. Without turning, he took my hand in his and squeezed. "Why are these trees in a circle?" It seemed a little unnatural for them to not be in the shape of an actual orange grove.

When he started to speak, his voice became strained. "I think one of the locals may have wanted to grow and sell oranges and probably didn't have the land to plant the trees, so he just came out here and did it where he thought no one would ever find them. I can't really think of any other reason myself. I came across them when I used to ride four wheelers out here with Mason." Jake turned to face me. "I wanted to choose a beautiful place for her."

"Who?"

With his hands in his pockets, Jake dropped to his knees and pulled me into the same position in front of him. He cupped my face in his hands, touched his forehead to mine and took a deep breath. "I don't know what you think of me now, but I know after what I told you yesterday you might not even want to look at me anymore. I wouldn't blame you if you decided to hate me for what I am. I just need you to hear all of it, and if you want to run away as fast and as far as you can once you know everything, then that's something I'll just have to deal with."

"I'm here." I placed my hands over his. "I'm here." I don't know what I was trying to tell him. I didn't know if that meant that I was there to listen, or that what he was going to tell me didn't matter. Honestly, I didn't know if it would or not.

He looked into my eyes, then started his story.

"This is where I buried my first body."

He watched me intently as he waited for me to react to what he'd just said. I was waiting for the shock to settle before saying anything back. Questions sprang up everywhere.

He killed someone here, in Coral Pines?

Who could it have been?

Does it even matter to me?

I already knew what he did. Would the details make a difference? "You don't have to tell me if you don't want to." What I didn't tell him was that my understanding of what he did scared me. What was wrong with me that I was so willing to accept someone in my life who admitted to killing people on a regular basis?

"Yes, I do." Jake sat down under the tree and pulled me into his arms like I was a small child. "You need to know all of it, Bee." He rested his chin on my head. "I was fifteen, and Sabrina was sixteen. We weren't in love. We weren't even dating. We just fooled around after parties sometimes. I was a stupid kid obsessed with girls. She wasn't even the only girl I was messing with at the time."

He took a deep breath and looked up to the sky. The moon was already showing through the trees, though the sun hadn't fully set. They were sharing the sky.

"She got pregnant, told me it was mine. I believed her because I was her first, and I'd known her most of my life. She wasn't a liar. We didn't know what to do. We were just kids. She said she wanted to keep it. I kept telling her that it would ruin her life, but being a stupid prick, I was more concerned that it would ruin *my* life. Sabrina finally made up her mind and told me she wasn't getting rid of it. I panicked. Even though I knew better, I told her it probably wasn't mine anyway and that I didn't want anything to do with her."

"I didn't talk to her for months after that. I saw her at school, wearing baggy sweatshirts to hide her stomach. I'm pretty sure she was keeping it from her dad because I know they would've been banging down my door and beating in my head if they'd known. I was such an asshole to her, and I regret that every day of my life."

I could feel his tears pooling on the top of my head as he silently cried into my hair.

"One night, Sabrina knocked on my window. She was freaking out. The baby was coming, and she didn't know what to do. She was only seven months along. I told her I was calling an ambulance, and that she needed to go to the hospital. She refused. She didn't want anyone to know. She made me promise I wouldn't take her there, no matter what. Her face was so pale already and all she wanted was my help. So, I helped her."

"We went out back to my dad's shed, and I put down a blanket. It was hours of her screaming and wailing. I held her hand all the way through. It was almost light out by then, and there was still no baby. I told her I was done. I was taking her to a hospital. She screamed at me, told me the least I could do for getting her into this and being an asshole all those months was to listen to what she wanted."

Jake wiped at his eye with his sleeve.

"So, I did as she asked and stayed put." He shivered now, both his words and his body. "When the baby finally came, it was a girl. She was so small, and I could practically see through her skin. She was so quiet...so still. I knew she'd probably been dead long before she came out. I think it was just Sabrina's body finally giving it up."

"I wrapped the baby up in a grease towel and handed it to her. Sabrina was so pale, and there was blood everywhere. I panicked. I told her she needed help and now, but when I got up, she grabbed me by the shirt. She said, 'Jake, when I die, don't let them find me. I don't want them to know.' Then, her eyes rolled back in her head and the baby's body fell from her grip onto the floor. I was alone, fifteen, and incredibly stupid. I had done her wrong in every possible way. I used her, ignored her, and when she needed me most, I left her to suffer alone. The least I could do for her was honor her wishes."

"You buried Sabrina here?"

He nodded. "And the baby. I thought they would like it here. I didn't want to just throw them in a swamp, or weight them down and drop them out in the Gulf, although I considered doing both."

"Is Sabrina the *S* on your tattoo?" I asked.

"Yeah, she is." Jake held me tighter and kissed my head.

"Who is the *L* then?" I traced the intertwining letters on his forearm with my fingers.

"Sabrina's mama had died a few years before, from some sort of cancer. Her name was Laurelyn. While she was in labor, Sabrina told me if the baby turned out to be a girl, that's what her name would be."

"Wow." It was all I could manage. The mystery of the *SL*

tattoo had been solved and the truth behind it was more incredibly sad than I could have imagined.

"I should have gone for help, and I regret it every day that I didn't," he admitted. His usually strong voice was weak and mild.

"It was what she wanted Jake," I said. "You were young. You did what you could."

"No, I could have done more. I could have done so much more."

"I think what you did was brave. Anyone could have just called an ambulance and gotten her to the hospital. What she asked of you was not what was expected. But it was what she wanted. I think it took a lot more strength for you to honor that."

"I don't know about strength. I was scared shitless."

"What do people think happened to her?" I asked.

"They think she ran away. It was well-known that her dad was a really strict religious sort, and from her constant bruising I suspected he beat the shit out of her on a regular basis, but I was too much of a coward then to even do anything about it. Sabrina's brother had run away when he was fifteen, so her dad assumed she either went to find him or followed his lead. Honestly, I don't think he ever really looked too hard for her."

"I know what that feels like."

"Why do you say that?" Jake asked.

"Right after Nan died, if I'd just disappeared. People may have wondered what happened to me, more for the sake of the gossip. But, no one would've looked for me."

"If you ever disappear on me, I would track you to the ends of the Earth and back. I will always find you, Bee. Always." He held me tighter.

"I'm not going anywhere," I assured him. And it was in that moment that I meant it. I wasn't going anywhere... though Jake would be. I had to remind myself again and again that our time together had an expiration date.

"I would kill for you, Bee. Happily." He ran his fingers down my cheek. "I need you to know that."

"I know." Not only did I know, but as odd as it sounds, it flipped something on inside me. I suddenly had a deep and powerful need to be taken care of by someone who would do anything for me—even if that meant taking a life. It may have been there all along, but only now that I had someone who actually felt that way would I allow myself to feel it.

Sick, twisted Abby was in love with the sick, twisted, beautiful Jake.

Jake ran his fingers through the grass beside him and patted the ground.

"The first blood on my hands was theirs. Somehow I knew it wouldn't be the last." He took a deep breath. "Which reminds me of something else I need to tell you."

"There's more?" There had already been so much. "If you tell me more now, what will we talk about tomorrow?" I smiled. Jake laughed.

"Sort of. I have to leave next week."

I knew he'd be leaving, after I'd heard him on the phone, but I hadn't known when it would happen.

"Leaving?" The word still made my heart jump. It was too soon. He couldn't leave yet. This was why I shouldn't have let him break through my barriers. This was why I should have stayed numb at all times. I felt myself putting the walls back in place, brick by brick.

Stupid, stupid Abby.

"Not *leaving* leaving. I have to go do a job, I was going to back out, but they've already sent payment and cut communication, so saying 'no' at this point really isn't an option, unless I want people looking for me."

Apparently, I was just overreacting. *Stupid Abby.*

"How long will you be gone?"

"There is some tracking involved with this one. The guy isn't exactly on the radar. Could be a couple weeks. Maybe a month."

A month?

"Then, what?" I asked.

"What do you mean?"

"I mean after you come back. How long until you leave again? You've told me Coral Pines isn't permanent for you. I can't help wondering when you actually do plan on *leaving* leaving." I needed to prepare for when that time came. I needed to be numb Abby for it.

Somehow, I knew I was fucking kidding myself.

"Not too long," Jake said. "This place doesn't exactly have long-term appeal for me."

"Where will you go?"

"It depends." He leaned in and rested his cheek on mine. His breath tickled my ear when he spoke.

He wasn't going to make this easy on me. The little hairs on the back of my neck stood at attention. "On what?"

"On where you want to go." He kissed my neck, getting bolder with each one. Closer and closer his little kisses crept towards my mouth and the excitement over my very first real kiss grew in the pit of my stomach.

Wait.

Where I want to go?

"Me?" I asked.

He nodded. "I've been thinking that this is my last…gig, for lack of a better word. At least for a while. It's not exactly a permanent job. After time, people find out who you are and what you do, and they come looking for you. The amount of payback and retaliation start to add up after a few years. So do the amount of people gunning for you."

An orange fell from the tree next to us. One little bounce, and it gained enough momentum to roll right out of the little orange grove.

"I have money—from this gig, and the money I've saved from the others. It should last us a long time. I don't generally stay in the same place for too long, but we could go somewhere and stay for as long as you want. You could take a photography class, or we could rent a place by a school and you can do the traditional college thing if you wanted to. I've got it covered. I just need you with me."

My heart was stuck so far in my throat I didn't know if I would be able to shake it back down into place.

"I don't need an answer now. Think about it while I'm gone. Use my laptop to look up some places you might want to go. I don't take electronics or phones with me when I'm working anyway. That's how people fuck up. The computer is all yours."

Jake yawned and stretched. After such a heavy conversation, his mood was surprisingly laid back and casual. He spoke of us leaving town together like he was talking about the afternoon rain. "My only requirement is that we have to be able to ride there by bike. We can go to Canada and Mexico, too… eventually. But it'll take a while to get you a passport. Since you're traveling with me, you'll need a fake. Even though I'll be technically retired, I don't like to take any chances."

"You want *me* to go with you?" My attention was still at the beginning of what he'd just said. It was still sinking in.

Jake cocked an eyebrow at me. "You're not a very good listener."

That wasn't true. I'd heard everything he said. It was more that I wasn't a very good believer.

"Once I'm eighteen, you won't be legally responsible for me anymore. You're not obligated to take me with you." He'd already done too much. He didn't need me in his way any longer than he had signed up for.

Jake laughed. "I don't give a shit what my legal obligations are, Abby. Do you think I wanted you to stay with me because I felt it was my civic duty or something? I wanted you to stay with me because the second I knew you needed that – the second it crossed my mind—I couldn't think of you staying anywhere else."

He *wanted* me with him.

It would have been so easy to say yes, so easy to jump on the back of his bike and leave everything behind. Then, what? What would happen when he realized I was incapable of a normal relationship, incapable of something so basic like sex? What would happen when he got bored and tired of my sickness, of my sadness and sorrow?

All I knew is that I didn't want to find out.

Chapter Thirteen

THE WEEK FOLLOWING Jake's revelation flew by. We fell into a comfortable routine. Jake made dinner, and I did the dishes. Then, we'd watch a movie on the couch before going to bed and falling asleep in each others arms. He never tried for anything more. He was giving me time, but he didn't understand that even a lifetime may not have been enough. I wasn't ever going to be normal. No amount of time could make me that. From the outside, we looked like quite a normal domestic couple.

The very opposite of what we really were.

After a long day of sorting through purchase orders and receipts at the shop, Jake brought me to the beach so I could take pictures of the coming sunset. It was the third time we'd gone for that reason. My camera quickly became an extension of my arm and my vision. I took it everywhere.

Jake and I walked hand in hand along the shore. I was getting used to the way he was always touching me, and I was filled with dread whenever I thought about the time not too far off when I would no longer be able to reach for him in the middle of the night. It had been only days, but already I didn't know how I would ever sleep alone again.

Had we only known each other for less than two weeks? It seemed like there was never a time when I didn't know Jake.

The night breeze pricked at my skin through my shirt as I

pulled my camera out of the bag and flung it around my neck. I was glad Jake hadn't gotten me a digital camera. I couldn't wait to develop the negatives myself in a real dark room. Jake had told me that when he was back from his job, he would set up a makeshift dark room for me wherever we ended up.

I practically just met him and he was making arrangements for me in his life and in his home. I'd never had that before.

Jake was sitting in the sand with his face to the sky, eyes closed. I took the opportunity to get some candid shots of him. "Don't you have enough pictures of me already?" he asked, without opening his eyes. I had taken a bunch of him this week. My favorite was one of him with a cigarette in his mouth as he pulled up to the apartment on his bike. I couldn't wait to develop that one. The sight of him made all sorts of crazy shit happen inside of me, which made me both incredibly happy and scared out of my mind.

"Nope," I answered. I would need to remember what he looked like when he left for good. I needed hundreds more.

Maybe thousands.

I pushed myself between his legs, and he opened his eyes. "Hey babe," he said, spreading his arms to me.

I sat facing the sunset with my back to him, wrapped up in Jake and the comfort of our silence. His cheek rested on mine as we watched the last of the sun disappear into the horizon.

"Oh, I almost forgot," he said. "I made this for you." He reached into his jeans pocket and pulled out an ornate metal charm attached to a simple stainless steel chain.

"You made this?" The pendant was a collection of interwoven silver wires. If I looked closely at the middle of the pendant, I could see his initials *JFD* where the wires connected. "It's beautiful," I told him. And it truly was. In fact, it was the most beautiful piece of jewelry I had ever seen.

"I made it for you a while ago, but I was afraid to give it to you."

"What's a while ago?"

Jake's face reddened a little. "Shortly after I met you that night in the yard. I couldn't get you out of my head. I asked around about you a little bit, too, and before I knew it, I was standing there with a welder in my hand at the shop, making this."

"Why did you want to make this for me back then? We never even talked that night." I thought back on the night just two weeks ago that involved me being homeless and Jake threatening me with his gun. "It was more like a fight."

"It was the best fight I've ever had." Jake opened the clasp and motioned for me to turn around. I lifted my hair so he could put the chain around my neck and close the clasp. His fingers brushed against the back of my neck. Goose bumps popped up all over my legs from the contact, and I shivered at the sensation.

I held my new gift between my fingers and inspected it. I wouldn't have believed he was so talented. His work was so detailed and delicate. "Thank you," I said. "For everything. I mean it. You've done so much for me." Jake lifted my chin to him and looked me in my eyes. "You deserve way more than I could ever give you in return." I meant it. He deserved more than me, I had nothing to offer him. Nothing he would want anyway.

"Why does this sound sort of like a goodbye?"

"It isn't... not yet anyway."

"I'm not leaving until tomorrow, Bee. Let's save it for then." Jake didn't understand that I wasn't talking about this trip. I was talking about him leaving for good.

Without me.

His beautiful blue eyes sparkled. He looked at me with such intensity, such fire. I wanted to know what he saw in me that made him look that way, because I didn't see it. Maybe, he was delusional. He turned me to face him, tilted my chin up, and slowly, very slowly, closed his lips over mine.

My very first real kiss.

I didn't pull away. Instead, I surprised myself and leaned into him. I closed my eyes, the sensation was like nothing I'd expected. The feeling didn't end where our flesh met. It was so much more than mouth-on-mouth.

It was like our kiss had started a wordless conversation between our bodies.

It turned out that desire was a funny thing for me. In all my seventeen years, I never thought I'd be able to feel it. I always thought it was one of the feelings that's been dead inside me. It wasn't that I was searching for it. I didn't want anything to do with it. But it was within me all along, I guessed. I'd just never met anyone capable of stirring it strongly enough to break through my determination not to feel it at all.

Until Jake.

He kept the kiss soft but short. I had a feeling that was out of consideration for me. I knew he didn't want to push me, but when he pulled away, I felt the empty space between us. It was like a crater had been left in the space he just occupied, cold and dark and empty. The rush in my veins was similar to the feeling I got after riding his bike wrapped around the back of him.

I wanted more.

More what? What was I capable of giving him? Could I take it further?

I had no idea. I just knew I wanted more of him.

"Jake, what are we doing?" I asked, breathless from the smallest of kisses.

"I am sitting on a beach, holding a very beautiful girl," he said. I don't think I was ever going to get used to him calling me beautiful. I had to remind myself he was only calling me beautiful because he hadn't seen all of me. "And you?"

"No, really," I persisted. "What are we doing?"

He was still confused. "Kissing?"

"Jake."

He smirked. "I like the way you say my name."

And, I thought I was the President of the United States of Avoidance.

"You know what I mean. With us. What's going on with us? It's important. I need to know now because at some point I'm not going to be able to give you what you want. And then what?"

He nuzzled his nose into my neck. "What is it you think I want?"

"Normal boy-girl stuff," I said throwing my hands in the air. I felt defeated before this line of conversation had even gotten started.

"That's where you're wrong. I don't want normal. I want you." He smiled down at me. "And we do normal stuff. We kiss." To prove his point he gave me a quick peck on the lips and smiled.

"What happens when a kiss isn't enough?"

"Abby, just a few days ago you flinched anytime anyone touched you, and look at us now."

I did look at us. I was sitting in between his legs, his chin rested on my shoulder, my hands on his thighs. "I still flinch when it comes to other people," I said. My aversion to Jake may have no longer existed, but I still wanted to stroke-out if anyone else came within my personal space.

"But you don't flinch when I touch you anymore, and that's what counts."

"I like it when you touch me," I whispered, the very words were hard to say. "But I can't even…" I pulled at the hem of my sleeves. I didn't know how to tell him that I didn't know if I would ever be able to allow him to see under my clothes.

Naked.

Ever.

"You can't even what?"

"Show you," I said. "I can't show you… *me.*"

"Why don't you just tell me about it, talk to me? Will that make it easier?" He was so much more understanding than I thought he'd be. "Instead of showing me what you think is so bad, you can just tell me."

"I can't," I said. It was locked so tight in my memory it was a floodgate I wasn't ready to open. Not just for Jake, but for me. It needed it to stay where I'd stored it for the last eight years.

"You will when you're ready," Jake said confidently.

"I'm not sure I'll *ever* be ready," I told him. "There is a possibility that I'll just be broken forever. I'm not just hiding my body, Jake. I'm pushing the memories out by not showing you what my past has done to me. It's my way of holding on." I shivered. "I'm not sure I'll ever be able to just let it go."

Jake smiled like he'd just accepted a challenge. "Bee, if you feel even a tiny bit of the attraction I feel when I'm around you, just a small amount of how bad I want you…" He kissed the spot behind my ear and flicked his tongue on my neck. Tingles traveled through my skin, sending messages to every part of my neglected body. "Then, taking our clothes off in front of each other is inevitable. It's human nature. It's us." Jake seemed so sure of himself, but what he was saying sounded almost impossible to me.

"I think we both know we don't exactly fit the human nature mold."

"No, we don't fit *any* mold. But, where you are concerned, it's simple." He kissed along my jaw line. "I want you, Abby. No bullshit. I want you just the way you are." He moved his lips to the corner of my mouth and brushed them over my face as he spoke. I closed my eyes and my lips parted in anticipation. "I would very much like to see that body of yours, but there is no rush. We won't do anything you're not ready for." He moved his hands to cup my ass through my shorts. "But *damn*, baby, waiting will be brutal." He kissed me again.

"What if you don't like what you see?"

"I don't know how to explain this to you to make you understand. You're beautiful, baby. Inside and out. I know this without having to see you with your clothes off."

"*You're* beautiful." God, I said such dumb shit around him sometimes.

"Not on the inside I'm not." His eyes grew serious. "I'm not stupid. I know it's a dark place in there."

"*Walking with a friend in the dark is better than walking alone in the light.*" I said.

"What's that from?" Jake asked.

"Hellen Keller. It makes me think of us."

He smiled. "Yeah, I like it. It works." He held me tighter. "You're under my skin, Bee. I really don't care what's under your clothes." Jake thought for a moment. "Scratch that. I'd be pretty pissed if it turns out you have a dick."

I burst out laughing.

"No, no dick," I assured him. He sure knew how to break the tension of a serious conversation.

"So to clarify, you do, in fact, have a vagina?

"Yes, I do."

"And you do not have a dick?" He was trying not to laugh as he asked.

"Yes, this is the case."

"You sure? Not even a little dick?"

"Nope. Just standard issue female parts, as far as I know anyway."

"Then baby, I really don't see what the problem is here." He grabbed me by the waist and stood. Picking me up in one quick motion, he lifted me above his shoulders and swung me around in the air. He let me slide back down against his body. When our mouths lined up, he held me in place and pulled me to him for another kiss. With one hand on the back of my head, he opened his mouth to me, deepening it. His tongue danced on mine. I moaned into his mouth as he pulled away and placed me on my feet. "You are going to be the death of me," he said.

I could have lost myself in those blue eyes. I was pretty sure I already had.

I picked up my camera bag, and we turned towards the parking lot hand-in-hand as a group of people approached us. There were about twelve of them, some familiar. Owen was among them. He led the group with his arm around a small brunette girl wearing itty-bitty white jean shorts and a red bikini top that did nothing to cover her huge breasts. Big Willie Ray was at his side, dragging a cooler on wheels through the sand. Several girls—including Alissa—hung to the back of the crowd.

I tensed when they spotted us.

Alissa was the first to acknowledge us... or the first to

THE DARK LIGHT OF DAY

acknowledge Jake, at least.

"Hey baby," she said, eyeing our joined hands skeptically. "Where you been?"

She reached out to put her arms around him, but he stepped back and pulled me in front of him instead. He wrapped both arms around my waist. Alissa looked at him with her jaw open and her eyes wide.

"Home, mostly we've just been hanging out at home. Right, baby?" he asked me.

I didn't get a chance to answer before Alissa interrupted. "She *lives* with you?"

"Technically, we live *together*," he clarified. She looked like she was going to be sick.

Owen left the brunette and strode toward us, stumbling in the loose sand, a beer in his left hand. He had a soft cast on his right hand and wrist. I was glad to see I'd done some lasting damage. Alissa backed away when Owen approached. "You get tired of fucking all the other whores in this town, Dunn? You gotta make a move on my sloppy seconds?" Owen was either looking for a fight or just very, very stupid. I was thinking it was a bit of both.

Jakes clenched his fists. He was ready to fight back, but I'd been fighting my own battles my entire life.

"Nice cast, Owen. Seems like you might be the one who needs a whore now, seeing as how your right hand appears to be out of commission for a while. How'd you hurt yourself, anyway?" I asked.

"Shut up, you fucking freak. Why don't you take that shirt off and show everyone what you're hiding under those sleeves? 'Cause I tell ya, I got a glimpse, and it ain't fucking pretty under there." He turned to Jake. "Good luck with that shit, brother. Hope you don't mind losing your hard on. When she takes that ugly hoodie off, she's even uglier underneath."

My face flashed hot. I didn't think Owen had seen me. When I'd woken up, all my clothes had been in tact. He obviously had seen something. All the blood rushed from my face. Jake tightened like a bow being drawn back. His eyes darkened and he reached for the back of his jeans. Before he could make a very huge and very public mistake, I reached over and held my hand over his and the gun.

"Not worth it," I whispered. I was trying to keep calm when all I really wanted was to set Jake loose on Owen.

Jake looked at me like I was crazy. "It's worth it to me."

I shook my head. "Too many people around. Too impulsive." I was reasoning with him on a level I thought he would understand. What was I going to tell him, that it was wrong to take out his gun and pop Owen right there on the beach?

How do you reason with someone who kills people for a living? All I knew was that I was talking him down from a ledge I didn't want him to be on.

Jake released the hold on his gun and closed his eyes for a few seconds. He was fighting for control. When he opened his eyes again, he looked down and smiled at me.

Control in tact.

"Why are you smiling, motherfucker?" Owen taunted him. "You can't be too happy about fucking a freak. If you haven't tapped that yet, you should reconsider now. The shit she's got going on under there is a cock-blocker, for sure." Owen winked. "Somehow, it didn't keep me from getting the job done though."

Jake squared his shoulders and grabbed me by the waist. He walked me right through Owen's group of friends. Just as we passed Owen, Jake pushed me to the side and landed a punch squarely across Owen's jaw. He went down hard. His eyes were still open when he crashed on his back in the sand. Jake didn't miss a beat. He just kept on walking, grabbing my hand and towing me away from the gawking crowd.

"So, that's it?" Alissa ran to catch up to us, keeping pace alongside. "You're just with *her* now?" She looked me up and down like she smelled something foul.

"Yes, Alissa. I'm with *her* now." Jake stopped in his tracks and turned to flash her with a look of pure anger, strong and stern. Alissa looked scared, I could see her shaking. Her mouth was open like she was trying to speak but couldn't. "You should know that if I find out you're talking shit about Abby, I'm not above laying you out, too."

I could still see Alissa in the same spot we'd left her, gawking at us with an open mouth as we rode away on Jake's bike.

THE SECOND THE door of the apartment closed, Jake turned to me. There was fire in his eyes. "You need to tell me what happened with Owen the night I picked you up by his house. I need to know because I'm about to blow his fucking head off as it is, and I don't need my imagination making me trigger happy right now."

I didn't say anything.

"Did that motherfucker touch you?"

"You believe him? He was just trying to get a rise out of you."

"*Did he fucking touch you?*"

"Don't you trust me?"

"I've got trust issues like you wouldn't believe, baby. But this is about more than what I believe or what I don't. So, for both our sakes right now, just fucking tell me if that motherfucker touched you."

"Yes," I answered quietly. I sat on the floor next to the couch and rested my head on my knees. Jake paced in front of the TV.

"Did you want him to touch you?"

Did he not know me at all by now?

"Why are you asking me this? Why do you care if he touched me? Let me remind you that when I first met you, you were being sucked off in a junkyard," I spat. "By Alissa."

"Just answer the goddamned question!" he yelled so loud the sliding glass door shook. I flinched as if his words had landed on my face.

"No," I whispered. "I didn't want him to."

"I fucking knew it!" he roared, drawing the gun from the waistband of his jeans. He headed for the front door.

I threw myself in front of him, blocking his exit. "Do you want to know what happened, or not?"

He put his arms around my head on the door, and pressed his chest up against mine, caging me in. "I know all I need to know."

"You can't kill Owen," I said sternly. "They'll catch you and put you in jail."

"Never been caught before."

"There's always a first time."

"This is what I do, Bee."

"Killing Owen isn't like whatever it is you do at your...job." I didn't know what else to call it.

"No, you're right. It isn't. It's more important. Because it's about you."

He still wasn't getting it. "Listen asshole! I don't want you to go because I don't want to lose you!"

It was true. I wanted to care about what happened to Owen, but the honest truth was that as little time as we'd spent together, I'd already gotten used to life with Jake in it. I couldn't afford to lose him. Not now. "Owen turns up dead on the very night that you knocked him out in front of a ton of people, and everyone will know it was you."

I wasn't sure he was listening, until he repeated my words. "You don't want to lose me." He softened his stance over me, his hands coming down to rest on my shoulders.

"No," I sighed. "I don't."

"Bee…" He squinted his eyes together and pressed his fingers on the bridge of his nose. "Did he rape you?" His breaths were short and shallow.

"No."

"How do I know you're not just saying that so I don't go after him?"

"Did you see his hand?"

"Yeah, it's in a sling."

"I did that. I slammed his hand in his own door when I ran out." I sounded proud of myself.

I *was* proud of myself.

"*You* did that to him?" Jake sounded impressed.

"Yes," I confirmed. "Owen didn't rape me. He just got touchy-feely while I was sleeping. I put a quick end to it, though."

"Baby, I hate that he touched you, that he thought his privileged ass was good enough to get to lay hands on you." He paused and rubbed his knuckles down the side of my face. "I don't want anyone to touch you but me." Jake smelled like the beach and leather. His breath was cool as it came in heavy quick bursts. "I'm not good enough to touch you either, but that's not enough to make me stop."

My own breathing quickened.

"Just you, Jake."

"Why didn't you tell me then? That night?"

"What was I supposed to tell you? I was embarrassed, I was tired. I didn't know who to trust or what to do." I held his gaze.

Jake pulled me from the door and sat me on the couch. He laid his gun on the coffee table, making sure to keep it pointed away from us. "I didn't just find you by accident that night."

"What do you mean?"

"I was looking for you. I just needed to see you. I didn't like the feeling I got when I saw you with Owen. I barely knew you, but I had this overwhelming feeling that I wanted to help you. I wanted you to need me." He shifted me to face him, our chests pressed up against one another. "Originally I was just going to make sure you were safe—even if it was with Owen. Then, I saw you walking down that road and I was just so happy to see you. When I saw the bruise on your jaw, I told myself it was from an accident. I wanted to concentrate on you and not killing the person who hurt you." He sighed deeply. "I'm so glad he didn't."

"No, he didn't, but I feel kind of guilty, anyway."

"Why would you feel guilty? He was molesting you as you were passed the fuck out."

"Because I liked it," I whispered. "While I was dreaming, before I realized it was him touching me."

Jakes jaw clenched, then relaxed. I could tell he thought hard about what to say next. "It's okay to like to be touched." He intertwined my fingers with his.

"Not for me it isn't. I mean, I liked how I felt when I woke up, but mostly because at the end of my dream I saw your face and…" I hesitated before telling him the rest. "…I imagined it was you making me feel that way."

Jake looked puzzled. "You were imagining it was me?"

I wanted to lay it all out for him. I was tired of tip toeing around my physical feelings for him. "Jake, the *only* person I've ever been physically attracted to, the only person I've ever wanted to ever touch me at all, and especially the only person I've ever wanted more from is you."

Jake still didn't know everything about me. I wanted to tell him all of it and just rip it off like a bandage, but *wanting* to and *being able* to were so far apart. I wanted him to help me heal, and for him to heal with me.

I wanted to take on his pain because he'd taken mine so completely.

I had let him into my life, into my secrets and my wounds, but the thought of letting him into my body still panicked me. I wanted him, so very much. I wanted his mouth on me and his hands on my body, and I wanted to feel what it would be like to lay skin to skin with him. I wanted him more than I wanted to breathe.

It wasn't a question of what I wanted. It was a question of what I was capable of.

As if he'd read my mind, Jake grabbed the back of my neck and connected my lips to his. His lips were soft, but his kiss wasn't. It was demanding. He pressed harder, asking for more. His lips a perfect mix of hard and soft. He opened to me, deepening the kiss, his tongue finding its way into my mouth as I pushed my hands into his hair.

I wanted this with him. I wanted him to kiss away the past and fill me with only new and amazing memories. Our breathing became labored, and for just a moment, I thought I could really give myself to him in every way.

It was only when he reached around to my waist and pulled me across his lap so my legs were straddling him that my chest constricted.

I could feel the blood rushing from my face, my palms started to sweat. My breath was still ragged, but I couldn't pull enough of it into my lungs. A type of dizziness started to take over.

I had to get out of there. So I did what was most familiar to me.

I ran.

In a flash, I had untangled my legs from around him and hopped off his lap, running to the bedroom and slamming the door behind me. I dove into the bed and buried my face in the pillows, trying to catch my breath.

Jake didn't come in after me. Instead, I heard the front door slam.

He left me.

Why can't I just be normal?

Jake was capable of sharing with me his deepest, darkest shit, and I couldn't just forget that I was a freak for a few minutes and let us enjoy one another. All I wanted was him, his touch, his kiss—his everything. But I had no clue how to get around the barriers I had created for myself.

I was so afraid that, just as it seemed like we'd been getting it all together, I had gone and torn it all apart.

Chapter Fourteen

THE CEILING FAN clicked and rocked as it spun around and around. With each wobbly rotation, the chain danced and jingled. The pale light of the moon shone through the open window, casting the shadow of a palm tree onto one of the bare wall of Jake's room. Its umbrella-like leaves looked like long teeth, rocking in unison with the fan.

The air was thick and hot around me. My long sleeved shirt clung to my skin like a wet paper towel. Moisture beaded on my forehead. I felt almost feverish. Hot, cold, hot, cold. Trying to find some relief, I kicked off the sheets and pulled off my pajama pants, tossing them to the floor. I laid back down on top of the damp sheets in only my long sleeved shirt and panties. The air from the fan felt cool on my wet skin, licking the length of my bare legs. My nipples were already aching. Now, they became painfully hard.

It had been hours since Jake left.

It was going to be a long, long night.

Had my crazy pushed him away so soon? He was supposed to be leaving in only a few hours. Maybe, he'd already left without saying good bye.

I had sprung from Jake's lap like he'd repulsed me when the truth was just the opposite. My body was more alert and alive with him then it had ever been. I could still feel it, too.

I was about to scratch my tingling skin right off my bones.

My fear, my body, and my aversion to sex needed to get together and figure their shit out.

For the first time in my life, my body craved touch. But, my past wouldn't allow me to lower the wall between us—the wall that kept me at a safe distance from everyone, including the one who made me feel safest of all.

I tried to sleep, but I knew it would bring with it dreams of Jake's beautiful face, his calloused hands, his soft lips, the way the harsh lines of his face softened when he laughed. I knew most of all I would dream about his eyes. Those sapphire pools had woken me up and reminded me of what it was like to *feel*— just feel, something anything. Everything. Jake had broken through all my numbness and reminded me that I was okay, just as I was, and that I was human after all.

Damaged, but human. Just like him.

I realized then, in the very short time that I'd known him, that I loved him. I loved all of him, the good and the bad, the light and the dark.

I promised myself that when—*if*—he came back, I would lay all my cards on the table. I would show him the Abby I'd been hiding. It was possible that he'd run. He might be disgusted with me by that point, but I was always going to be me, flaws and all. Holding onto my secrets for the sake of a few more days with someone I know I didn't deserve anyway suddenly felt over-whelmingly selfish.

It was time.

Ready or not.

Definitely not…but whatever.

I was in love with the angel and in lust with the devil. If I were honest with myself, I'd have to say that I was in love with the devil, too.

The bedroom door slowly creaked open. Jake's massive shadow covered the shadowed teeth on the wall as he moved toward the bed. He was wearing his black sweats and a black wife-beater. He paused and looked me over from head to toe before crawling onto the bed beside me. He pulled me into his arms, drawing my back against his hard chest. He softly kissed the back of my head and sighed into my hair.

I sighed, too. From relief. "You came back."

He used his fingers to make circles along my naked thigh. I tensed, aware now that I was wearing only panties, and we were on top of the covers. I checked to make sure my shirt was in place. Thankfully, it was.

"I didn't leave. I just took a walk to cool off." His voice was tired and raw. "I promise I will always come back to you. Always." He lifted my hair off my neck and kissed my bare shoulder. "It's time for you to share your final secret with me, Abby."

"Now?" I didn't know if I could.

"Yes, now." It was a demand, but a gentle one. "It's the only thing left between us. I'm not going to push you for anything but your words. The rest is up to you."

Words.

They'd sat heavy on my tongue for almost nine years. They'd never gone any further than that. It was time. I knew it was. I wanted to be unburdened of it now, and I let that feeling lead the way. It felt right to have Jake know all of me.

I was as unsure of his reaction as I was of myself.

Darkness quickly freed me of my fear.

The words surprised me when they started to flow out of my mouth and into the shadows. I closed my eyes as I told him about the last night I'd spent in my mother's house before I was put in foster care. He listened as I told him how I'd eaten the neighbor's dog's food, though only when I'd been hungry enough not to think about feeling bad for stealing it from the dog. I even told him about running from the constant open-door orgies and endless parade of vile "aunts" and "uncles" who came and went with the same frequency as their highs and jail sentences.

I described in detail how I'd used the shard of mirror to stab the man who'd come into my room in the eye. "I might have killed him... there was so much blood." My eyes spilled with hot tears, but I wiped at them before they had a chance to fall. "I asked the social worker who picked me up if he was dead. I don't think they tell eight-year-olds if they've killed someone, though."

Jake was quiet as he listened, but he continued to trace around my upper thigh with his fingers, blazing a trail of fire on my skin everywhere he touched. But, it wasn't like the fire of a few weeks ago.

This fire was built out of want, not fear.

"That's not all." I braced myself as I began to tell him the rest.

Suddenly, I am nine again. I am naked and crouching in the field. The winds have died down, and now, it's just the cold rain pummeling my skin.

I am free. I am free of the jail I never committed any crime to be in.

The home that held me prison would soon be a memory. I will work my way through starvation. I will never eat dog food again. I will find a family who will love me.

I am still worth loving.

A strong hand is on my arm, hoisting me up from the ground. A bitter voice in my ear: "Now you're really going to find out what happens to bad girls, you little shit."

With one hand wrapped in my hair, she is dragging me through the tall grass, sand spurs clinging to my legs. "You think you can defy me? You think you can say no? I own you and that scrawny, little body. If you don't want to give it up to who I fucking tell you to give it up to, I'm going to make it so no one will ever want you again."

Back in the house. Handcuffed to the radiator. Each burn of her cigarette. Each stab of her knife. Every time she slowly drags the rusted blade across my body, I jump back against the steaming radiator she's purposely set on high.

I am waking up.

I am passing out.

I am waking up.

I am passing out.

I wake, and my mother is no longer over me. She's across the room on the couch, tying a tube around her arm and shooting the needle into a vein by her elbow.

"Abby has been a bad girl, Vinnie. She screams when I punish her."

My mother nods to a man sitting on the floor, leering at me. He isn't wearing a shirt. He smiles and his front teeth are missing, the rest of them a mixture of yellow and black.

"She needs to learn how to shut that mouth of hers. Think you can help?"

The man stands and throws me onto my back, my hand still cuffed to the burning radiator, blood drips down my arm. "Come here, darlin'," he says. He smells like the bottom of the trash can behind the Chinese restaurant. The one where I've looked for food.

He slowly unzips his jeans, and before I can wonder what he is doing, he shoves himself into my mouth, pressing his hands against the back of my head. He holds a knife at my throat. My screams are muffled. I choke once, twice, three times. Then, I'm throwing up, but he won't pull out of my mouth. He just laughs. The vomit spills out the sides of my mouth and splashes down his legs.

Suddenly, I don't care what happens to me. A feeling of not being meant for this world washes over me.

I bite down. I bite down so hard my teeth meet in the middle. The man jumps back and screams. Blood and vomit coat his lap. My mother is passed out, her chin on her chest.

The man lunges at me, knife raised and sinks it into my shoulder so deep he hits carpet before standing and running outside.

It takes me a few minutes before I am able to calm myself from the nauseating pain and remove the blade from my arm. Strings of flesh and thick carpet fibers cling to the rusty blade.

I look over at my mother, and for a moment, I contemplate shoving it deep into the back of her neck while she sleeps.

Instead, I run. As fast as I can I run into the night, down the road, three miles to the fire station. Naked, covered in blood and vomit, I knock on the door, and when it opens, I fall into the arms of a large black man wearing a blue t-shirt and red suspenders.

I went for help.

I was hoping for death.

Jake needed to know all of it. He needed to *see*. I sucked as much air into my lungs as I could. "Can you turn on the lamp, please?" I asked. While Jake leaned behind him to do as I asked, I lifted my shirt over my head and tossed it to the floor. I wasn't wearing a bra, so he could clearly see all of me. I sat on my knees on the bed and waited for him to see who I really was and what I really looked like.

No more hiding.

When he turned back from the lamp, his eyes went wide. Matching slashes covered the tops of both of my breasts. The redness of the injuries never truly faded to white as I had hoped they would. Burn marks, patches of uneven and stretched looking skin—from cigarettes, from cigars, from lighters and the steaming radiator my mother had once handcuffed me to—ran down the length of my right arm and my upper back. In contrast, my left arm was virtually mark-free. My biggest scar was a jagged, red scar that ran from below my left breast down to the top of my right thigh, traveling through the inside of my legs, only a half an inch or so away from doing real damage.

My injuries hadn't been inflicted to cause me to not function physically. They'd been meant to scar my body.

I held my breath.

"These are my punishments," I said. A hot tear ran from the corner of my eye. Jake leaned into me and licked the line it left on my face. He was trying to take on my pain, consume it.

He sat up on his knees and reached out for me. Slowly, he ran his hand over each of the scars on my right arm. He bent his head and kissed along the lines marring the tops of my breasts above each of my nipples. They weren't kisses meant to titillate.

They were meant to heal.

"Mom's in prison. She got life for what she did to me and for the drugs they found on her. She had a ton of priors so they threw the book at her, no parole." I exhaled and closed my eyes.

I was done. Exhausted and done.

Jake cupped my face in his hands. He looked me right in my eyes when he finally spoke. "You are so fucking beautiful," he whispered.

It wasn't what I expected him to say. I expected him to run.

"Just the way you are, Bee. These scars don't make you ugly. You don't need to hide them from anyone. Fuck anyone who thinks anything on someone like you could ever be anything but beautiful. You should be proud of them, baby."

"Proud?" How could I be proud of the ugliness on my body, left on me courtesy of the ugliness in people?

"Yes, proud. They make you powerful. Each line is a road traveled, an experience you had, whether it was good or bad. Each mark is proof of pain in the past, not the present. You are a survivor, you are a warrior. These are the scalps hanging from your fucking belt. You took the beatings and here you are, in front of me." He kissed me softly on my lips and my mouth opened to him before he pulled away again. "You are fucking amazing."

What?

"How can you not see how fucking beautiful you are? He lifted my right arm to his mouth and trailed kisses and caresses from my shoulder to my hand, like he needed to experience with his lips each every mark, dent, line, and poorly-healed patch of skin on my body. My mind reeled from bringing to the surface the memories I had pushed deep inside since the very night it happened.

Jake didn't hesitate. He pulled me into an untamed embrace. "She should die for what she did," he said.

I nodded. She should have. I wished I would've killed her then. I wished it every day.

Jake held me tighter, but we weren't close enough. He raised himself up, just enough for him to remove his shirt before pulling me into him again, with my back to his chest. He leaned into me and pulled the tip of my ear into his mouth. He gently sucked and licked, working his mouth and tongue down to the sensitive spot right behind my ear. I closed my eyes, relishing the feeling of his mouth.

"Do you know how proud of you I am?" he whispered. "That you got away? That you defended yourself against those sick fucks?" His tongue was in my ear, his cool breath danced over the hairs on my neck. "My strong girl." His hand moved from my stomach, traveling further up, his fingertips grazed the underside of my breast. I couldn't hold back the long moan that came out if I'd tried. Jake responded with a groan from deep within his throat. "If I knew who those guys were—" He tried to pull me even closer. "—the one you stabbed in the eye—" I felt his hardness against my leg through the thin fabric of his sweat pants as he pressed against me. "—I would find out if you really had finished off that fat fuck." His hand moved further until he was cupping and massaging my breast in his palm. "If you hadn't and I found him alive—" He brushed his thumb over my nipple and back again. I writhed against him, arching into his touch. "—I would tear that one-eyed bastard limb from fucking limb for you." In one quick motion he had ripped my panties off, tossing the scrap of fabric to the floor. "Then, I'd end him with a bullet through his fucking skull. Would you like that baby?"

"Mmmmmmmmm......" My body released a flush of wetness between my legs.

"Answer me, Bee." He kneaded my breasts in his palms then rolled my nipples in between his fingers. "I need to know if you would like knowing I put him to ground. For you."

No secrets. No lies.

"Yes," I answered honestly. I arched my back into him.

Jake moaned into my neck. He pulled on my shoulder and positioned me onto my back. He lowered himself over me, holding my face in his hands. We were looking right into each other.

Broken soul to broken soul.

Jake's bare chest pressed against mine, his hardness and my softness finally together. "Now that we know all of each others secrets…" He dipped his fingers below my belly button, teasing my skin until he made his way in between my legs, cupping my mound. All I could do was moan.

I was done with words anyway.

All my hesitation was gone. The voice that had always told me to run was a distant memory. I had lost my ability to have a conversation sometime after he ran his thumb over my nipple. A pulling sensation in my lower stomach had already started.

Jake pushed his hand down lower, until his fingers found my wetness and spread it over my sensitive nub. At the same time, he sucked my right nipple into his mouth, lavishing his tongue over and over the hardened peak as his fingers stroked my tender flesh.

My body had never been so alert. It was as if his mouth was right on my core. Every lick, every gyration, every sound he made sent me further and further toward a place I wasn't familiar with.

"You are so fucking beautiful," he said again. He covered my mouth with his, stroking my lips with his tongue, urging me to open for him. When I did, he tasted my tongue in long slow strokes before breaking our kiss to lavish his attentions on the nipple he hadn't yet tasted.

"You know I've never done this before," I whispered. Since I'd never just come out and said it, it felt foreign to me. I guess I was technically a virgin, although I never really felt like one.

I may have never have had sex, but I'd lost my innocence a long time ago.

Jake looked up into my eyes while he pressed two fingers inside me, pushing them in as far as his hand would let him go. I gasped at the new sensation while he watched my reaction, a sly smile on his face. He slowly and expertly pumped his fingers in and out. His thumb circled my clit in a torturous rhythm of fast and slow, hard and soft. I bucked my hips at the sensation of him touching the most sensitive part of my body. The pulling inside grew stronger and a pressure had started to build low in my stomach.

"I know," Jake whispered. His beautiful lips were curled up in a crooked grin.

"I may not be any good at this," I said.

"Not fucking possible," Jake said.

"And you still want to? Even though I've never..." I trailed off. The pulling was building faster, and I had forgotten what I was about to say.

"Fuck yes." He circled my clit faster, applying more pressure. I bucked under him, writhing around for some sort of release. He continued to fuck me with his fingers.

"You see, Abby, a respectable man would probably not want to take your virginity. Some guys, the kind with manners or morals, would even be turned off at the thought of being your first, but like I've tried to tell you–" He leaned in closer, and his lips brushed against my neck when he whispered in my ear. "I'm not like those men." He pressed firmly on my clit. The pressure that had been building exploded in a blinding white hot release, sending shock waves from my toes to my neck, my insides pulsed and clenched as I rode out the new waves of sensation that just kept coming.

I didn't know how much time had passed when I could again open my eyes. "That was..."

"Nothing yet," Jake finished for me. He looked downright wicked, sinful, amazing, I could go on forever. "I've never wanted to be inside someone as much as I want to be inside you right now, baby. I want to feel you come around my cock."

I shuttered in anticipation.

Holy. Fuck.

Jake reached over to the nightstand and pulled out a foil packet from the drawer. I watched him intently as he sat on his knees next to me and opened the package. He never took his eyes off mine as he rolled the condom over his thick length. I was in pure awe of him. I could feel the power radiating off of him. The moonlight highlighted the shadows of his hard biceps and abs. His beautiful black and gray tattoos glistened with sweat.

He positioned himself between my thighs, pressing his hands on the insides of my knees and spreading my legs. As I gazed at the raw power and beauty of his naked form, I realized something.

"Fuck. This is going to hurt isn't it?" I asked, panting with need and a little bit of fear.

Jake flashed me his most wicked grin. He ran his hand through his hair and smiled down at me. "Only in the best of ways, baby."

With the base of his cock in his hand, he rubbed the tip over my clit, creating an all new pressure inside me. He crawled up my body and kissed me. Not an *I'm going to be gentle with you* kiss. It was an all-consuming kiss. I returned it with the passion that had been simmering at the surface since the day I met him. My hands linked on the back of his head as I pulled him to me. The vibration of his moans in my mouth sent an electric pulse right to my core.

Jake didn't break our kiss as he pressed himself into me. My body stretched for him, but not enough. "Shit, baby. You're so tight." He groaned into my mouth, pushing my knees further apart. "Spread your legs for me baby. Let me in."

When I obeyed and had spread my legs as far as I could, opening myself all the way up to him, he surged inside me like he had been waiting to do it his entire life, taking the last traces of my virginity with him. He pushed right through the quick pinch of pain, without pausing his movements even when I flinched.

It was the best pain I'd ever felt.

We were just us. Broken and bruised. Fucked up and messy. And together we were everything we never thought we could be. We didn't need sweet and gentle. I didn't need to be coddled. I needed Jake, and he gave himself to me just as I gave myself to him.

"I need more," he said, his voice strained. I lifted my hips to give him further access, and in an instant, he was buried inside me to the hilt.

The unexpected fullness and the sweet stretching of my body as it accommodated Jake was like nothing I had thought it would feel like. He thrust into me as if he was trying to climb into my soul. Each time he pulled out and pushed back in, I felt his urgency grow. I raised my hips to meet each of his thrusts. The friction on my clit, along with Jake's cock massaging a place so deep inside of me, was overwhelming.

My legs tensed.

"Relax, baby. Just let it happen," he pled. "Please… I need to feel you."

I relaxed my legs as Jake reached his arms around my neck and pressed down on my shoulders, driving into me over and over again. His strokes were hard and furious. He filled me as deep as he could and when he couldn't get any deeper he'd circle his hips like he needed even more of me.

We had all of each other, and yet still we wanted more. So, I asked for it.

"More," I begged him. I squeezed him with every muscle I had inside. I'd been waiting so long to feel again, I needed it all.

"I love it when you beg." His words were like another set of fingers massaging all the right places.

"More," I said again. Louder this time.

"Always." Jake gave me all he had, picking up his pace and slamming into me, sparking the flame between us with each wild stroke until we were both yelling into the night. "Come, baby. Let me feel you come around my cock," he growled.

My legs shot out from beneath me as I felt the pressure start to take me under. Jake held my gaze as the white hotness returned, this time even bigger than before, rolling in on waves that never seemed to end until the flames ignited in one powerful explosion. I pulsed around Jake until he pushed deep into me one last time. I felt his ass clench under my hands. He hardened even more, if that was even possible, and twitched inside me. Then, he held my gaze and cried out my name as he spilled himself into me.

Before that very moment, I had thought the sight of Jake on his bike was the sexiest thing I'd ever seen. That was no longer true. From that day forward, nothing could compare to the sight of Jake coming.

And nothing ever would.

Our bodies throbbed and hummed together as we came down from the high of our orgasms. Jake was still inside me when we fell asleep.

I felt his heart beating though the pulsing of his cock.

"I love you, Bee. So much it fucking hurts." It was the last thing he said before closing his eyes and giving in to his exhaustion.

Chapter Fifteen

FEAR KEPT ME from looking up. I was afraid if I glanced into his eyes I would throw myself at his mercy, beg him to stay here with me and lose my shit entirely. I looked at the shell driveway instead and shuffled my feet nervously, tucking a stray hair behind my ear. Jake ran his knuckles down my cheek. I leaned into his touch that just weeks ago would have sent me running at full speed.

It was still dark out—only one a.m. according to the alarm clock when we woke up. I was standing outside in my orange pajama pants and a white tank.

No hoodie.

No sleeves.

I was tired of hiding, at least in front of Jake. How I felt in public remained to be seen.

"I like this look," Jake said, smiling down at me.

"Yeah, I was thinking tomorrow I would just wear a thong and nothing else."

Jake raised his eyebrows.

"You fucking save that shit for when I get back." He winked at me and went back inside to grab the last of his things from the table. When he came back out the old screen door creaked the protest I felt. "You know what I was thinking?"

"What's that?"

"You know how much you love my tattoos?" Where was he

going with this?

"Yeah."

"Why don't you just embrace your scars and work them into some tattoos?"

"Jake, it's most of my body. I would be one of those freaks on the believe-it-or-not shows."

He laughed and shook his head. "I'm not saying get a full body piece, wise-ass. And I'm not saying you have anything to cover up or be ashamed of. I was just thinking instead of wearing sleeves, you could just get a full tattoo sleeve on your arm… make the scars part of the story, on your own terms."

"Really?" I'd never even thought of inking over them.

"Just something to think about. Besides, it'd be kinda hot."

"I knew you had another reason." I pretend punched him in the arm.

Jake put his hands in the air like he was surrendering. "No other reason. I just want my girl to be as comfortable in her own skin as possible. I want you to be happy."

"You know what? I think I'm actually getting there." I smiled and I felt it all the way to my toes. It was the closest I'd ever been to being happy in my entire life. I had some work to do, but I was getting there slowly, with Jake's help. I saw a light at the end of the tunnel I'd never seen before.

I closed my eyes. I didn't want to be stuck with the mental image of him leaving to play over and over again in my brain until he returned.

He walked over to me and tilted my chin up to him. "Hey," he said. "Open your eyes."

Reluctantly, I obeyed. Jake stared down at me with a smile that reached all the way to his ears. There was no monster lurking in his eyes now, no sign of the killer within. He didn't have the look of a man who was leaving me to complete a kill contract.

But he was.

"I'd prefer it if you kept your eyes open," he joked. "Walls tend to move into your path when you're not watching."

"Oh, they're open all right." I couldn't help but to lean in to kiss the beautiful blue eyed man who I loved.

Jake pulled away with a sigh and continued to pack the saddlebags of his bike. When he was done, he leaned back against the seat and even in the light of the single bulb buzzing from the porch I could see how beautiful he was. I loved everything about him, from the way he hooked his thumbs into the belt loops of his jeans that hung low on his hips to the way he ran his hand over his short goatee when he was thinking about something. There wasn't a sight I wanted to see more on Earth than what was right in front of me.

But, he *had* to go.

Life or death. Kill or be killed.

In every sense, the burden of those words was upon him.

Jake ran his hand over his goatee, I smiled and my heart pounded like a steel drum in my chest. It was nearly drowned out by the sensation of ache and need in my sore body, a reminder of how we'd spent the last few hours.

I wondered if it was like this for everyone. Maybe, Jake felt this way with every girl he had fucked. Maybe to him, ours was run-of-the-mill stuff.

Jake gathered me into his arms until I stood between his legs. He kissed the top of my head and breathed into my hair. "Is it always like that?" I asked hesitantly, my voice a cracked whisper. I had to know.

"Is *what* always like that?"

"You know." I tilted my head back toward the house, hoping the dim light hid the redness I felt creeping up my neck and onto my face.

Understanding and amusement mingled on his face. "No, Bee," he laughed. "It's not."

For a split second, I thought he meant I'd been a disappointment, that he was used to better than what we'd shared.

He must have read my thoughts, "Bee," he started, "it's never, *ever* been like that for me. I'm not exactly a word person, but let me put it this way: I don't think most people ever get to experience something that fucking amazing—" His gaze deepened. "—some*one* so amazing." He leaned down to me. I could feel the brush of his goatee lightly graze my chin and cheek before his lips covered mine. Slowly, the heat that never had enough time to die down started to build again. His tongue gently parted my lip. When it met mine, our breathing became labored and my hands moved into his hair.

Jake pulled his lips away, but stayed close enough so I didn't have to release my hold on him. "If I don't leave now, young lady, I'll be dragging you back to my bed and never, ever leaving."

His hands rested on the nape of my neck as he pressed his forehead to mine. "That doesn't sound so bad."

He growled in frustration. "Go!" he commanded, pointing to the apartment and placing an innocent final kiss on my forehead. I still didn't move. I couldn't.

"Abbbbyyyy," he said, playfully warning me. I liked that side of him.

It almost made me forget what he was heading out to do.

Not that his work itself bothered me. I was worried about his safety, not his job. For once, I wasn't going to question my feelings, or the black-and-white of what they should be.

"I'm going. I'm going," I said, as I peeled myself away from him and slowly turned toward the door.

"Hey Bee!" he called when I had almost reached the front door.

"Yeah?" I asked and turned to see him already mounting his bike. His goggles were in place, and he adjusted the strap on his helmet.

Damn sexy.

"I'll be back as soon as possible. I promise." His face was a mix of happiness and dread.

"You better," I said, trying to keep a light tone to words that sat heavy on my tongue. I took a deep breath and summoned control I never knew I had. Then, I turned and walked back through the front door.

I sat on the floor with my back against the door until I heard the roar of his bike coming to life and the clattering spray of the gravel from under the wide tires as he pulled out onto the main road. I sat there long after the sound faded into the distance, Jake along with it.

"I love you," I whispered to no one.

It wasn't just that I had lost my virginity. It was that, other than with Nan, I had never felt so needed, so wanted, so sure of something in my entire life. What happened to mean, angry Abby Ford, with defenses stronger than Fort Knox? Who was this girl who had actually managed to let someone into her life besides her grandmother? For the first time since Nan died, I didn't feel alone. I didn't have to be Mean Abby with Jake. I didn't have to put on a front and show him how tough I could be. I was softer around the edges. He challenged me in the best of ways. I even loved that he was just as stubborn as I was.

I would rather fight with him than have a normal conversation with anyone else.

It was at least an hour before I got up. I needed something to distract me, so I turned on Jake's laptop and typed *tattoos and scars* into the search engine. I was shocked at the images that came back. Thousands of pictures, mostly of women, with colorful flowered tattoos inked over c-section scars, or in places where their limbs had been amputated. I spent hours looking at them all. The breast cancer survivors were what really caught my attention. So many had opted to embrace their scars – some with a full design filling their whole chest. They didn't cover their scars. They decorated them.

It wasn't just what I wanted now.

It was what I needed.

If the apartment phone hadn't rung just then, I would have already been pulling up images of what I wanted depicted around my scars. I would have been up the rest of the night contemplating the new Abby, someone I was actually beginning to like.

I crossed the room reluctantly and picked up the phone. I didn't even get a chance to say hello. "Abby. Thank fucking God you answered," Reggie said. "Listen, I know Jake is out of town, but the motor on the Morgan crapped out on us again, and we are stuck on fucking Cabbage Key in the middle of the damn night. Just now got enough cell reception to call you. Bo lost his keys for the three hundredth fucking time, and the moron waits until *this very moment* to let me know he left everything open at the storage unit! He's about as useful as a trap door on a canoe."

Before Reggie could ask me to head over to the storage unit to lock up, I offered to do it. I wasn't like I could have slept, even if I'd wanted to. The short walk would help me work off some of the energy that was still humming through me.

"It's no problem, Reggie. I'll head over there now and get it all locked up for you."

"You're my lifesaver, Abby. The sea tow is going to take forever and cost a fortune, so we won't be back until morning. Thank God it's only Sunday. See you at the office Monday. Thanks again." The line went dead. I grabbed the spare keys off the hook by the fridge, shoving them in my shorts pocket before I left the apartment and started off down the road on foot.

The storage unit was only a half a mile up the road, so I didn't bother putting on a shirt to cover my scars.

I was testing myself.

The full moon seemed even brighter than it had been the night before, and for once, the wet thickness of the air didn't feel like it was going to choke me out. Even the smell of butchered fish, a stench that usually stuck to the inside of my nostrils, didn't bother me as much as it usually did.

The lights from the construction on the bridge hummed in the distance, the generator running them sounded like it was powering up for lift-off, drowning out the sound of the river crashing gently against the seawall. In the distance I heard the waves of music and laughter as people went in and out of the ever-revolving door at Bubba's Bar.

I thought about Nan as I walked, up in whatever heaven may or may not have existed for her. I hoped it was the one she whole heartedly believed in, and convinced myself that in some way that she was the one who'd sent Jake to me. She would have liked him so much, regardless of his flaws—and maybe even because of them. I imagined if she were still alive she would demand I bring him home to meet her properly. She would probably make him dinner, insisting he take a second helping of her famous mustard greens potato salad and forcing him to take all the leftovers home. She seemed to believe that no one in town ate unless she fed them. I chuckled aloud thinking about Jake trying to answer the barrage of questions Nan would've surely had for him. We would leave out the part about him being a contract killer.

I don't think that would go over big.

I could taste the salt in the air on my tongue as I walked across the bridge, swinging my arms and whistling.

Whistling?

Who was this girl?

I knew one thing: the new me was almost happy… and that was okay with her. For once, I wasn't going to stand in my own way.

Once I was clear of the blinding lights hanging from the construction cranes, I relaxed under the comfort of the thousands of stars occupying the sky, reminding me of thousand of winking eyes. The moon hovered like an old friend wanting to know the news of the day.

I knew for sure Nan was up there watching me, rooting for me to have the life I never thought I could. I was so close. In less than a month, Jake would be back and a new chapter would officially start for both of us. Together. I was going to go with him. I could be normal with him. I could have a life with him. As soon as he got back, we would start planning where we would go first. I was thinking New Orleans, but New York was on the list, too. I'd never been anywhere besides Georgia and Florida.

My life finally had possibility.

I was grateful for the first time since Nan took me in. "Thank you, Nan," I whispered, hoping my message would reach her somehow. The very first happy tear I've ever cried in my almost eighteen years on this earth slid down my cheek.

"Nan don't need no thanks from a fucking whore." A deep, slow, slurred voice growled from somewhere in the dark, startling me.

"Where are you?" I asked. "*Who* are you?" My heart thumped out an uneven warning like Morse code.

"Aw, baby." Owen stepped out from shadows under the overhang of the bait shack and into the moonlight. "What's the matter? You don't recognize my voice no more? Tsk tsk tsk. Now, that hurts my feelings." He took a swig from an almost-empty glass bottle, wiping the dark brown dribble from his chin with the backside of his grease-stained hand.

"What the hell do you want, Owen?" I crossed my arms over my chest and tried to push out the little voice in the back of my head telling me I should freak the fuck out.

He motioned his bottle to my exposed arms. "Looky here. Someone decided to come out of hiding. It's about time you showed off those fat tits." I remained silent. I didn't want to make more trouble with him. I just needed to get the fuck away.

"What do you think your Nan would say if she knew you'd taken up with a junkyard dog like Jake Dunn? You really think she'd be proud of you for fucking that loser?" Owen took another slow menacing step toward me. "You lied to me." There was an edge to his voice I'd never heard before. His white tank top was stained brown and red with what I could only guess was a mixture of bait and fish guts. Even from a few feet away, I could smell the liquor wafting off him.

"How the fuck did I lie to you, Owen?" I asked, trying not to show my growing unease. I started to walk casually toward the storage unit door next to the bait shop. My plan was to run in and lock it behind me as quickly as possible. I could hear Owen's foot steps on the gravel quicken as I tried to pass him.

He closed the gap between us.

"Yes—LIED! Look it up!" he yelled, furious. "You told me you weren't fucking *no one,* weren't wanting *no one.* Truth was, you just didn't want to fuck *me!*"

I'd never heard him talk with this much hatred and pain behind his words.

He drained the bottle and slammed it against the seawall rocks lining the road. The glass exploded like fireworks. He let out a laugh like a machine gun. "I thought you were different, but you ain't no different then all the other sluts in this fucking town, are you?" A cruel smile hung on his lips. His eyelids were puffy; thin, red veins swam in the whites of his eyes.

"Owen, you don't know what you're talking about. Get your drunk ass home." I tried to play it off, walking faster toward the door of the unit. The handle was just steps away from my grasp.

"Now Abby, why would I go home to my empty bed when I've got you right here?" He caught up to me and grabbed me by the back of my tank top, spinning me around to look him in the face, my ankle twisting on the unevenness of the road, sending a shock of pain up my leg. I regained my balance and took a step back, but Owen held on. "Especially since you're game now," he added. The venom in his voice more potent than any rattler.

"Owen, stop! I have to go. This ain't funny!" I tried to turn back around, but his hands shot out and caught me by the shoulders. The burning I hadn't felt in over a week was back in an instant. My entire arm was engulfed in flames. His grip was tight, unclipped fingernails dug into my flesh. The stench of rotten fish and whiskey made my stomach turn.

Owen glared into my eyes, talking between gritted teeth and spraying saliva on me as he spoke. "So let me get this right, you have time to fuck Jake Dunn, who you ain't known but for a minute, but you ain't got no time to for your dear friend, Owen?" An involuntary gasp shot out of my mouth like the blast from an air gun. He breathed in my ear, his grip tightened, I was sure he was drawing blood. He pulled me closer, running the back of his dirty index finger down the side of my face, leaving an icy chill on my cheek. I recoiled from his touch. "You know, I saw you two tonight."

"Owen, stop. You're scaring me." I struggled to free myself.

"Oh no, you don't, Miss Abby," he seethed. "Not this time." The dip he had tucked into his lower lip sprayed out of his mouth with the emphasis of each of his words, chunks of it sliding down his lip to his chin. Owen crushed his cold, wet, tobacco spit covered lips over my mouth. My face ignited at the sensation. I managed to get an arm free, and as soon as I did, I cocked it back, and slammed my fist straight into his jaw.

Owen's head snapped to the side. He dropped me and rubbed his face, which was already red from the blow. I turned and bolted, but in no more than three steps, he'd caught me again, pulling me into him with one hard muscled arm and crushing us together, chest on chest. I felt his erection through his jeans, pushing against my stomach. He might as well have doused me in gasoline and set me on fire. But, I wasn't about to let the unwanted heat weaken my resolve to fight him off. I tried to kick at him, aiming for the very area of my concern. He laughed at the attempt. "Fucking stop it, Owen!" I screamed. "Get off of me, you *asshole!*"

This wasn't just Owen teasing me. This was Owen taking what he wanted. I was just an outlet for his anger. The object of his revenge.

I had to get out of there.

"Now now, Abby. You know I like it when you struggle a little. It isn't fair that little bitch Jake gets to have all the fun, now is it?" Owen trailed his tongue over my earlobe, his hot breath almost making me wretch. I stretched my neck aside, pulling away as much as I could. I screamed until he covered my mouth with one large filthy hand and began to pull me backward into the dark. I pressed my feet down into the dirt, trying to hold my ground.

Where was he trying to take me?

With his hand still over my mouth, he hoisted me up with his forearm under my breasts, dragging me over the jagged rocks of the seawall. I lost one boot, then the other. My knife was securely tucked in the last one. Still, I refused to let up on my struggle.

The rocks sliced painful cuts on the soles of my feet. With my arms locked to my sides, I tried to use my elbows to dig into his ribs. It did nothing more than annoy him. He was too big, too powerful. He just turned and lifted me, carrying me like a suitcase tucked under his arm. His other hand never left my mouth.

My heart raced. Every vein inside me throbbed in panic.

Jake! I need you! Was my primary thought.

I did the only other thing I could think of, I bit down as hard as I could, digging my teeth all the way into the flesh of Owen's hand. His blood instantly flooded my mouth, tasting of liquor and copper.

"*Motherfucker!*" he shouted. But, he never loosened his grip, and he never missed a step.

Hot tears streamed down my face.

"You think that's going to change anything?" He spoke with playful tone piled on top of his menacing laugh. I knew now that this was just a game to him, with rules I didn't have any hope of understanding.

I screamed into his hand, blowing his blood into my nose, breathing it into my lungs. I coughed and choked but didn't stop the onslaught of teeth into skin. I bit into him again, only this time he released me. I spun around, trying to gain some footing on the uneven sand only to be met with the wrecking ball of his fist smashing into my right cheek. It crunched under the pressure of the blow, spraying the blood from his hand all over my face. It was like nothing I'd ever felt before. My head felt like it had exploded. My entire body vibrated as my legs collapsed under me and I fell onto the beach.

"Fuck, Abby. Look at what you made me do!" Owen scolded me like I was a child who'd knocked over my dinner plate at the table. "If you'd just behave yourself, it wouldn't have to be like this."

Words I'd heard before and had hoped to never hear again.

Owen paused and let out a deep sigh. "Either way, baby, it's gonna be real special."

I drifted in and out of consciousness after that punch.

Truth be told, I wished he would have knocked me out cold.

Owen took both of my feet in his hands and dragged me under a palm tree leaning over the water. I couldn't open my right eye, the vision in my left had begun to blur. I kicked my legs aimlessly as hard as I could, hoping to hit something or anything of Owen's that would cause him to stop. Either my kicks were so weak they had no affect on him, or my perceived kicks were purely a product of my subconscious still willing me to fight.

He dropped to his knees, hovering over me. His sweat dripped onto my forehead like water torture. His pungent body odor mixed with the smell of the salt in the air. I spent the last bit of fight I had left trying to keep my knees together when he pushed my shorts down off my legs, shoving his hands between them and holding my thighs open with his elbows. He hooked his fingers through the crotch of my underwear, ripping them off in one swipe, groaning when his fingers brushed over my sex. He brought my panties up to his nose and sniffed. His jaw tightened. The thick vein in his neck throbbed. His rage erupted.

"I can fucking *smell him on you, you fucking whore!*" he roared.

He tossed them blindly into the canal. He used his knees to keep my legs spread open, then positioned himself between them.

This is really happening...

I tried to scream, but all that came out was a weak groan. A wave of nausea washed over me. I turned my head to the side, and I threw up into the sand, choking on the chunks of fried chicken as they came back up.

Had it been only an hour since I was with Jake? Was it possible?

Because now I was in hell. With the devil himself.

Owen didn't seem to notice the vomit, and if he did, he didn't seem to care. With one motion, he pulled down his jeans and freed himself of his boxers. He forced one hand under my back, yanking me closer to him, and with the other hand he thrust himself inside me. I could feel the grit of the sand from the beach tearing at my insides like shards of glass. The burning was like nothing I'd ever experienced from external touch. This wasn't like my skin was being ignited.

I cried out.

This time, I was the flame. The pain was blinding. All I saw was white.

I couldn't make myself believe what was happening. As a product of the most fucked up home in some deviant God's creation, I was being faced with the one thing I'd managed to avoid. *This can't be happening.* I kept telling myself over and over again. *This can't be happening.*

Only, it was happening. There was nothing I could do to stop it.

The pain was worse than when my mother carved me up like a fucking Thanksgiving turkey. It was worse than being stabbed.

Worse than being beaten.

Worse than anything.

I cried out again and again as he entered me. Every sound from my mouth was answered with a blow from his closed fist. "Don't fucking cry, you *bitch*," he spat, thrusting harder, punishing me. "I know you like it."

He closed his eyes and moaned. When he opened his mouth, I could see strands of saliva connecting his top and bottom teeth. I tried to scream again, I wanted someone to hear me, but this time, no words came out. "I heard you moan like the whore you are when you fucked Jake tonight. I know this shit turns on girls like you. So, moan, you *fucking bitch!*" With a twist of his hips, he sliced into me like a serrated knife. The more I tried to resist, the more forceful his thrusts became.

I could no longer feel my limbs.

Owen suddenly pulled out of me, scraping my insides like sandpaper, flipping me over onto my stomach like I was a rag doll. With one hand on the back of my head, he shoved my face into the wet sand. "That's what you fucking get for trying to scream." His next thrust sent painful shockwaves through my body, I'm pretty sure I lost consciousness for a minute or two.

I was being torn apart from the inside.

I didn't know how much more I could take. My body was shutting down. I wasn't gasping for breath anymore. Only small pulls of air kept my heart pulsing slowly, deep within my chest.

"It fucking hurts, doesn't it?" he hissed through gritted teeth. "Bet Jake didn't fuck you in the ass!" Taking fistfuls of hair, he yanked and pulled for leverage until he yanked hard enough to rip out patches of hair and scalp. It made the same sound as a stubborn zipper. "You see now, don't you? A part of you is mine now." He almost giggled when he whispered those words. I could smell him even through the sand. I could smell and taste my own blood and vomit. I could actually feel my insides coming apart as every grain of sand ground against them.

My mind wandered to the news reels I've seen where people describe the aftermath of a tornado: *It was a surprise... sounded like a death train... left everything broken and twisted in it's wake... almost killed...scared to death...lost everything...would never be the same...*

I'm not going to survive this.

I opened my mouth to scream into the dirt. Instead, I welcomed wet sand into my lungs, gagging until I dry heaved and forced even more of the beach into my throat.

I'm going to die.

I was never going to see Jake again. Just when I thought I finally had something I could trust, something real, it was all being taken from me.

By force.

How stupid I was to think I could ever be happy. I was being punished for wanting more than what I had been dealt. I was going to die here. I lifted my head from the sand in one last attempt to stay alive.

Owen flipped me back over and pressed his hands into my chest forcefully to steady himself. I felt the crack of my ribs and heard bones snap. He kept talking, but now, his voice was just a muffled sound in the distance.

Smaller background noises seemed amplified. A nearby cricket chirping. The rustle of palm fronds in the wind. The splash of mullet jumping into the canal.

Help, please someone… help.

Instead of help, I received only more blunt force, more blinding agony across my battered face.

And then, I died.

Chapter Sixteen

D EATH DIDN'T DRAW me into its embrace that night, although I truly believed that it had. I'd rather have been dead than have to be the fucking victim again. I'd rather have been dead than hold the knowledge of what happened, to have the power to see those images whenever my thoughts felt like wondering beyond the walls I'd built. All the reminders of the blows to my face and body would come with them, the revisiting of the horrific intrusion inside of me.

It was too much to ever think that I could be happy.

I wasn't the happy ending type, after all. I was the fucked-up kid that fucked-up shit happened to. Why had I ever thought I deserved more?

I didn't know how long I'd lain there, didn't know if it was day or night. I didn't open my eyes for hours. I kept them shut and wished for a quick death. I thought if I concentrated hard enough I could will myself into oblivion. People like me were only meant to feel pain and suffering, I opened my eyes—or, I should say, I opened my *eye.*

And pain I felt.

I was in my room. Jake's room. *Our room.* That was all I could make out before having to shut out the harsh rays of daylight. My mouth was dry and cracked, and seemed glued shut. One of my nostrils was clogged. I couldn't catch my breath. I used my swollen purple fingers to pick the dried blood and scabbing from my lips so I could open my mouth to take a deep breath. It felt like glass shattering inside me.

How did I get back here?

Did someone save me?

No, someone hadn't saved me. Someone *moved* me.

He moved me.

A wave of nausea came over me. Unable to stand and run to the bathroom, I tried to wretch onto the floor beside the bed, in the process unclogging a dried blood-filled nostril, sending chunks of black and streams of fresh red into the bile on the side of the mattress.

So much for puking on the floor.

Exhausted from what couldn't have been more than a few minutes of consciousness, I drifted back off to sleep lying upon the mess I just created.

The next time I awoke, it was night, and I needed to use the bathroom. My legs wouldn't cooperate. The second I tried to stand, I started to go down again. I tried to catch myself on the nightstand, but my arms weren't strong enough. I fell chest-first onto the floor. A tingling sensation in my spine erupted into a tearing sensation from my neck to my ass. There was no way I was going to be able to walk the twenty feet or so to the bathroom.

So, I crawled.

With only the support of my forearms, I slowly dragged my own meat-bag of a limp body across the cold ceramic tile floor inch by agonizing inch. I left a bloody dirt trail from my bed to the bathroom. I don't know how long it took. It seemed like days, years, an eternity. In another turn of universal cruelty, once I finally got there, I discovered that the bathroom door was shut. I summoned every inch of determination I still had to reach a shaky, nearly-useless arm up to the door handle. I leaned on it, forcing the door open and falling to the bathroom floor like a broken rag doll.

I needed to see what he'd done, to know what I was dealing with.

I gathered my strength and slowly pushed myself to my knees. In one huff, I launched myself up onto my feet, grabbing the countertop to regain my balance and hold myself up. I had to lean into the counter so far my chest was almost in the sink. I used my elbow to nudge the light on.

What I saw in the mirror, the girl staring back at me, wasn't me at all.

My eyes were both as black as night, with smudges of purple and yellow. My usually-pale skin was unrecognizable under the red stains of blood, and the blue and yellow bruising that extended all the way down my cheeks and along my jaw. My copper hair was slicked back and caked with dark crimson chunks. I ran my fingers over my lips, flinching at my own touch. The tank top I wore was smeared with dirt and vomit. I was naked from the waist down. Streams of red ran along the inside of my legs, like thick veins that spilled over onto my feet. I opened my mouth as much as I could in order to press a finger inside to feel for my teeth. As far as I could tell, they were all there.

I need Jake.

When I was eight years old, my mother's drug dealer beat her to within an inch of her life. She looked very much like how I looked now, except she was unconscious and in a hospital bed for over two weeks. When she was released, I was so happy to finally have her home. To have her all to myself, sober for once. That had to be her rock bottom. Almost dying had to be reason for quitting and even more of a reason to start being a real mom to me. I convinced myself it was going to be a new start for all of us.

I sat on the front of their yellow station wagon on the bench seat, between my dad, who was driving, and my mom, who was in the passenger seat, on the way home from the hospital. I was beaming. After everything we had been through, I had reason to believe that we were going to be a real family.

We were three blocks down the road from the hospital when Mom asked me to hold one end of a rubber tie-off while she shot up right there in the front seat.

That was the first and last time I allowed myself real hope for a family...until Nan.

Nan..

I let out a scream that could have woken the dead, igniting the fire of pain within every cell of my body. I didn't care. Pain was what I was used to. Hurt and disappointment and fucked-up-ness were normal for me. I screamed louder. Something in my throat felt like it popped, and blood rose in my throat and into my mouth. I sank down onto the floor of the bathroom and curled up in fetal position. The blood, too much to swallow, flowed out from my mouth and onto the tile, creating rivers of red in the grout. I wasn't throwing it up. I was just releasing it.

Dragging myself up onto the toilet wasn't an option. I had no strength left. Urine came out of me in burning waves of agony, causing me to see what looked like TV snow behind my eyelids.

My life *was* my pain, and there was so much more to come.

It was then that I made the decision. A decision I always knew I might have to make at some point in my life, but had somehow doubted I'd ever have the strength to actually carry out.

Owen was going to die.

When Jake returned, I was going to tell him what happened. Every explicit, gory detail. I was going to awaken the monster within.

It wasn't like I could call the authorities. In Coral Pines, Owen's family *was* the authorities. The mayor, the DA, the county judge, the lowly sheriff—all were Fletchers, born and bred. They wouldn't help me.

Jake would.

My breath quickened – not from the pain anymore, but from the dark satisfaction of my decision. A small maniacal laugh escaped my lips, and I clutched my ribs that felt like they were being broken again and again with each sound I made.

I let it all come.

Jake is going to kill Owen.

In between the throws of unbearable agony and the fits of insane laughter, the thought was comforting. It made the pain almost bearable.

Almost.

Chapter Seventeen

I T WAS TEN o'clock p.m., and all of the lights inside Coral Pines High School were off. I didn't want to turn any of them on for fear of drawing attention to myself. What I was there to do didn't require light, anyway. The red glow from the exit signs above every doorway and my tiny keychain flashlight allowed me to see just enough for to find my way through.

Even in the absence of students, the school still smelled the same as it always did: like chemicals from the dry erase markers mixed with stale air and a faint smell of body odor wafting from the gym. It would be another couple of months before the students returned to school, it was as if I'd hear the bell ring at any moment, the sounds of the students' laughter echoing through the halls as they spilled from their classrooms, slamming lockers and shouting over one another.

I navigated my way down one dark hall and then another. Most of my soreness was now replaced with a constant state of 'uncomfortable' that I felt in each and every step.

The towering locker system looked very much like rows of silent soldiers lining every open section of wall from the floor to ceiling. When I reached the closet-turned-darkroom that Mr. Johnson had built for his photography class, I used the knife from my boot to flip the flimsy latch.

When I was sure the room was light-tight, I turned on the safe light and went to work pulling the negatives from my camera and filling the trays with processing chemicals. It took longer than I thought, but when I was done, twelve black-and-white photos hung on clothespins on the drying line across the room, each one a different angle of the same subject.

Me.

Looking at them made me feel as if not even a second had passed, let alone a few weeks. I was right there again. I closed my eyes to fight off the intruding memories, but they wouldn't relent.

Again, I felt every blow, every bit of force he used when he pushed himself into me. I felt a sudden panic rise in my chest that radiated down my body to my toes.

I was afraid to leave the apartment in those first couple of weeks, not just because Owen was out there somewhere, but because I didn't want anyone to see me. I'd called Reggie and told him I was violently ill and didn't want to get the rest of the guys sick so he slipped invoices and receipts under the door of the apartment for me to organize at home until the bruising on my face faded.

When I did make it back to work, I'd heard that all the Fletchers were spending the rest of the summer at their cabin up in Jackson Hole.

Owen would be gone until Jake came back.

I could breathe for the first time in weeks.

The smell of the chemicals in the small space, mixed with the heat of the non air-conditioned room, must have been too much for my fragile state of being. I grabbed an empty mop bucket from the corner and threw up the contents of my stomach until nothing was left, and I was just dry heaving.

I'd come to develop the pictures knowing how I would feel. I knew what my reaction would be. I didn't want to remember what happened. I didn't want to acknowledge it at all. But, this wasn't for me. This was for him. I would be strong for him. I had to show him everything. He needed to know.

I barely had the strength to hold my camera when I took them. My wrists had shaken under its seemingly enormous weight. That shake could almost be seen within the photos themselves, causing fuzz around the edges instead of solid lines.

I saw so much more in them than I'd expected to.

In the first, I was staring straight ahead, as if I was looking at someone else's reflection. I held the camera down by my side so I could capture all of my naked body. Every bruise, every bit of dried blood, every swell and scratch was picked up by the camera's lens and magnified in the truthful light and shadow of the black and white image. The next was similar. In that one, my body was turned as if I looked over my own shoulder at the spreading bloodstains under the skin that covered my ribs. The next was similar, too, but slightly different.

And the next one.

And the next one.

And the next one.

Each was a haunted, battered version of me, taken from a different angle.

In the very last one, I was on the floor with my legs spread out in front of me. My knees were pushed open wide as I could make them go. I was wincing from the pain of the position, but the camera I'd raised above my head in both hands had captured my determination to take the photo.

This photo wasn't taken to document what Owen had done. This one I had taken for me. Fresh wounds mixed with old scars. A portrait of my life in pain. Proof that I had been beaten, but I wasn't broken.

They couldn't fucking break me.

My photos reminded me of my favorite painting by an unknown artist. It depicted a woman lying naked with a huge red scar running down the length of her body. Her mouth was open, like she was screaming. Just like her, my photos represented my abusers ill-fated attempt to cut me open and gut out my secrets. She'd been cut but not opened.

Just like me.

I looked at the line hung with square images of my battered body, my blackened eyes and my swollen mouth spread in a wince, and realized: *all of this was a consequence.*

I was a consequence.

These photos were just one side of my story. There was a cause behind the consequence. I imagined the moment one day when there would be similar photographs of that cause, of the man who made this misery for me.

That became my hope.

I took a photo folder from the cubby behind the safelight and placed my dry pictures inside. I spent extra time cleaning the dark room and putting away the chemicals so there wouldn't any trace of my presence left behind.

As I walked away from the school grounds, an idea came to me. Maybe, the woman in the scar painting wasn't screaming in pain. Maybe, she was laughing.

Maybe, she, too, was plotting her revenge.

Chapter Eighteen

I STOOD ON the very top of the Matlacha Pass on a day with no clouds. The only visible reminder of the nightmare from five weeks earlier when my life changed forever once again was a small, bright red scar on my lower lip. I found myself wanting to spend more time in the sun than I had in the past. I relished the feel of a sunburn now. It was just enough discomfort to remind me that I was still alive and to kill the numbness that threatened to take over every day that Jake was away.

I let myself sit in the blazing heat, my eyes closed and my face turned upward to the sky. I watched the colors move around and dance behind my eyelids while I imagined what it would be like when he returned.

I'd spent the last few weeks planning my tattoo sleeve and pinning cities on the map on Jake's laptop of where I wanted him to take me. The day before, I'd even bought a sundress. It was green and strapless and stopped mid-thigh. I didn't have the nerve to wear it in public. In addition to my scars, the bruises on my inner thighs hadn't quite healed all the way. Wearing the dress had become my goal.

Maybe, I would wear it on the day Coral Pines disappeared in the rearview mirror of Jake's bike.

I watched a tourist boy try to pull up a massive grouper that he wasn't prepared for or even skilled enough to catch. The boy was a teenager and a very small one at that. I guessed he couldn't have been more than fourteen. After more than twenty minutes of battling his catch, he finally reeled in the enormous fish just enough to break the surface of the water, exposing the full figure of what looked to be a forty pound catch. He didn't have time to celebrate. The second the creature's tail lifted off the top of the water, the tip of the boy's rod broke from his pole, and his line snapped, sending him backwards on his ass to the sidewalk and the grouper back home to the river floor with a free meal of Spanish mackerel in its belly.

I imagined I was that boy. I had something so massive and wonderful just within reach. I was starting to believe my line was ready to snap just like his did.

I missed Jake.

It had been weeks since he left. I was starting to lose faith that he would come back to me. I tried to be strong, to believe in him in the same way he seemed to believe in me. I knew how he felt about Owen, even before he'd done what he had to me. I knew how strongly he'd react when he heard what had happened, but I wasn't sure how he'd feel about me once he knew. As difficult as it was for me, I had to believe we could make it through. After all, he was the one who'd taught me to trust him with my pain. I just hoped that he would trust me with his.

I didn't know how I would find the words, so I decided I'd speak through my pictures instead.

The moment the afternoon storm clouds chose to block out the sun before delivering their usual torrent, I felt him. Even before I saw him.

I was still on my bench but had just shifted my focus from the tourists to the weather when the awareness of him washed over me. My skin prickled with anticipation, and my heart fluttered in way I wasn't used to at all. I smoothed my hair with my hands as I stood and walked off the bridge, hoping that when I got back to the apartment, he would be there, and that the feeling wasn't just some misguided intuition.

I had only taken a single step when I saw him. He stood at the bottom of the bridge in all his black leather glory.

Jake.

I tried to walk and not run toward him, but as I got closer, I couldn't help picking up my pace. By the time I was halfway to where he was, I'd broken into a full-on sprint. I flung myself into his arms and wrapped my legs around his waist. His smell was intoxicating—leather and sweat and pure man. I couldn't help running my hands through his hair and taking a deep breath so I could take him all in.

I molested him this way for a while before I realized how stiff he was. His arms hadn't come around me. His lips never touched my face. When I finally pulled back, I realized his gaze was as hard as stone and focused sternly on his feet.

I didn't know what he would be like after he finished a kill. Honestly, I had been through so much of my own shit that I hadn't spent any time thinking about it, either. Now, I realized that he'd been through something incredibly dark while he was gone. Maybe, he just needed to ease back into the reality of his other life.

I touched his chin with my fingers and raised his face. His beautiful blue eyes met mine, but they were cold and distant. I softly ran my lips over his, giving him time to react to my nearness. But when he stayed stiff and still even after all that, I knew there was something more happening.

"Jake?"

He took a step back and my feet met the ground.

"What's wrong?" I asked. Now, I was confused. What could

have happened to make him this cold to me when he'd been so hot and affectionate before he left?

He shuffled his feet and pinched the bridge of his nose before he spoke. His words were horrifying. "I'm just going to ask you this once, Abby." His voice sounded shaky and gravely, and his nickname for me went noticeably unused.

I nodded. I would answer whatever he needed. Of course, I would. "Okay."

"Did you, or did you not, fuck Owen Fletcher while I was gone?"

My stomach turned sick, my arms so heavy I wasn't sure my frame would support them. They hung limply at my sides as I tried to form a coherent thought.

"What?" It was all I could manage.

"I asked you if you fucked Owen Fletcher." He said it through gritted teeth, with his fists clenched at his side, his steel face blushing slightly. I could see his jaw clench and his pulse beating quickly within his temple.

"I know what you asked me." I tried to sound angry, but it didn't work. My own voice sounded foreign to me. I heard a higher-pitched, more terrified version of myself. "I want to know why you would even think to ask me that."

"Because a reliable source said that he saw you go under the fucking bridge with Owen right after I left, and when he went to find Owen, that prick had your fucking *underwear* in his pocket and was bragging about how you finally gave it up to him."

As soon as he said it, I lost all hope for what could have been. The accusing look in his eye. The cold, hard stare burning a hole right through me. The way I felt like a slut under his gaze, even though I hadn't done a single thing to deserve such a look. What I believed Jake and I had didn't really exist after all. His look told me that. He'd heard a fucking rumor from some ignorant asshole friend of Owen's—like the rumors I hear every day—and he assumed it was true. He believed I was capable of betraying him so easily. I felt my walls going up. I was building it, brick by fucking brick. The old Abby was being put back into place. Part of me was heartbroken about it, but part of me couldn't help but feel relieved. Deep inside, no matter how much faith I let myself have in Jake, somehow I'd known this moment would come eventually.

I just didn't think it would've come so soon.

"So that's what you really think of me?" I said in almost a whisper, sinking down to the curb of the sidewalk.

Pelicans dove behind us for live bait in the fisherman's buckets. Children laughed hysterically when they pulled up pin fish on their lines. People buzzed by on scooters, the inexperienced drivers spinning past us without so much as a glance in our direction. It was like we weren't even there, like none of it was really happening. All around us, life was still going on. But inside, it felt as though my heart had just stopped. It stood as still as Jake did.

"Just answer the fucking question." His voice was angry, but there was something pleading about it, too. He wanted the truth but only on his terms. He wanted me to tell him that I hadn't done anything and that he had nothing to worry about. He wanted me to tell him it would all be okay.

But, beneath that, he doubted me. He doubted *us*. He questioned it even though I had freely given him all of me.

Every broken part of me was his.

Somehow he thought that after what we'd had together the night he left, I could run to the nearest bed—Owen Fletcher's bed—and dive right in.

It dawned on me then why this was so significant. Why I couldn't just tell him it hadn't happened and move on.

I had been questioned by people my entire life.

Nobody had ever believed my word as the truth. No matter what happened to me—even the most unthinkable things. When I'd told anyone about them, nobody had ever trusted that what I was saying wasn't a lie.

I'd thought Jake was different than everyone else. I thought what we had was actual trust.

I was wrong.

The clouds released the first of the afternoon rain, soft at first then harder, until sheets poured between us. Tourists screeched and scattered for shelter. Jake and I just stood there and stared at one another, the water dripping off of us as if it wasn't happening, either.

"Abby, just tell me!" He was frustrated now. His forehead was furrowed, and his eyes looked hurt and concerned, but his voice sounded like pure vinegar.

"I would never do that to you."

"Wouldn't you?" I couldn't believe he would ask me that, after everything I'd shared with him.

The rain concealed my tears. I looked down at my boots to compose myself.

"You can believe whatever you want," I told him.

"I want to believe the truth," Jake said.

But, it was the truth. Whether he believed it or not.

"No, you don't. You heard a rumor, and you immediately believed that I fucked Owen." I shook my head. "You doubt me. I let my walls down with you. I showed you how much you meant to me. I told you things I've never told anyone else." My voice cracked. "I showed you my scars."

He would be the last person to see them.

"Doesn't matter, though. A few minutes after you ride back into town, you accuse me of screwing someone else. You don't know me like I thought you did. You're not who I thought you were." I didn't wait for him to answer. I just started walking past him, toward the apartment.

"Bee." He grabbed my elbow. I looked up at him so I could see his beautiful sapphire blue eyes for what I imagined was going to be one last time. His lips were tight and his grip on my arm was even tighter.

I shook him off and kept on walking.

I was glad for the rain now, to cover my tears so Jake couldn't see them. He didn't deserve my tears. He didn't deserve my pain, or the faith that I'd placed in him.

I heard his boots on the gravel trailing behind me.

"Bee!" he yelled.

Each time he said it, it felt like he was stabbing me one more time, letting me bleed out and suffer a slow, agonizing death. When I couldn't take anymore, when I needed the torture to be over, I stopped walking and turned to face him. I steadied my gaze and looked him right in the eye.

In that moment, it wasn't red that I saw. It was blue. Radiant blue, like the color of his eyes. I don't remember the look on his face. I just remember the beautiful color blue clouding my vision.

Before I could say anything, he jumped in. "You were my *only* reason to come back here."

"Well, ain't nothing holding you here now."

I turned and started to run. I had no destination in mind. I just needed to get away from the hurt. But, it traveled with me.

I ran faster.

There were no sounds of boots on the gravel behind me, no smell of leather or of sweaty man. No beautiful blue eyes to make it all stop. It was just me, left alone again with all the pain I just couldn't seem to get rid of.

It would have hurt less if he'd just shot me instead.

Chapter Nineteen

OUR TOWN MAY have looked like the Mayberry of tourist destinations, but if you were to come inside and stay a while, it wouldn't take you long to learn that filth, decay and darkness were the glue holding it all together.

It was time for me to get the fuck out. Every reason I'd ever had to stay put in that town had left.

I shoved the few things that I owned into my backpack. I needed to get out of there, and I needed to do it as soon as possible. Even though I had nowhere to go, I was still in a rush to leave. It's not like Jake would be barging through the door at any moment—I knew that much. I'd heard his thunderous bike fading into the distance over the bridge minutes before.

I knew it would be the last time that comforting sound ever touched my ears.

I left my keys on the rack and swung the door open to leave. I wanted to turn around, to take one last look at the rooms where we'd shared so much happiness in so short a time, but I couldn't let myself bring that to the surface. The air in the apartment was sticking to me, suffocating me.

I had to get out.

I grabbed my hoodie and stuffed it into my bag before gunning for the door.

I was in such a hurry to leave I ran right into the doughy chest of Sheriff Fletcher. He was standing on the porch, his fist raised in the air, about to knock. He didn't react to me slamming into him or ask me what was wrong when he saw my tear-stained face. In his suspicious, coal-colored eyes, I saw a flash of knowledge, of recognition, and I knew that he knew everything.

Owen. Jake. Everything. He knew what his monster of a nephew had done.

The sheriff handed me a thick yellow envelope and walked away without uttering a word.

I closed the door and sat back down on the couch, losing my will to flee. I dropped my backpack onto the floor beside my feet and examined the envelope in my hands. It was too thick and heavy to be a letter. My name was written in feminine handwriting, in large black marker across the top flap. I opened the seal and poured the contents out onto the coffee table.

What little there was left of my heart nearly stopped.

It was money—stacks that had bands around them, labeling how much was in each. I had never seen so much money in my entire life. I prodded around inside the envelope. There was no note—just a business card. It read *Bethany Annabelle Fletcher, ESQ, Attorney at Law*. Owen's mother. And on the other side, in the same handwriting as my name on the envelope it read:

To ease your troubles…

The Fletchers were trying to clean up Owen's little mess. This made them as sick and twisted as Owen. At least I knew then where he got it from. The money—ten thousand dollars from what I estimated—was hush money, meant to keep me quiet. The Fletchers obviously didn't want people to know that their golden boy was really a sadistic rapist. The thought made me gag.

I wondered how many times he'd done this before, how many times this worked for them in the past.

It sure as shit wasn't going to work with me.

Bethany Fletcher was trying to give me money *to ease my troubles*. Like money would undo the damage Owen had done to me, over and over again. There truly was only one thing that could *ease my troubles* completely. Since Jake was gone now, it was no longer an option.

But if Jake were here…

He wasn't, though, and he would never be again. I would never experience his reassuring touch. I would never again see his stone face turn soft when he looked at me. This kind of pain, coming from a heart that I thought I had successfully closed off to the outside world years ago, was worse than any physical pain anyone could cause me. It was worse than what I'd experienced the morning after Owen attacked me.

I would go through what Owen put me through me a thousand times over to have Jake be the person I thought he was.

Jake would put Owen to the ground if he knew, and I would want him to. Frankly, I didn't care if that thought made me a bad person. Bad, good. Right, wrong. The lines were so blurry lately. I was in love with a killer, and I wanted Owen dead.

When I thought of it as simply as that, maybe it wasn't so blurry after all.

The money on the coffee table mocked me, and I could feel all the pent up anger that had been distorted by the sadness from losing Jake rise to the surface. No matter what they tried to pay me, I wasn't going to say anything to anyone except Jake, anyway. Did they think I'd be seeking justice from a failed system? That I'd tell people what their precious son did to me? Little did they know Jake leaving had just bought Owen a reprieve from his almost guaranteed death sentence. Something clicked inside me. I wasn't sad over losing Jake, or upset that

Bethany Fletcher thought I was poor, stupid white trash who could be bought.

I was fucking enraged.

I couldn't remember a time in my life when I'd been so angry. The heat from below the surface of my skin felt as if it had been dropped in oil. I wanted to jump out of my skin and harm someone, throw something. To destroy for the sake of destroying.

The hair on the back of my neck stood up. My heart rate went from normal to borderline cardiac arrest in a matter of seconds.

Fuck. This. Shit.

This bitch thought she could buy my silence? Well, she was dead fucking wrong. All the Fletchers were. And, I was about to show them how dead fucking wrong they really were.

The argument Jake and I had in the kitchen over me paying him back for the camera he'd bought me played in my head. *"I'll just burn the money,"* he'd said, when I insisted on paying him back.

I stuffed the bills back in the envelope before grabbing Jakes truck keys from the rack. My move to nowhere would have to wait a little while. I grabbed a half empty bottle of lighter fluid from the shelf over the barbecue and a pack of matches from the drawer below it.

I got into his truck and drove. I tried to ignore the part of me that was thinking about how much the truck smelled like him, how his old black baseball cap was still sitting on the dashboard, and how much all I wanted to do was curl up into the back seat and sleep surrounded in his smell.

The misery wasn't going anywhere, either.

I became more and more heated as I drove. I saw red again.

The anger poisoned my blood, and I was drunk on it. High on my hatred. My heart pounded in my ears the closer I got to my destination. I didn't follow a single traffic law. The gas pedal was squeezed between my foot and the floor board the entire way.

What was it about me that made people think I was for sale?

My mother thought I could be used as payment for her fucking habits. Owen and his family seemed to think that ten thousand dollars could buy him a night of rape and attempted murder at my expense. Owen may have seen the shy Abby in the past—the one whose skin was always covered, who kept to herself out of self-protection. He had no fucking clue who he was dealing with now. I wasn't going to curl into a corner. I was done feeling sorry for myself. This shit wasn't my fault. It wasn't something I'd asked for.

I was no fucking victim, and I refused to be bought.

Fuck. This. Shit!

I peeled down the shell road that led to the Fletchers' compound. The Sheriff's squad car was already parked on the driveway by the main house. Owen's blue Chevy was on the side of the house by his private entrance.

A chill ran down my spine at the thought of them witnessing me making it clear that I wouldn't be purchased, by them or anyone else. Ten thousand dollars may have bought the Fletchers a lot of things, but it couldn't buy me. I knew one thing for sure at that point: Owen was determined to treat me like the whore he thought I was by taking what he thought he was entitled to and then making sure he paid for it.

I didn't take my foot off the gas when I tore into the Fletchers front yard. I started with a few 360s, making sure I used every bit of the thick heavy truck tires to destroy Bethany Fletcher's award-winning roses, plant beds, retaining walls, and manicured lawn. I hit a few sprinkler heads and mini-geysers of water shot out of the ground and into the sky, raining a thick muddy fountain down onto the windshield. I turned on the windshield wipers, spreading the mud over the windows before clearing enough of it to see through the blurred coating of brown sludge.

I kept going even after there was no grass left. Each turn of my wheel kicked up more mud, caking it onto the sheriff's car and the pristine white siding of the house. By the time I pulled back onto the road, the front yard looked like a good ol'-fashioned redneck muddin' hole.

I threw the truck in park and grabbed the envelope, the matches and the bottle of lighter fluid from the passenger seat. The envelope felt hot, as if its evil intentions were burning a hole in my hand. I laughed.

It was about to get a whole lot fucking hotter.

My heart beat with a speed I've never known, like I'd taken a shot of pure adrenaline. I didn't care if they came outside and saw me. In fact, I hoped to fucking God they did. I wanted them to know it was me who was telling them to go to hell.

I grabbed a freshly-rolled joint from my back pocket and held it in my mouth.

I picked up a rock from what had been the garden and dropped it into the envelope with the bills. I doused it inside and out with the lighter fluid, tossing the bottle to the floor when it was empty. I folded over the flap of the matches and lit the entire pack in one strike. Then I lit my joint, and I set the envelope on fire.

I let it burn, and when I couldn't hold onto it any longer, I cocked my arm and launched their blood money through the front window of the Fletcher family home.

Fuck you, motherfuckers.

The window shattered. Bits of glass dangled from the broken aluminum window frame. I stood back and watched as the living room curtains caught fire, framing the window in flames and black smoke. This picture perfect house, the home of all the power in the town, was now going up in flames. Flames that I caused. Flames those bastards would eventually see again if they believed in any sort of hell.

I blew out my long-held drag, and then I heard the first high-pitched scream. It brought me a satisfaction that ten thousand dollars certainly couldn't. I didn't run this time, and I didn't look back. That would have suggested that I cared what happened next, and really, I didn't care if their propane tank exploded and they were all blown to Kingdom Fucking Come.

These were the thoughts of someone with nothing left to lose.

Sheriff Fletcher was already standing next to the driver's side door of Jake's truck waiting for me. He stepped forward as I approached. I didn't see his right hook coming straight for my cheek. The fat fuck made contact with the side of my face, then managed to grab me by my shirt and shove me up against the hood so he could cuff my hands roughly behind my back. He snuffed out my joint. I didn't see where it went, but it was a pretty safe bet he'd pocketed it.

He used his portly body weight, pressing himself up against my back to subdue me. He grunted. "You got some balls, Abby. I'll give you that. What you don't understand is that money was your final offer. From here on out, there will be no more money. No more chances. No more nothin'." Then he started mumbling to himself. "If I had the chance again—between taking you home or digging a hole—let's just say I would have done things a little differently."

I knew Owen had help moving me. Even as small as I was, my dead weight must have been difficult to lift and maneuver. It didn't surprise me that it had been the sheriff. It surprised me more that he hadn't just let me die. It would have been less work on his part.

There was nothing the sheriff could say to me—not even the confession of his decision to keep me alive rather than let me die—that could have killed my adrenaline rush, my high. The Fletchers had brought my madness upon themselves. They shouldn't have covered for Owen. They shouldn't have protected him when it was me who needed the protecting. They certainly shouldn't have thought that ten thousand dollars would have bought my silence or in any way, would have made me whole again.

They didn't know they were dealing with someone who'd never been whole to begin with.

The sheriff was right. He should have dug the hole and fucking buried me deep. No good could come of who I was becoming. Jake had once told me that the most dangerous people are the ones with nothing to lose.

I'd already lost it all.

"MISS FORD, PROTOCOL requires for me to ask you if you would like an attorney."

Bethany Fletcher stood and tapped a long red fingernail on the scratched wooden table. We were sitting in a small room with no windows and bare green walls, stained with god only know what. My hands were cuffed to the chair behind me.

"Protocol?" I asked. "That's funny. I'll have to remember that one." The woman had some nerve. She furrowed her brow in warning.

Owen had the same look.

With their green eyes and dark hair, they could almost be mistaken for siblings instead of mother and son. Bethany looked sharper though, like a knife with a new blade. She wore a fitted black power suit. Her heels were four inches of pointy, red patent leather.

"Abby, you are being charged with a class A felony of arson, as well as driving without a license, destruction of property over twenty-thousand dollars, and possession of marijuana. You have priors for breaking and entering, petty theft, possession of marijuana paraphernalia, resisting arrest, disorderly conduct, and battery. You should really take your situation more seriously, sweetheart, because you're looking at ten years without sunlight in a nice, cozy cell all to yourself." Bethany was taunting me. The way the word *sweetheart* melted from her lips, it could have been mistaken for an endearment. Southern women used it when they couldn't come right out and call you a cunt.

"So what, then? Rape and attempted murder are just misde-meanors? 'Cause I got a feeling that kind of thing goes unpunished around here." I looked her right in her eyes.

She parted her shiny red lips and chuckled.

Bethany circled around the desk, unbuttoning the jacket of her suit, and knelt down next to me. "I'm glad you decided to have your little episode today, because now you need my help, and I am the only one who can make all these unfortunate charges go away. I felt bad for you, Abby. I really did. That's why I sent you the money. Too bad you fucked up a good thing. Now, we play it my way." Bethany flashed me a fake smile.

"Now, you're blackmailing me?" I asked. Bethany stood and took a seat opposite me, propping her briefcase up on the table.

"Not blackmail sugar. An agreement." She pulled papers from her briefcase and set them in front of me. "This is your account of what happened that night: you were mugged. You don't know who did it. You didn't get a good look at your attacker. The police report will make it seem as if they searched heaven and hell for the assailant but have ultimately come up empty-handed, and the case will be shelved."

"You're out of your goddamned mind."

"Now, sugar, don't go using the good Lord's name in vain. It's not the Christian thing to do. This is a business transaction—your account of what happened in exchange for me dropping the charges for torching my house. You're the one who ruined this, Abby. You could have taken your money and gotten out of town, but instead you chose to go all avenging angel on me."

"Fuck you." *I'll go to jail,* I thought. *After what I've been through, jail would be like summer camp.*

Bring it bitch.

"Doesn't matter to me, darlin'. It's not like you can prove anything, not like Owen will ever be charged, what with his father being county judge and all. It's a simple decision really." She leaned over the table and propped her chin up on her elbows. "Jail, or your signature. You make the call."

She was right, but I didn't care. This wasn't about making sure Owen was prosecuted for what he'd done to me. This was about not letting these people own me.

I wasn't a piece of land or livestock.

They could take their power and shove it up their asses.

Bethany had a victory smile already plastered on her overly botoxed face. It was time to rip it the fuck off.

"I don't think you quite understand something, Mrs. Fletcher." I mimicked her posture, leaning and pressing myself as close to her as my cuffed hands would let me. "The last thing you want to do is fuck with someone who has nothing to lose. I want your entire family to leave me alone, and I want Owen to stay at least one hundred yards away from me at all times. I mean it. If he sees me on one side of the street, he needs to cross to the other."

"This isn't a negotiation. I've laid out your options so you pick. Jail or signature. End of story." She placed the papers back into her briefcase and clicked the locks shut. She stood. "What will it be, Miss Ford?"

"Fuck you."

She shrugged and turned to leave, but before she could twist the knob on the door, she turned and looked at me. "Enjoy jail, Abby. It's always nice when a daughter follows in her parents' foot steps."

Bitch.

I had to pull out the only card I had left to play.

"Hey, Bethany." She glanced at me over her shoulder. "Did you know that photography was a hobby of mine?"

She froze and turned all the way back around. Her face had gone pale.

I felt a tickle on my nose and bent over to scratch it on the table. "I'm more of a documentary kind-of photographer, really. I like to tell a story with my pictures, you know? It's amazing what the camera picks up when you're naked in the mirror. Even in black and white photo, you can see where the purple of each bruise looks gray, where the dried blood looks almost black. You can almost see the yellow tone in the swelling of a black eye... or two."

She crossed the small room in two strides leaned over the

table, bracing both arms on it for support. "All that proves is that someone hurt you. It doesn't prove who did it."

"I have copies of the pictures and my statement of what happened that night in three different locations. If something were to happen to me, if Owen does this to someone else, or if you don't follow through with my demands, there is a plan in place to send them to every newspaper and media outlet within a hundred miles. I won't be the one rotting away in a jail cell. Owen will be. I'm guessing shortly after that, I won't be the only rape victim in this whole situation, either."

I was bluffing about everything but the photos.

She tried to stifle her gasp. She shifted her grip on the table before making her decision.

"Owen leaves you alone, and the charges against you are dropped. Is that what you want?"

"Yes. And I'm not signing a fucking thing," I added.

She grabbed her briefcase and headed out the door. Sheriff Fletcher met her on the other side. A wicked smile crossed her lips. "I'll think about it. In the meantime, Carl," she said as she put her hand on Sheriff Fletcher's shoulder, "please take Abby to the infirmary. It seems she needs medical attention."

It was only a half-assed sucker punch to my cheek. It would bruise, but it didn't hurt. It was a mosquito bite compared to what I'd experienced at Owen's hands. "No need. I'm fine."

"Are you?" Bethany winked over her shoulder at me as Sheriff Fletcher entered the room and closed the door behind him. He pulled a night stick from out his belt.

Chapter Twenty

I AWOKE SO suddenly, it felt like I'd been launched into consciousness. I sat straight up, flinging some sort of ice pack off my forehead and across the room. My ribs protested. I clutched them in apology.

I was in a small sea foam-colored room, I assumed in the infirmary at the police station. Coral Pines didn't even have a real hospital, and the nearest emergency room was over thirty minutes away in the next town over. So when people had non life threatening injuries—or were beaten by the sheriff with a night stick—they came here, like a bunch of elementary school kids at the fucking nurse's office.

The paper from the exam table crinkled under my movement as I slowly swung my feet over to the floor. There was a cotton ball with a small bandage over it stuck to my inner arm. I felt sore and woozy, and very much like I'd just gotten my ass kicked by a fat man swinging a heavy plastic baton.

I did a physical inventory. I started at my toes, wiggling each before I bent my knees and lifted my arms. I worked my way up, until I was pressing my fingers against my face to make sure my skull was still in tact. I was swollen and in pain, and I may have had a cracked rib or two, but this time I knew I was going to live.

Dammit.

An older woman in pink scrubs walked into the room, staring down at a manila file in her hands as she moved. I recognized her as Glinda Mallory, one of the ladies from Nan's church group. She flashed me what passed as a professional smile. There was little warmth in it.

"How are you feeling, Abby? Do you know where you are?" She moved right to the second question as if she didn't give a shit about the answer to the first. She pulled on a pair of latex gloves and tried to push me back down onto the exam table, but I dodged her. She reached for my face with one of her gloved hands, and I raced for the other side of the room, my head throbbing. "I can't care for you if you won't let me touch you."

"You examined me while I was unconscious, right? You lifted my shirt up, saw what I had going on under there? Does it look like being touched has worked out for me?"

She closed her mouth and shook her head.

"I'll be okay, really. Thank you for wanting to help." Oddly, I was trying to comfort the nurse who should have been comforting me. "Do you have anything for the pain?"

I held onto my head with both hands in an attempt to gain some balance. I didn't know if she knew what had just went on here, but I suspected that, as the nurse at the Sheriff's station, she knew enough not to ask.

She pulled off her gloves and tossed them in a red trash bin. "It isn't advisable to take pain killers while pregnant, you know."

She was just full of information I didn't need or care about. "I'll be sure to keep that in mind when I'm having a baby. For now, can I get some sort of drug to take the edge of off all this? My ribs are fucking killing me."

She grabbed her file and sat on a short rolling stool using her feet to wheel herself over to me. "I had suspected you didn't know, but it's proper procedure before administering any sort of narcotics to an unconscious person to test them for conditions such as pregnancy." She didn't even give me time to process that information before adding, "Do you know who the father is?"

"I'm sorry. What are you asking me?" I was trying to process the information, but between her cold distance and my throbbing head and ribs, it was difficult to understand her coded message.

"You may want to alert the father before you make any hasty decisions," she added while scribbling on her clipboard. "You can always come see the ladies group at the church. They are really good at handling cases like yours."

Cases? Like mine?

"Father?"

"Yes. As in father of your unborn child. You're pregnant, Miss Ford."

My chest tightened, the pain increasing with each breath as they got shallower and shallower. I couldn't hold air in my lungs. The room started to spin. The nurse came and went in my line of site. Seconds earlier, I was holding my head in order to ease the ache. Now, I was just trying to hold my shit together. I had to think.

Jake and I were careful. We used condoms.

The only thing Owen had used was me.

My life was more than just a single disaster. It was many disasters, all happening at the same time. It was a tsunami after a hurricane after an earthquake happening in the middle of a tornado, while a wildfire blazed in a circle around me. I waded through the wreckage of one and right into the next.

I was pregnant, and Owen was the father.

TWO MINUTES CAN be a lot longer than most people realize.

Two minutes was all it took for me to move from liking Jake to loving him.

After I was released from the jail on my own recognizance, pending Bethany's decision to send me to prison or not, two minutes sitting in front of that plastic fucking stick was torture.

I'd decided to take a home test to see if the nurse had lost her goddamned mind, or if I'd lost mine. I lifted it from Sally's Corner Store on the way back to Jake's apartment. But I left exact amount of money for the test on the shelf where I found it, right after I'd shoved it into the front pocket of my hoodie. I wasn't ready for the town to know something I wasn't sure of myself.

After counting down the ticks the second hand on the old wall clock above the desk, I took a deep breath. I was probably just over reacting. I was sure I was going to laugh about how stupid I was being in just a few more seconds. I knew the universe was cruel, but I didn't think it could be this ridiculous.

I didn't think that, after everything I'd already dealt with, I could actually be carrying my rapist's child, too. I was only seventeen. I prayed to a God I wasn't sure existed.

Please no... please no... please no.

When the second hand hit the twelve for the second time, I lifted the white stick and gazed into the little window.

I had never seen a more menacing pair of parallel lines.

JUST A LITTLE while longer and it will all be over with...

"Abby Ford?"

It was another nurse in pink scrubs calling my name, measuring me, making me pee in a cup and giving me the once over.

Only this time, it wasn't in the Coral Pines police station.

A doctor with salt-and-pepper hair introduced himself as Doctor Hodges and promptly asked me to lie down and put my feet in the stirrups. He looked to be in his mid-fifties. He was calm and friendly, but wasn't going to be performing the procedure just yet. He explained that it was just the initial exam before *the big show.*

My words, not his.

I closed my eyes and took deep breaths as he poked and prodded with cold instruments and intruding fingers. It was so uncomfortable. The burning inside me built to epic proportions. My eyes watered and a tear ran down my cheek. I had to power through. I tried to sing in my head to distract myself from what the doctor was doing.

When that didn't work, I thought of Jake.

I wonder if Jake would have gone with me if he knew the truth. If he knew that I loved him and hadn't willingly let Owen do what he did to me. I couldn't let myself linger on those thoughts. I was pregnant with another mans baby, and I needed not to be anymore.

"Miss Ford, I know you already spoke to the counselor so forgive the repetition here, but may I ask, what brings you here today?" He gestured for me to sit up.

Relief flooded me instantly.

"I don't want to be pregnant anymore." I wondered if that wasn't the reason that every seventeen year old came here.

"How did you get pregnant, Miss Ford?" His voice was steady and professional, but I sensed something else lingered behind his question.

"Is there more than one way?" I faked a laugh to distract him.

He looked at me skeptically. "Miss Ford, I am going to be honest with you. I see scar tissue within you that suggests you've been through a *traumatic* injury recently." He took a deep breath and flicked his rubber gloves into the trash bin. "Frankly, I am surprised a pregnancy resulted or survived such trauma."

It was a statement, but he looked as if he wanted me to confirm his suspicion.

"Resulted," I blurted. I instantly regretted telling this stranger anything that wasn't his business.

"Have you filed a police report?"

"No." *But, I'm facing some pretty hefty charges myself.*

The Doctor didn't press me why I hadn't. He just nodded as he placed a manila file on his knee and started to write with a fountain pen from his lab coat pocket. He shook his head from side to side, like something he was writing was almost unbelievable to him. "Strong fetus you've got in there." He looked up from his file, his embarrassment written all over his face. "I'm sorry. That was entirely insensitive of me. My apologies."

"It's fine." I wanted to silence his rambling. I hated being apologized to. After all, he was right. This thing in me had such a will to be in this world, it had found a way to exist during the worst of the worst of conditions.

It was a survivor, just like me.

And I was going to kill it.

I SPENT THE next three days searching for a new job with no luck. Bubba still wasn't hiring seventeen year olds. Sally's wasn't hiring. The bait shop wasn't hiring.

Jake's home was no longer my home so I was back to sleeping in Nan's old Chevy, the same one Jake had caught me in all those weeks ago. I'd put his keys on the counter, locked the door, and shut it behind me.

I didn't want to live there anymore anyway. Just being there long enough to grab some of my shit and lock the door was painful enough. A few times I could've sworn I'd heard his bike pulling into the drive. I had to remind myself it wasn't him.

He was gone.

The Chevy couldn't be home forever, but it was all I had for now. I'd made a little money working at Jake's shop, but the hotels on the island were tourist traps, and a single night's stay was more than half of what I had to my name. I tried to rent a room, but being seventeen and jobless wasn't exactly an attractive mix to potential landlords.

I lay in the Chevy, tossing and turning.

It wasn't just the stagnant heat of the night air that kept me restless.

Has it really been only days since I had last seen him, since I let him walk away? Where is he? What is he doing?

Jake had assumed the worst of me, and with that assumption he revealed that we didn't have what I thought we did. He didn't love me the way I loved him. As far as he was concerned, it was all or nothing.

I promised myself I'd push all thoughts of Jake out of my mind, in hopes of pushing him from my heart.

Yeah, right.

Even I didn't think that was going to happen. In time, I hoped he would become just a distant memory. Now, though, his memory was so strong, if I allowed it just a moment to occupy my mind, it consumed me. I closed my eyes and could still feel his breath on my cheek, his skin on my skin. I would never again be able to let myself be as free as I was with him.

That girl was gone.

Survivor Abby had returned, boundaries and walls firmly back in place.

Choosing the comfort of being numb over the pain of heartbreak.

On what was to be my third night of sleeping in the Chevy, I climbed in through the driver's side door and plopped myself down on the bench seat to get some much-needed sleep. I'd spent the entire day walking up and down the island looking for work and was just drifting off when I heard something jingle. There in front of me, reflecting the light of the full moon, was a key ring with two small gold keys and a large silver Ford emblem key chain hanging from it. The keys were attached to the steering wheel by a large janitor-style hook. A Dunn's Auto Repair sticky note was attached to the center of the wheel. The note on it appeared to be written by a child:

abby

the apartment is urs fer as long as you need. yu can use the truck too it needs to be run ery once in a while and settin in the lot aint doin it no good. I dont no what happened with jake and I dont care but I know he dont want you sleeping in the fucking truck like a dam hobo. reggie is pissed you aint showed up fer work so be there in the morn. sorry about the punching ur face thing. Im a drunk asshole most of the time.

sorry again.
frank dunn

Tears stung the back of my eyes. Despite the fact that he'd called me a hobo, it was by far the greatest note I had ever received. I held the necklace Jake gave me in between my fingers, as it had become my nature to do when I was thinking. It would be my constant reminder he wasn't just a dream.

It had certainly felt like one, though.

I hadn't even been sure that Frank remembered who I was, especially under the circumstances of our first encounter. But there I was, reading his offer of salvation.

The Dunn men may have seen themselves as being worlds apart in every way, but when it really came down to it, both men were deeply troubled by pasts they'd rather forget, and they both had laid themselves on the line for me when I really needed it.

Selflessly. Easily.

It was in these acts of kindness that I saw the similarities in them for the first time.

I laughed to myself because Jake would shit a brick if I ever told him that he and the man he hated most were in any way similar.

Mr. Dunn had just offered me the chance to save money and have a place to stay when the baby came.

The baby...

I didn't know if I would be a good mom, or if I would even be able to be one at all under the circumstances. But when it came right down to it, I couldn't bring myself to kill someone who didn't even know they were the product of a hateful act, especially after he or she had been created despite the horrible condition my body was in. This baby was a fighter, a survivor like me.

We were already kindred spirits.

It was because of, not in spite of, the life growing inside me that I was able to move forward, a little at a time.

I had the chance to have a real family, for the first time in my life.

I was going to try my damnedest to protect it.

Chapter Twenty-One

Four years later

I T WAS SEPTEMBER when Mr. Dunn's already weak body gave out and was crushed under the heavy weight of his addictions.

Leave it to the people of Coral Pines to turn what should have been a small simple service into an event that could rival their annual mullet-toss festival.

Every meddling church lady and bored husband within twenty miles dressed to the nines to pay their "respects" to a man that they didn't really know, and certainly didn't respect.

A group of chatting woman smiled and laughed on the top step of the church before the service started. They all clutched handkerchiefs as if letting everyone know they were capable of springing a leak at any moment. Although a lot of people had cared about my Nan, more people had come to her service as an excuse to finally dust off their best mourning outfits and compete in a *Who's Sadder* competition than to celebrate her life.

This felt just like that had.

Mrs. Garrith, a woman with white blonde hair and bright pink nails, was getting ready to jump into the fray as I approached the steps. "And when he lost his sweet Marlena I made sure to bring him a casserole every day for a month. I could tell he really appreciated my gesture of kindness... told me so himself. Those casseroles were a lifesaver to that man." She adjusted the fingers of her short black laced gloves.

"Well, bless your heart, Mary," Mrs. Morrison added. Everyone knew it was Southern slang for *Go fuck yourself.* "Did you know that Franklin asked me to go steady with him in high school? Practically begged me, really, before he and Marlena became an item of course. That boy was sweet on me, I tell ya." She fanned herself with one of the funeral programs handed out by choir boys.

I took a program from one of the boys and pushed passed the crowd into the church. Loud whispering had always followed me wherever I went, and today was no different.

Mrs. Morrison might as well have been speaking into a microphone. After she spotted me, the comments about my inappropriate funeral attire began. She leaned in close to her cohorts and whispered, "I think that Abigail Ford and Franklin had a 'special' relationship." She had the balls to quote the air when she said the word *special.* "It turns out the girl helped plan this entire service. Don't you think that's odd?"

That statement was met with gasps and exaggerated sighs from the clones that surrounded her. The group added their own speculations, fueling the rumor. It was like listening to creation itself in the beginning, where it all started, with these dumb bitches poisoning the water.

I don't know how Nan ever got along with those ladies. It never seemed to me that she ever really fit in with them. Nan was someone who would show up to a funeral wearing her brightest floral colored sundress instead of a black funeral gown. I don't know how she did it all without drawing all the negative attention I seemed to attract, or maybe she did draw negative attention and I just never really noticed. Maybe, I was too wrapped up in my own self pity and bullshit to notice that these ladies hurt her, too.

I'd thought about her a lot when I got dressed that morning. Her funeral was the last one I attended, over four years earlier. It was in her honor that I wore a bright coral colored spaghetti-strapped sundress that crossed in the back with a long-sleeved white cardigan over it and wedge sandals instead of the black mourning uniform of the gossip mafia.

Not because I was ashamed or afraid anymore.

I just thought it was more appropriate for church.

It was those people, those nasty two-faced women who preached their impossible morals about town to whoever would listen, that pissed me off the most. Those women didn't live the lives they preached about anymore than the people they shunned for it. They just knew how to hide it better. The more I heard them talk, the more I realized they weren't speaking about Frank's life. All their stories or revelations were about their attempts to associate themselves with him. They wanted to paint themselves into the picture of his life for the attention only.

The truth was that, even with all his problems, Frank Dunn was someone who would be missed, even if it was only by me. The know-it-all church ladies on the steps were just selfish bitches.

Those were always the worst kind of bitches.

So, I was going to have a little fun with the ladies.

I squared my shoulders and walked back out of the church and right to the center, where the coffee klatch from hell was taking place. Before they could pick their jaws up off the floor or squawk out a fake greeting, I spoke first, laying on my Georgia accent much thicker than usual.

"Why, hey y'all," I started. I smiled at the two ladies who seemed to be the leaders of the group. My voice dripped so much false sugary sweetness, I probably made their teeth ache. "Thank you so much for comin', I know that Mr. Dunn would have appreciated his dearest friend—" I gestured toward Mrs. Garrith. "—and his high school sweetheart—" and I gestured toward Mrs. Morrison. "—goin' out their way to pay their last respects."

Mrs. Garrith looked me up and down like I was wearing fishnets and nipple tassels instead of a simple sundress and sweater. She opened her mouth to speak, but I cut her off.

"Honestly, toward the end there, he didn't know if y'all would show up. Especially since the three of you have such *history* together."

The smiles from both their faces melted into frowns. One of the other ladies from the crowd questioned this new found piece of information out loud. "History?"

"Oh sure. You know that these ladies and Mr. Dunn go *waaaaay* back." I winked.

"Not really." Mrs. Morrison protested while smoothing the collar of her dress before looking down at her feet. She knew what was coming next. I knew all their secrets, and now they would know that I was the wrong person to fuck with.

"Oh sure, he said that in high school the three of you had quite the *connection*." Their faces paled, and Mrs. Garrith looked down right gray. "Oh, don't be modest, ladies. It's perfectly natural to want to experiment at that age with your alternative feelings."

Alternative feelings was a phrase the church ladies made famous when speaking about the immorality of homosexuality.

Frank had let that bit of information slip to Reggie one day when Mrs. Garrith had come in for an oil change. I just happened to overhear.

"Abigail!" Someone faked shock and shame, though her voice said very clearly that she was truly entertained by this bit of information. I kept my smile big. Laying into those parasites was more fun than I'd thought it would be.

I was about to finish them off with some inside information about Mrs. Garrith using store bought orchids for her entry in the flower festival—which, believe it or not, would probably have been considered the biggest secret of them all—when the reverend opened the doors of the church and told us that it was time to find a seat. The service would be starting.

I went in first, but not before looking back over my shoulder at the visibly shaken women. I turned to go in, satisfied that Nan would have scolded me for chastising the church ladies in public, but I also knew she would have been holding back a laugh.

I sat in the first row marked "Reserved for Family", but since Mr. Dunn didn't have any that would be attending, I figured it was a space that needed to be filled. There were quite a few whispers directed at my bold seating decision.

The reverend tried to speak about Mr. Dunn, but I could tell he was struggling to find anything positive to say about a man he barely knew. Frank rarely left his house, and when he did it was only to work at the shop. Even then, he kept mostly to his office, keeping the blinds shut and the world out. It wasn't as if he'd even needed to be at the shop, but he made it a point to come in when he wasn't sinking too low. I paid his bills, both business and personal, and between me and Reggie, we had Dunn's Auto Body running like a…well, like a well-oiled machine.

The reverend began speaking about life and death and the rewards waiting in heaven for those who lived their lives by the light of God and the good book. It made me wonder: even if I did believe in God or religion or the power of the "good book" did I know anyone who qualified?

Not in Coral Pines.

The reverend asked for a moment of silent prayer, bowing his head and folding his hands in front of him as the crowd followed suit. I did, too, but my mind was not on prayer; it was on what I was going to have to do next.

I wiped my sweaty palms on my thighs. When the reverend said "Amen" and the crowed echoed him, he gestured to me. I took out the piece of wrinkled yellow notepad paper from my pocket and ironed it out on my knee before heading up the steep steps to the pulpit.

It was a packed house, and all eyes were on me. They were probably wondering why the hell I was up there.

I cleared my throat and stared at the paper in front of me. My opening paragraph was about why I was the one up there, explaining the nature of my relationship with Frank.

Suddenly, I didn't feel the need to explain anything to these people. This wasn't about them. It was about Frank, a man who, over the last few years, helped me in more ways than I could have ever repaid him. I had written the words in front of me and had even practiced reading them aloud at home, but for some reason, I was having a problem reading them now. Instead, I decided to tell them about the Mr. Dunn I'd known.

Straight from my battered and broken heart.

I cleared my throat again and took a minute to gather my thoughts. Every small movement from the silent audience caused the old wooden pews to creek and groan. I took a deep breath and started to speak, the squealing feedback from the microphone caused a few shocked noises from the congregation. I waited for another moment before continuing. This time, the sound system cooperated.

"I'm not going to stand up here and say Frank was a saint, because it's not true," I started. "He was a troubled man. He turned to his addictions to numb his pain when he thought he had nothing left. There were plenty of times when, after not seeing him for days, I would go over to his house and find him passed out on the floor. I cleaned him up, put out the cigarettes, emptied the ash trays, and threw away the empty bottles. I wouldn't yell at him. I wouldn't tell him how badly he was messing up. Instead, I told him how much his help meant to me, what a difference he made in my life. Then, I would beg for him to find his way out of the fog. And he would, for days at a time, sometimes even a few weeks."

I paused and smiled.

"Those were some really great weeks. There were plenty of other times, actually, when he shouted at me and cursed me to the devil for trying to help."

I laughed nervously and the audience laughed with me. The double doors at the back of the church opened. A petite blonde woman entered, and some of the standers parted to let her by. She held the hand of a little red headed girl with long braided pig tails. All my nervousness dissipated.

"But he had a good side. A *great* side really." I smoothed my hair behind my ears and grabbed both sides of the podium to steady myself. "Mr. Dunn—"

My heart twisted in my chest.

"Frank was a person who made great mistakes—too many mistakes, and he knew it. He was also a man who crumbled under the weight of tremendous grief." I took a deep breath. "But only because he had experienced tremendous love. When you experience love as greatly as he did, it's easy to let the sadness and anger consume you. It's easier to turn away from those you still have left and give yourself over to the numbness. He invited the pain in because it helped him remember, and he numbed it with whiskey when it all became too much. He once told me that he was afraid he would forget what Marlena and Mason looked like if he ever tried to move on. Sometimes, he talked about them as if they were in the very next room."

Everyone knew who I was talking about.

"Now, y'all have had your own different experiences with Frank. Some good, some bad... some God awful."

More chuckles from the congregation. The blonde woman walked up the isle and sat her self and the little girl in the first pew. Her bright smile urging me to continue. I smiled back at her.

"I can only tell you about the Frank I knew. He was a man who put a roof over my head when I didn't have one. He was truly the only person besides my grandmother who never judged me and never assumed the worst of me. He never made me explain myself, even when I owed him an explanation. In his own quiet way, he accepted me into his life without question. In some ways, I think he was trying to make amends. He saved me because he couldn't save his wife and son from death, and he couldn't save his relationship with his living son. Frank never asked me questions he knew I didn't want to answer."

I took a deep breath, my eyes started to fill with tears as the memories started to flood into my mind of the last four years.

"But his tremendous love wasn't gone. It didn't die with his wife and son. It survived, in the way he felt about the son he pushed away, and in the way he cared for me...for us."

There was a shuffle in the back of the church when the doors briefly opened behind some standers, but I continued on.

"His biggest regret was not the loss of the dead, but the loss of the living. Frank loved his son, Jake, but pushed him away because he reminded him of his loss, and he didn't know how or where to channel all the pain."

I held in the tears. These people needed to know about Frank, they needed to know he was a person who should be mourned in death, not made into a freak show legend. My voice was raspy, but I pressed on.

"I'm not making excuses for him, and I'm certainly not saying drinking himself into oblivion was the right way for anyone to handle anything. But, it's what happened. It's his truth. Frank died full of regret but certainly not alone. He was a man that you may have known as Ol' Man Dunn or Mr. Dunn or Frank… or even 'Bubba', for those of you who played football with him in high school." More laughs. "In the end, though, you didn't know him at all."

I noticed that some of the church ladies were pressing their hankies to the corners of their eyes, their tears looked real. I was glad to see I'd gotten my point across.

"Franklin Dunn was a troubled man who lived a troubled life. To me, he was a friend, a father figure in his finer moments, and someone I wanted to help when he was in the throes of his agony."

I paused for a breath.

"I couldn't save him," I said. I was holding back the sobs that threatened to come out after every sentence. "But, I like to think I offered him some sort of comfort in these last few years because he sure as hell gave me the same." There were a few gasps at my use of the word "hell" in church. But most people seemed to understand the point I was trying to get across.

I looked again toward the little girl who was beaming in the front pew, her coppery red hair swinging over her shoulders with ever move of her little freckled head. Her sundress was the same coral color as mine. After I had gotten dressed, she'd insisted we match. "Actually, I like to think *we* offered him some comfort." I looked directly at her.

At the mention of *we*, she crawled over the blonde's lap and spilled into the aisle. She dashed up to the pulpit, took a running leap and flung herself into my arms. I gave her a squeeze and set her on my hip. I looked at her and asked "Because what did we call Frank, baby girl?"

"Gampaw Fank!" she exclaimed. The whole church laughed at my excited little girl.

"That's right, baby girl. We called him Grandpa Frank. Did you love your Grandpa Frank?"

"Yes, mama," she said timidly, earning *oohs* and *aahs* from the crowd. She'd melted my heart every day of my life. These people were lucky to even get a glimpse of what she was capable of.

I turned my attention back to the congregation. "I think we should remember Frank for who he was, not for who he *wasn't*. He was as much of a Grandpa to my little girl as she's ever going to get. He was a friend to me when I needed it most, and he was a father who loved his family enough to let their loss destroy him. He loved his son Jake more than anything." My heart skipped a beat when I said his name, even after all this time. "And he lived with regret every second of every day, right up until the day he died, for not fixing what they once had. Frank may not be missed by everyone here." I looked at my little girl and planted a kiss on her forehead. "But my daughter and I will sure miss him. Won't we, Georgia?"

"Yup!" she shouted and clapped her hands together.

Before I could set Georgia down and walk back to our pew,

there was another commotion at the back of the church. Both doors swung wide open and the blinding light of midday invaded the small space of the dimly lit church. I covered my eyes with my free hand to block out the light. My daughter buried her head in the crook of my neck.

I caught a glimpse of the person who made the dramatic exit. An awareness washed over me. I could only see his back because he was already halfway down the front steps. What I did see stopped the very breath in my chest.

The familiar site of blonde hair and black leather was all it took.

The doors slammed shut with a bang so loud. It echoed throughout the church and shook the stained glass windows.

Once again, Jake was leaving.

Chapter Twenty-Two

B Y THE TIME the service had ended, Jake was long gone. The sad truth of it all was that, if it hadn't been for Georgia, I would have run after him, right out of the church. I was glad that I hadn't. I didn't need another image of his beautiful face haunting my every move. I had enough to last a lifetime as it was. Even if I had gotten the chance to talk to him, what would I have said? He hated me because I'd let him hate me. Because it was easier to have him hate me than it was to deal with allowing someone in my life who I believed didn't trust me, or what I thought we'd had.

The empty space in my life Jake once occupied would've only been made even bigger if he stayed.

I skipped the customary cake and coffee they were serving in the meeting room after the funeral. Tess, Georgia's babysitter and my assistant at the garage had to get back to the shop to process a new shipment of parts, and I wasn't about to expose Georgia to the wicked ton for the rest of the afternoon. I'd told her if she was good at church I would take her over to the new playground at the elementary school.

That's exactly what we did.

Tess had been a godsend since she moved to town from Gainesville. She happily took Georgia at every chance she got so she could spend time with her, which allowed me more time to work on my photos.

It was nice having a friend around again. Someone I could trust with my daughter, anyway.

I lifted my squirming little girl from her car seat and set her on the grass, her little legs were running at full speed before I even had a chance to put her on the ground. "Be careful, Georgia!" I shouted after her as she made her way to the swings and pulled herself up on the lowest hanging one. She held onto the chains and kicked and kicked her legs, but the swing didn't move.

She was going nowhere fast.

The playground was crowded with children and their families. I worked my way through a sea of running and screaming little folk. I ducked under a stray soccer ball whizzing by my head. It took me twice as long to reach the swings as it took Georgia.

When I reached her, I stopped dead in my tracks.

Bethany Fletcher, Owen's mother, was pushing Georgia on her swing. Georgia was squealing with glee. "*Higher...higher!*" she shouted.

"Not too high," I said, making my presence known.

Bethany gave me a courteous nod. "Hello, Abby." Her smile slid into a straight line. Bethany wore a light beige suit jacket with a white blouse and a matching knee length flowing skirt. Her signature bright red lips were no more. Now, they were just glossed over, neutral. Her once-severe bun had been replaced by soft dark waves falling around her face and shoulders.

She looked almost human.

"What can I do for you, Bethany?" I asked. I kept my tone even. I didn't need her using the anger or anxiety I felt in her presence against me.

Before she could answer me, Georgia interrupted. "Mama,

the nice lady pushed me on the swing!"

"That's great, baby!" That girl could make me smile through a plane crash. "Why don't you try out the new slide, okay? Mama will watch you."

"Okay!" She squealed. Bethany held the chains on her swing still so Georgia could jump off. She took off running toward her next adventure on the shiny red slide.

"Can we talk?" Bethany asked. She sounded hopeful and even a bit kind, nothing at all like the Bethany who'd ordered my beating four years earlier. Her voice was calm. There was no hatred radiating off of her. I'd only seen her in passing since the day she dropped all the major charges against me. Only the marijuana possession charge had been kept. I paid a three-hundred dollar fine and served six months probation for that one. She could have easily dropped all the charges, but keeping one was her way of letting me know who pulled the strings in Coral Pines.

I was all too aware.

I sighed and took a seat on the bench facing the jungle gym. If Bethany wanted to talk, Bethany was going to talk. My saying *yes* or *no* had never made a difference to her before.

She took a seat next to me. "I've been wanting to tell you something for years now, and have never had the opportunity, and really didn't know how to say it. I didn't want to reach out because I didn't want to scare you away." She wrung her hands in her lap and nervously continued, shifting her focus from her feet to where Georgia was playing. "It's just...I'm so tired." She took a deep sigh and finally turned to look me in the eye. "I'm so tired, Abby... of everything." Her bright green eyes that used to stare daggers into my own, were now softer and watery.

"Excuse me?"

"I've been cleaning up messes my entire life. Sweeping things under the rug, justifying horrible things on a regular basis. Not just in my practice, but in my life, in my own family. Had I known you were pregnant, I would have tried to stop that, too."

I had thought of that, and it was the reason I'd hid my pregnancy for as long as I possibly could. Nobody knew until Georgia was already here.

I didn't even list Georgia's father's name on the birth certificate.

"So, I'm done now. I'm not doing it anymore and haven't for a long time," she announced, like it was something she'd been thinking about for a while. "I know you could never forgive Owen, and I don't blame you. I can't forgive him, either. Our relationship hasn't been the same since this happened if that makes things any better." She looked up from her hands at my raised eyebrows, realizing how weak that sounded. "Of course it doesn't."

"What did you really come here for, Bethany?" Avoiding one another for four years had been downright peaceful.

"I know I don't deserve it. I don't deserve anything after the way I treated you, and you should know that I am so, so sorry for that, too. I don't even recognize the person I am anymore, and it makes me sick to think of all the things I did to hurt people back then, what I did to hurt you." She shook her head as if she was shaking the bad memories from her brain. "I want to get to know Georgia," she said. "I'm willing to work for it, to gain your trust. I know you've never come right out and said who her father is, but I saw her with her babysitter in the grocery last week and got a really good look at her. She's got those green Fletcher eyes, although they are a little brighter than everyone else's." She cleared her throat. "I would really like a chance to get to know her."

I was shocked to hear that she wanted anything to do with Georgia, and my instinct to fight her off from four years ago bubbled at the surface.

Bethany did look tired though... hurt, even. The harshness of four years ago was gone and in her place was a woman whose sharp edges had been softened and rounded down with time.

Shortly after the secret was out that I had given birth, Owen had come to the apartment demanding to see *his* daughter.

I had slammed the door on his face and called over to Frank's office in the adjoining shop. Thankfully, I'd caught him in a run of sobriety, and he was in that day. Within seconds I'd heard a scuffle outside, and then a car pulling out of the gravel lot. Frank didn't come over to check in on me afterwards, he waited until he was back in his office before calling me back on the phone to let me know the problem had been taken care of.

The morning after, there was a note from Frank on my desk about a new alarm system being installed in the apartment that very afternoon, and a loaded .22 on my keyboard.

Owen never bothered me again, but with my .22 at the ready, I kinda wished he had.

"You want to bring my daughter around Owen?" I asked Bethany. I tried to rein in the panic in my voice, but I know she'd heard it.

"No, no. It would be just me," Bethany assured me. "I haven't told anyone about this—not even my husband. I'm not asking to take her anywhere, either. Maybe, we could just meet up at the park, just like this, and I could play with her a little...get to know her." She looked like a woman who was desperate to form a relationship with someone—one that didn't take everything she had to keep it from falling apart.

Bethany let out a long held sigh. "You know, I tried to have him put away, but Owen's father wouldn't have anything to do with the idea. Instead, I had Cole lock him in a cell for a few days to calm him down after he'd had a fit. That's what we called his behavior, anyway. I started recognizing the similarities between my son and my husband. Jamie's never been a gentle man." Bethany's eyes glazed over. "He is very much like my son. I think he's just better at covering his tracks." She crossed and uncrossed her legs.

I couldn't figure out why she was telling me any of this.

"If I had to pinpoint a time when it all started to go wrong, I would say it was when Mason died."

"Mason? Mason Dunn?" I asked.

What did Jakes brother have to do with the Fletchers?

"Yes. They grew up together, practically shared a crib. Marlena was my oldest and dearest friend. I think when both Mason and Marlena died, Owen started to lash out. He blamed everyone and anyone for Mason's death, especially his brother Jake."

"Why?" I asked. "It was an accident."

"Yes, well. Jake was supposed to be with Mason that morning, but he was still a teenager and probably didn't want to be on a boat in the middle of the river at five a.m. on a Sunday. So in typical teenage fashion, he didn't show up at the docks. Mason went out alone. Nobody knows what happened to capsize the boat. The waters were due to be rough, but nothing more than usual. Owen just assumes if Jake had been there with him, then maybe Mason would still be alive."

"Or they both could've died," I said. At least now, I knew why Owen and Jake had hated each other from the very beginning. That hatred hadn't started with me. I'd just added to it.

"I know that. But Owen couldn't see it that way. I felt so helpless, he was hurting so much. Instead of getting him help to work through it, I justified his behavior. I enabled him. Instead of making him realize he was wrong, I made excuses." She gave me a sad smile. "I helped to make him what he is."

"Has he hurt anyone since me?" It was something I wondered about almost every day.

When she nodded, I almost fell off the bench. I clutched my stomach. "The Preston girl. Stacy, I think her name was. Owen gave her a black eye and roughed her up a bit. We also think he might have sunk the Prestons' shrimp boat, but he denies it, and they have no proof." She wiped her palms on her skirt. "Nothing compared to what he did to you, though."

No. Nothing did.

She cleared her throat. "I know this doesn't mean shit to you, Abby, but I think you are doing a great job as a mom, a much better job than I ever did." Bethany's eyes had started to glaze over. Was hell freezing over, or was Bethany Fletcher—formerly Satan's right hand man—actually about to cry? And in front of me, no less. "Is Owen her father, Abby? I mean, I know you were living with Jake for a while..."

It was time to tell someone about it.

I would never have dreamed in a million years it would be Bethany Fletcher. But, she happened to be the one who was asking.

"When I first found out I was pregnant, I was sure she was Owen's, but then she was born with bright blue eyes, and I thought for a second there was a chance..." I shook my head and laughed. "I was so young. I didn't know most babies born with blue eyes changed color over time. One day I was staring at my six month-old baby girl and her eyes were as green as the freaking Emerald City. That's when I gave up all hope that she was Jake's." It was difficult to admit out loud.

"Oh, Abby," Bethany said. "That must have been hard for you."

I nodded. "It still is."

"Will you at least think about letting me get to know my granddaughter, about giving me a chance?"

"I can't promise you a yes or a no, but I can promise you I'll think about it," I said. Bethany may have been ready to let go of the person she was, but I couldn't forget so easily. That person caused me too much pain to be given a do-over and a free pass to form a relationship with my daughter.

"That's all I'm asking." She got off the bench to leave. "Thank you." It was said so softly I could barely hear her over the parents calling to their children from the benches next to us. "Thank you," she repeated and walked away.

Had I just agreed to think about letting the most evil woman I've ever known have a relationship with my daughter simply because she no longer looked like the devil and had spewed some sincere-sounding words?

Apparently, I had.

I sighed and looked over at Georgia, who was showing a little brown haired boy how to position his feet in front of him before sliding down the shiny new slide. "Hey Bethany?"

"Yes?" She turned around, her cheeks flushed red.

"You know what Owen did to me. You know how badly he hurt me. But what you haven't said is *how* you know."

Her face paled. "Abby..." She started, her voice shaky and unsure. "Owen was in terrible shape afterwards." He wasn't the only one. "He drove two towns over and called Cole. Cole called me. I'm so sorry." She shook her head. "I helped Cole bring you home that night." Tears streamed down her face.

And then she was gone.

Chapter Twenty-Three

I TRIED NOT to think about Bethany and her request from that night, or her revelation that she had more to do with covering up Owen's sick behavior than I had initially thought. But, I did tell her I would think about letting her get to know Georgia, and I meant it. I wouldn't do it right away. I had other issues on my mind.

Tall, blonde and leather issues, to be specific.

My housing situation had changed, too. I had that on my mind more than anything else. After Nan's house had been foreclosed on, it sat empty for years as the economy continued to slide downward. Eventually, the bank sold it to some big time investor who fixed it up and turned it over to a property management company to find a renter. When I passed the window of the Matlacha Realty office and saw the familiar pink siding and white shutters on the picture taped to their window, I ran inside to sign the lease right then and there. After a few phone calls to the owner, they accepted my check and handed me the keys.

I didn't even have a chance to tell Frank about the house before he died. I knew he would have been really happy for us though.

Georgia and I had officially moved in a few days earlier. There were still boxes piled in the corner of her room that I hadn't had a chance to unpack yet. Actually, there were boxes I hadn't unpacked in *every* room.

I gave Georgia a bath before tucking her into bed in very same room where Nan had so generously given me the deadbolt I requested on the very first night I'd stayed with her. I'd felt safe there, like my heart could finally lay calm and quiet. Now, the framed photo above my little girl's bed made my heart skip a beat and my stomach double over.

I wish she hadn't asked for me to hang it up for her.

A few months earlier, I'd been sitting on the couch in the apartment sorting through some old photos in my scrap box when Georgia turned from the cartoon she was watching and asked if she had a daddy. I had no idea how to answer that. Telling her about Owen was out of the question. I was trying to figure out the right way to tell her she actually *didn't* have a daddy when she pulled a picture from the bottom of the box I was sorting.

"Mama, is this my daddy?" She had asked, holding up my favorite picture of Jake. He was on his bike, a cigarette hanging from his mouth. He had just parked in the lot and pushed his sunglasses to the top of his head. He wasn't quite smiling, but there was happiness there. It captured exactly who he was. My heart fluttered just looking at him. I had almost forgotten the effect his appearance had on me.

Almost, but not quite.

My childhood had been built on lies and mistrust. I decided then that I wasn't going to continue that cycle with my daughter.

"No, baby girl, he's not," I answered. "I wish he was though." My eyes watered.

"Don't cry, Mama. We can pretend he is. Okay?"

"Pretend?" I asked. Georgia had such a huge imagination.

"Yeah. We just pretend he's my daddy."

I couldn't say no to her liquid green eyes. "Just for pretend though, okay, baby girl? He's not your daddy. Not really."

She looked down at the picture then back at me, smiling like she'd just ransacked an ice cream truck. She also lost all interest in knowing anything more about who her father was. She was satisfied with her new picture and the promise of a game we could play together.

"Yes, Mama. Just pretend." Then, she ran off to her room with her picture in hand. It wasn't until I changed the sheets on her bed a few days later when I realized she'd kept it under her pillow.

The day we moved into Nan's house she requested a frame for her picture and announced she wanted it hung over her bed. I didn't want to do it. It took the pretending a little too far for my liking. But, the picture went up, and each night when I put Georgia to sleep I came face to face with what almost had been.

Before I started tackling the boxes in the kitchen, I changed into shorts and a tank top. I was in need of some comfort, so I threw my old black hoodie on top of it all.

I wondered what Nan would have said if she could have seen all of the changes her little house had been through. I was sad to see the old avocado appliances and white cabinets were gone, but I wasn't about to complain about the stainless steel and cherry wood that had taken their place. The stained and ripped linoleum floors had also been replaced with a dark hard wood in varying shades. Nan's home, even in its new and improved state with its landscaping overhaul and new coat of paint, still looked like Nan's house...just mixed with an ad from Island Home Magazine.

I slipped out of the house through the back sliding glass

doors. The investor had torn out the old screened in lanai and built a new outdoor kitchen area, complete with a brick paver deck, state of the art grill, mini-fridge, sink area, and granite counter tops. But the view was as spectacular as ever, with the mangroves floating over the dark blue waters of the Coral Pines River River. It seemed to be the only thing left completely unchanged.

I opened the grill and felt around for the key I had taped to the inside of the hood. I used it to open the lock on the drawer below the grill meant to house cooking tools.

I had no such tools.

I retrieved the old tin pencil box I hid the day we moved in. The box had been doodled on and taped together more times than I could remember. It contained a small yellow glass pipe, a lighter, and a dime bag. I'd tried to be one of those women who had a glass of wine at the end of the day.

I'd never developed a taste for it.

I'd bought a couple of reclining chairs from a garage sale to use on the patio. Those chairs, plus a twin bed and mattress for Georgia and a mattress and box-spring for my room, were all the furniture we had. I had planned on buying myself a real bed, along with a couch and table for the living room by perusing the weekend flea market and swap meet the week before.

My plans for more furniture had been derailed when Frank died.

I had been calling him all throughout that day to tell him about having rented Nan's house, and to tell him that I would be by with his groceries a little later than normal. After two hours with no call back, I had a sick feeling that something was wrong.

I pulled up to his house and banged on the front door. When he didn't answer, I tried the door...which was already unlocked. As soon as I had entered the house, I knew he was dead. It seemed to radiate a chill throughout the space.

The smell only reinforced that.

I found Frank's body upstairs in the guest bathroom. He'd been sitting, fully clothed, in a pink tiled bathtub with no water, clutching a picture frame in one hand and an empty bottle of Wild Turkey in the other. His eyes were closed and if I didn't have that feeling of death all around me, I would have just thought he was sleeping.

I went downstairs to use the phone and called the sheriff's station. I waited upstairs, sitting on the bathroom rug on floor next to Frank. He'd been alone for such a long time. I didn't want him to be alone anymore.

It felt wrong to have them come pick him up with the bottle in his hand so I worked it out of his grip and set it on the counter. For a few minutes, I troubled over what I should do with the picture frame resting on his chest, clutched in his other hand. I finally decided not to take a chance with whatever it was getting lost when they moved him. I promised him then that I would make sure the frame would be buried with him.

I lifted his elbow just slightly and wiggled the frame free. I sat back on the fuzzy rug and flipped the frame over. It was one of those split frames that held three pictures. The first was of Jake, it looked to be right after high school. He looked a little younger than I remembered him and his hair was cropped close to his head. With a carefree smile on his face he held a fishing pole in one hand, and in the other he held up the end of his fishing line with a huge sail-cat dangling from the hook. I had touched the picture and smiled to myself. I loved seeing that he'd been happy once with his family. His life hadn't always revolved around the bad; there seemed to have been plenty of good in that house once too.

The middle picture was of Marlena and Mason, I had seen the same picture on the desk in Frank's office.

The last picture took me by surprise.

It was me.

I was sitting on the worn leather couch of the apartment, holding a very new born Georgia. I was smiling, but you could see the genuine fear in my eyes. Frank had taken the picture with my camera on the day I brought Georgia home from the hospital. I had it printed and hung it on the refrigerator of the apartment. I had no clue Frank had a copy, or how he went about getting it. It told me all I needed to know about how important we'd been to him.

I hoped he died knowing how important he was to us.

Frank had all three pictures tucked in his suit jacket when he was buried, along with a picture Georgia drew for him. I made sure of it.

I turned on the small radio I kept on the patio to my favorite country station, keeping the volume low so I wouldn't wake Georgia. I collapsed onto one of my new-old chairs and packed a bowl. I sat back, lit it up, and inhaled the smoke, savoring the familiar heat in my lungs. I held it inside as long as I could before exhaling it through both my nose and mouth.

I enjoyed my high, and allowed my mind to drift to the one person I tried so hard not to think about. I traced the design of the metal pendant around my neck. I'd never been able to bring myself to take the damn thing off.

I couldn't help but think about how great a father Jake would have been to Georgia. If he'd stayed that day, I doubt I'd have decided to keep her after all. The thought caused my heart to seize in my chest. I was definitely not going to let myself go there. Georgia was the best thing that ever happened to me, and I refused to think about a world without her in it.

I was lifted out of the comfort of my high by the sound of heavy steps in the grass beside the house. The small patio light only lit the immediate space I occupied, but it cast shadows over everything else.

"Who's there?" As soon as the words left my mouth, I knew the answer.

He stood as still as stone, just a few steps from the patio. I heard the familiar sound of his Zippo lighter and saw the red glow from the end of his cigarette. I was frozen in my chair. I opened my mouth to speak and nothing came out.

"Hey," he said. His familiar voice washing over me like comfort I hadn't known since he left.

I breathed deeply and gathered enough brain power to speak. "Hey," I responded, trying my best to keep my voice level. "You don't have to creep up on me in the dark, you know. You could get yourself hurt." I mustered as much false confidence as I could, but inside I was shaking like a paint mixer.

Jake stepped out of the dark shadows and into the light. The picture above Georgia's wall was nothing compared to the real thing. He was still dressed all in black, but the muscles beneath his tight t-shirt were larger than I remembered. They strained against the thin material. "Oh yeah?" he asked. "How you gonna hurt me?"

He flinched when he realized what he'd said. I pretended not to notice.

"With this," I said as I pulled my .22 from my beach bag.

"Wow. You're packing now?" He looked amused. "Let me see that thing." I handed it over to him, and he inspected it carefully, turning it over in his hand. "Nice. You do know you shouldn't hand your pistol over to someone just because they asked, right? You could be the one who gets hurt."

"Oh yeah?" I asked, using his words. "How you gonna hurt me?"

He laughed.

His hair was longer than it had been when he left. His face was harder and a looked little older than four years should have made it. But his eyes were as blue and amazing as ever. I had to squeeze my legs together to rid myself of the tingle that was happening all over me. "Maybe, handing over my gun is part of my whole plan of defense. I just give it to people and ask them to hold it for me. It distracts them while I run away."

For the first time in over four years, the smile I'd been seeing in my dreams was now right in front of me.

I almost fell over.

I was seventeen all over again.

"I would probably come up with a plan B if I were you," he said, pushing his hair behind his ear.

I liked the longer hair. It was hot… and *I* was getting hot. *Too* hot. I took off my hoodie and threw it on the chair next to me. The night breeze kissed my skin, and I sighed in relief. "That's better," I muttered.

"Bee!" Jake exclaimed. His eyes went wide.

My heart fluttered when I heard him say my nickname again.

"What?" I asked, hoping I hadn't dropped my pipe.

"Your arm. Holy shit, you did it." He reached out to me and right before he was to touch me he pulled back. "It's fucking amazing," he said softly.

My tattoos. He was gawking at my tattoos. After Georgia was born, I'd decided to get the sleeve Jake and I had talked about. It started at my shoulder and went down my right arm, ending at my wrist. I'd spent endless hours in the tattoo chair, starting with a recreation of one of my favorite sunset pictures I'd taken myself on my shoulder, followed by the angel of death riding a motorcycle down my bicep. Underneath that was *the scar* painting I loved so much, and on my forearm was The Hellen Keller quote I'd used to describe how I felt about Jake. Its winding script stopped just short of my wrist. Each line and mark offered by my scars had been used as part of the design. When people looked at me, they were looking at the marks I'd chosen for myself, not the marks others had forced upon me. It'd been liberating.

I wished Jake had been there to see what I'd done.

"Why didn't you ring the bell?" I asked as he handed me my gun. I checked to make sure the safety was on before placing it back in the pocket of my bag.

He was still gawking at my ink. "You're just...fuck." He rubbed his hand over his mouth and goatee, glancing toward the house and turning serious. "Oh, I didn't want to wake up..."

"Georgia," I finished for him.

"Georgia," he repeated. "Like your Nan." I nodded, happy he remembered Nan's name. "She's cute." He didn't look mad or angry when he said it. He just looked tired.

"Yeah, she sure is," I said proudly. It was thoughtful of him not to ring the bell and wake her up. I was surprised his bike hadn't already done that, though I hadn't heard it, either. "Did you ride here?"

"Nah," he said. "Bike's at the apartment. I walked."

"You walked all that way?"

Jake shrugged his shoulders and took a long drag of his cigarette. He shifted from one foot to the other, blowing the smoke out through his nose.

"Sit." I patted the empty chair next to me. "You wanna hit?" I handed him the pipe as he sat down. He hesitated at first, searching my face for something. I had no doubt he was wondering how civil we could be. The man had just lost his father, after all. It was the least we could be to each other.

Jake dropped into the chair, lit the bowl, and took a hit. I reached over to the mini-fridge and pulled out two Coronas, handing him one.

And just like that, it was back.

The silence.

I can't say it was as comfortable as it'd always been. But it was as close to comfortable as it could be under the circumstances. His face softened after a few minutes, and I knew he could feel it, too.

"I'm sorry about your dad," I said, taking the pipe from him and lighting it for my next hit. My hands shook. I was almost as nervous as the first time we were alone. I needed to be much higher to be this close to him.

Jake shook his head. "Seems like I should be saying that to you about him. Your words gave me a closure I didn't think I'd be finding. Ever."

I guess he'd heard my eulogy.

"Yeah, well… he helped me out when no one else would, and I honestly don't know where I would be now without him." I heard myself and hoped he wouldn't take that as an insult. I certainly hadn't meant it that way.

"How long have you been back here?" He gestured to the house.

"Just a few days."

"And before that, you were…?" His questions were cautious,

like he was trying to figure something out.

"The apartment at the shop. Your dad let me stay there when he found out I had been sleeping in the truck." The words slipped out, and I instantly regretted them.

Jake bent over and put his face to his knees, his hands cupping the back of his head. "Why the *fuck* were you in the truck again?" he asked. When he lifted up his face, he looked enraged.

"I had nowhere else to go," I said firmly. But, Jake seemed tortured in a way I didn't remember him being all those years ago.

"When I..." He halted, as if he were thinking these things for the first time as he said them now. His tone softened. "When I took off, I didn't mean you had to leave the apartment. You could've stayed there forever, for all the fuck I cared."

"Yeah, well, it was only a few days. And nobody blew anyone else on the hood this time." That broke the tension a little, and we both laughed. "Then, your dad left me a note, in the truck. He called me a hobo, and left me a huge set of janitor's keys for the apartment and for your truck."

Jake looked comforted by that. He relaxed and let his head fall back against the chair. "I saw your postcards."

For the past couple years, I'd been selling my landscape pictures as postcards in the gift shops around town. They were selling well, and recently one of my better-selling cards had been chosen for a state calendar. It wasn't going to make me rich. But with that in addition to my job at the shop, I could take care of my baby and myself. That was all that mattered.

"Where did you see them?"

"Reggie." He turned to face me. "He sent me a socket I needed to fix my bike. When I opened the box, there were your cards. He stuck ten or twelve of them in there. I didn't even need to see the signature in the corner to know they were yours."

"Oh."

"They're fucking beautiful, Bee."

I didn't know what to think of that. "Thanks." I could almost feel my heart beating back to life with each word he spoke. Soon, I would be back to where I was four years ago, melting in his hands. I couldn't listen to him be nice to me. I wanted him to yell at me, be cruel to me—scream at me if he had to. It would have been so much easier to let him go all over again if I'd hated him, if he hated me. Instead, his kind words caused so much conflict within.

I was so distracted with Jake I didn't hear the sliding glass door open. When Jake's gaze widened and focused past my chair, I knew someone was behind me. I turned to see Georgia, standing on the patio, rubbing her eyes with her fists. Her night shirt was tucked into her underwear, and her favorite Raggedy Ann doll was being strangled in the crook of her arm.

"Georgia, baby, what are you doing up?"

She came over and crawled onto my lap, almost knocking me over as she did. I was glad I'd already put the pipe back in its hiding place. I may not have been June Cleaver, but I did my best to keep up appearances.

"I couldn't sleep." She shifted around in my lap until she was facing away from me. She didn't even notice our guest until she'd stopped squirming. "Mama?" She tugged at my shirt and pointed to Jake.

"Georgia, this is an old friend of Mama's. This is Jake." To my surprise, Jake held out his hand, and she immediately took it.

"Pleased to meet you, Georgia." He looked her over cautiously. Neither of them took their hands away from the other. They were both smiling, like they were sharing a secret I wasn't in on.

Knowing about the pretending we'd done with his picture, I was nervous about what would happen next. She left my lap and crawled right into Jake's, as if she had done it a hundred times before. He didn't seem to mind. He studied her like she was a puzzle he was trying to figure out while she climbed all over him.

Georgia was comfortably snuggled onto Jake's chest with her head nestled in the crook of his arm before I could stop her. "Baby girl, why don't you let our guest relax on his chair by himself, and I'll tuck you back into bed," I said carefully. "You need to go back to sleep."

"But, Mama," she said as her eyes lit up. "I can't go to sleep now. Daddy's here!"

Fuck my life.

Chapter Twenty-Four

I TUCKED GEORGIA back into her bed and sang her to sleep. Lullabies? Not for my kid. The song of the evening, per her request, had been "Bennie and the Jets" by Elton John. That was definitely Frank's fault. He had given her an iPod for Christmas last year, pre-loaded with her favorite songs from his record collection.

I did my best, but I was no Elton.

Wherever Frank was now, I knew he was laughing at me.

Fuck you, Frank.

Jake was leaning against the counter when I returned to him. He had his legs crossed at the ankles, his arms folded in front of him and a huge, shit-eating grin on his face.

"What?" I asked.

"Nice song," he teased.

I felt redness creep up my cheeks. "That's Frank's fault. Him and his goddamned record collection." I laughed. "I've tried to just play her music at night, but she insists I sing to her."

"Smart girl."

"*Spoiled* girl." I looked around at my bare living room, suddenly embarrassed by my lack of furniture. "I'd offer you a seat, but there aren't any."

"Yeah, I noticed," he said, glancing around the empty space.

"The patio chairs are pretty much it for now, as far as furniture goes," I said. Jake nodded. I noticed that as he interacted with me, his gaze never shifted from the door of Georgia's room.

"How old is she?"

"Three," I answered. I walked past him through the sliding glass doors. He followed me back out to the patio, and we returned to our chairs.

"Three, huh?" Jake eyed me skeptically and took a sip of his beer. His elbows rested on his knees. "And you're bringing her up without her father?"

I didn't even hesitate. "She doesn't have one." It was the truth. As much as I hated saying it, there would never be a father in my little girl's life.

"I may have not done well in school," Jake said, "but I re-member sex-ed quite well, and I do recall that both a man and a woman are required to make one of those." He gestured to the house with his beer.

"Making a child doesn't make someone a father," I told him. I wished my beer was scotch. This wasn't a conversation beer could handle.

He shifted to reach into his pockets to retrieve his lighter, lit a cigarette and nodded. "Ain't that the fucking truth." He blew out the smoke and scratched the bridge of his nose. "You know, I didn't even know you had a kid until I saw her run up to you during your eulogy today." He shook his head. "It was the shock of my fucking life." He ran a hand over his goatee again. The gesture was so familiar. It brought me a little comfort being in his presence after all these years. It reminded me of the Jake I'd fallen in love with. "I wish I would have known, Bee. I mean, she looks a little like my mom when she was her age. Aside from the red hair. That part is all you. Fucking amazing really."

Jake kept talking, but I'd stopped listening. Between what Georgia had said about Daddy being home and my comments about fathers being more than a person who makes children, Jake somehow thought that Georgia was his.

"Oh wow. No, Jake." I tried not to be shitty about it.

"*No, Jake* what?"

"No, Jake, she's not yours."

He sat still for a moment, letting it sink in a little. Then he stood, like he was preparing for war. Everything about his squared-off shoulders said he was ready for a fight. He roared a stream of profanity into the air and launched his beer into the river. Then, he turned around, and with one swipe of his arm flipped over the little metal table between us, sending it rolling onto the grass.

"Explain to me how she's not mine, Abby."

"She's just not, okay?" I stood up and started to walk away, but in a few large strides he had closed the distance between us. The house stopped me from going any further. I turned and found him towering over me. He raised his arms and pressed his hands against the wall on each side of my head, his massive form caging me in. He pressed his chest into mine. I was surprised when he leaned into me and buried his face in my hair as he inhaled deeply.

He stood, breathing me in, until he remembered his anger. "Fuck, Bee!" His gaze met mine. His intoxicating smell filled my nostrils. I was turned on by it. There was no denying that. I'd never been attracted to anyone but Jake. Years, decades, even centuries could pass, and he would still be it for me. I would take him angry or sad, and there was definitely something madly hot in angry Jake at the moment. "Explain to me how your kid, who looks just like my mama, who is *three fucking years old*, isn't mine."

"Why do you even care?" I snapped at him. I tried to move

out from the cage of him, but he pressed his hips into me to keep me captive. I kept my expression hard, but the contact sent heat racing down my spine.

My face flushed.

"Just answer the fucking question," he growled into my ear. His mouth was only a breath away. Part of me wanted to run my hands through his hair and part of me wanted to knee him in the crotch just to show him who I was now, how strong I'd become while he'd been gone.

I spoke slowly, and kept my voice from shaking. "You have blue eyes right?" He nodded. "And I have blue eyes right?" Confusion started to replace the lingering anger written on the lines in his forehead. "Did you see Georgia, Jake? Did you see the color of her eyes?"

"Green," he whispered. His shoulders fell from their commanding stance and he backed away from me. He sank back into a chair and his face dropped into his hands. "And we used protection, so why would she fucking be mine." He sounded defeated.

I realized how painful this was for him now. "I looked it up. Two people with blue eyes only make blue-eyed children," I said softly. I remembered how, even a few months after her birth, I'd still held out hope that Georgia could have been Jake's. When I looked online and found a genetics eye color chart that said otherwise, that hope died.

It was a horrible fucking day.

I leaned against the house and continued. "She found a picture of you. When I told her she didn't have a daddy, she asked if she could pretend it was you. She loves that damn picture so much." I wrung my hands nervously as I spoke. "I thought I'd never see you again, so I let her pretend. She has the picture hanging above her bed. She says 'goodnight, Daddy' to you every night and kisses the picture before she goes to sleep. It breaks my heart every fucking time." I wiped at the tears I didn't realize had sprung from my eyes. "I'm so sorry. I never thought..." I slid down the side of the house until my ass reached the concrete. I pulled my knees up to my chest.

When he lifted his face from his hands and looked up at me, the anger was back in full force. "So why hasn't that cocksucker been a father to her? Why aren't you guys together raising her? Where the *fuck* is that pretty-boy motherfucker?" A thick vein throbbed in his neck. His eyes were dark and wide, they shone with each angry word.

"Jake! You're going to wake her up."

"Fuck this shit." He stood and started walking back into the darkness from where he'd appeared not long before.

"Wait!" I called after him. I stood up, but didn't follow him. He stopped, but didn't turn around. "You never answered my question. Why do you care who her father is? *You* were the one who didn't believe in me, or in us. *You* were the one who left. So, why does it even matter to you now?"

I was sure I already knew. I just needed to hear him say it.

"Because—" He cut himself off and started walking again. Just when I thought it would remain a mystery forever, he stopped again, and turned to face me. "Because I wanted it to be me, Bee."

With that, he disappeared behind the side of the house.

I fell. My ass crashed into the paver deck. I let my head fall back onto the siding of the house. "I did, too," I whispered to no one. One tear fell, and then another, until I couldn't control the flow. "I did, too."

It was quiet a while before I pried myself up off the patio and headed back into the house. I checked on Georgia and found her still asleep, her chest rising and falling evenly, her doll still suffocated at her side. Our argument hadn't woken her.

Had it been an argument, a fight?

It was the best fight I've ever had. Jake's words from years ago played in my brain.

I made sure all of the doors were locked and went room to room to turn off the lights. It had been the longest day of my life. All I wanted to do was try and get some sleep, although I doubted it was even a possibility. My mind was still reeling over what he'd said. He'd been hoping he was Georgia's dad. The thought made my stomach turn and my heart flutter all at the same time.

Several times during the night, I contemplated telling Jake just how Owen came to be Georgia's father. But then, I asked myself if his knowing the truth would change anything. I had no idea, and it just wasn't me I had to think about anymore. I had a daughter by another man. Jake hadn't trusted me or loved me enough to ignore the gossip four years ago, and according to the events of the evening, that hadn't changed.

I reached for the switch under the kitchen cabinet to turn off the lights when my eyes landed on a newspaper clipping stuck to the top of the refrigerator. It hadn't been there earlier in the day. The letter magnets Georgia liked to play with were holding it to front the fridge. Someone had spelled out the word LOVE with them. I didn't even need to read the article. The headline was enough for me to know who left it, and why:

ONE-EYED MAN FOUND SHOT AND DISMEMBERED
IN SWAMP

I remembered his words from the one and only night we'd

ever had sex, when I'd told him about the man who I'd stabbed in the eye with a shard of glass in my mother's house: *I need to know if you would like it if I put him to ground for you.*

I had told him yes then.

I read the rest of the article and clutched it to my chest. After the initial shock of it all, a kind of warmth spread throughout my body, and I knew without question.

I would have said yes all over again.

Chapter Twenty-Five

I HADN'T SEEN or heard from Jake since the night we argued. A few weeks passed, but I knew he was still in town. I'd seen his bike parked at the apartment occasionally. He never came to work at the shop. I wondered why he was still there. Frank was dead and buried. Reggie and I were keeping the shop running smoothly, but ultimately, we were waiting for Jake to decide what his plans were for Dunn's Auto Repair.

I dropped off Georgia with Tess early one morning while it was still dark, so I could photograph the sunrise on the beach. Sunrises were my best sellers, and at the rate Georgia had been growing I was going to have to sell a ton of postcards just to keep her clothed.

It was a really clear morning, not a cloud in the sky. The waves were small. Seagulls flew over my head, heading to the restaurants to steal bagels and eggs from the tourists dining outside. Conditions were perfect. I took some standing shots before lying on my stomach on the sand to make myself even with the horizon and taking a dozen or so more. Those always turned out to be my favorites, and it didn't hurt that they were also the ones the tourists wanted to shell out three bucks for.

When I was satisfied that I'd gotten what I wanted, I tucked my camera back in its bag, shook the sand from my long skirt and fanned out the inside of my tank top. A shadow fell over me and an eerie sense of unease pricked the hairs on my arm. An icy hot panic coursed through my veins. I looked up just in time to see Owen standing over me, gazing down my top. His eyes looked clear and his hair was tucked into a backwards baseball cap. He was wearing a clean yellow tee shirt and board shorts. If I hadn't known any better, I would have thought that he was just a cute, clean-cut local boy.

But I had known better.

And I'd known worse, too.

I didn't say shit to him. I just started walking away. I saw the Chicken or The Egg Diner in the distance. Its beach side tables were already filled with patrons, but it was too far for them to hear me if I screamed, so I picked up my pace.

Owen followed me through the sand. "I just want to talk to you, Abby," he said.

"You are not supposed to be near me!" I shouted without looking back. He was on my heels.

"I just want to talk about our daughter."

I heard those words leave his mouth, and suddenly I didn't give a fuck what he did to me. I stopped and turned on my heels, pressing my hand into his chest as he ran into me. I caught him by surprise, and he almost fell backwards.

"What the fuck did you say to me?" With adrenaline coursing through my veins I was no longer scared. He should've been scared of me, though.

"I want to know about our—"

"MY daughter, Owen—MY daughter. You have no rights, no claim—no *nothing*. You are a monster she never needs to know. Forget she fucking exists."

Owen grabbed my wrist and pulled me to him. A wave of nausea washed over me. I felt around the inside of my beach bag with my free hand. "I wasn't going to be rough with you," he spat, "but you seem to always bring out the best in me. I want to know her, Abby. She's my flesh and blood, goddammit, and I've waited long enough!"

"You can wait in hell motherfucker." I yanked my wrist from his grip, and just as he was reaching for me again the barrel of my .22 met his forehead.

"You've got to be kidding me," he said, straightening up to full height. He lifted both of his hands like I was robbing him instead of protecting myself.

"I'm so not fucking kidding." I kept the gun aimed at his head. I didn't want to have to shoot twice.

"All I want is to get to know her," Owen said.

"And all *I* want is to see parts of your head scattered across the beach."

"You'd really shoot me?" Owen had the balls to look surprised, and even a little scared. It made me visualize the way his head would look as it exploded at point blank range. I may have laughed out loud.

It was fucking funny.

"If you ever come near me or my daughter, I swear to God I will lay you out, and you will never even see it coming. Consider this my nice warning. You won't get it again."

"Abby," he pleaded. His whine made me want to kill him even more. I had no sympathy for him whatsoever. In fact, there wasn't a single place in my heart that felt the least bit of remorse for Owen Fletcher. "Please."

In one quick motion, Owen grabbed the barrel of my gun. I pulled the trigger, shooting into the sand. The gun fell from my grip, and Owen put his hand over my mouth. "You can't keep her from me," he whispered in my ear. "Besides, I know you'd never shoot me."

"But, I will." The cocking of a hammer brought my attention to where Jake stood. Even in the lightest light of day his normally sapphire eyes were as dark as night. His black t-shirt and jeans looked like hell against the heaven of the white sand. Owen released me instantly, and I instinctively ran to Jake. He took my hand and pulled me behind him. *Protected by a wall of Jake.*

I liked the thought of that. And the feeling.

"You again," Owen said. He looked pissed, but also very, very afraid.

"Me again," Jake said.

"I'd heard you were back."

Jake turned to me, the gun still aimed at Owen. "Your call, baby." He was asking me if Owen should die, right then and there. As tempted as I was to say yes, there was too much at risk.

I had my daughter to think of.

"Not today." It was my honest answer. I had dreamed about Jake taking Owen down for so long. I savored the sight of Owen quivering while he stared down the barrel of that gun.

Owen kept his hands in the air. "You two are sick," he said, as if he could read my mind.

Jake laughed out loud. "It took you *this* long to figure that out? You're fucking dumber than I thought." Jake tucked his gun in the back of his jeans and put his arm around me. "If I see you near her again, you're fucking dead – my choice, not hers. Simple as that." We turned toward the road and started walking. Jake turned to face Owen again. "And if you even think about going near Georgia, I won't just kill you. I'll cut you into pieces and scatter your parts."

We left Owen shaking in the sand. I may have just had a confrontation with my walking nightmare, but all I could concentrate on was the feeling of Jake's arm around me and his lips in my hair when he kissed my head reassuringly.

When we got to his bike, he handed me his helmet as if we'd done that very same thing every day for the last four years. I got on behind him, hugging him tightly as we sped down the road. It felt good to touch him. It had been so long. The vibrations of the bike had a way of making me remember that I was still alive. Through the good and the bad, and between all the very blurred lines in between, Jake had always made me feel that way.

I knew we would never be able to make us work. That knowledge didn't stop me from finally admitting that I was still madly in love with the killer in my grasp.

Chapter Twenty-Six

INSTEAD OF DRIVING me home Jake took me back to the clearing among the orange trees where he'd revealed his last secret to me, the place where he had buried both the body of his childhood friend and his stillborn daughter.

We didn't speak when he parked the bike or when he led me through the narrow path to the clearing. When we got to the spot under the same tree where he made his darkest confessions to me years ago, he pulled me down onto his lap and buried his face in my neck. His heart was beating so quickly. His breath was short and came in spurts. After what seemed like a silent eternity, he finally spoke.

"Bee, what happened between you and Owen, and why the fuck were you trying to shoot him on the beach?"

That question held so much more than words.

"Pass," I said, using the same rules of the game we used to play. I had a daughter to protect now. Jake knowing about Owen raping me would just make matters worse. "Why are you still here?" I asked him.

"What?" Jake asked. Confusion marring his beautiful face.

I thought the question was pretty obvious. "Why are you here with me? Why did you help me on the beach? Why are you even talking to me? I would hate me if I were you."

He looked at me just the way he used to: past my eyes and into the broken soul beneath. He brushed some stray hairs from my face and cupped my cheek in his palm.

"Pass," he said.

"Well," I laughed. "Looks like we're back to square one."

"We can just play again then," Jake said. "Four years adds a lot of new secrets, don't you think?" That was an understatement. "We'll start small." He reached for the pendant on my neck and ran his fingers over the ornate metal that held his initials hidden within the design. "Why do you still wear this?"

That was one I could answer easily. "I've tried to take it off. Several times. I even went a whole day without it once, but when I got home I went right for the dresser and put it back on, I didn't even stop to think about it. I haven't taken it off since." Jake lifted it and pressed his lips to my skin underneath. My breath hitched at the feeling of his warm soft lips on my chest. "My turn." He nodded and pulled his lips from me, creating an empty feeling. "Why were you at the beach today?"

"I was looking for you." It was a simple statement, and he didn't explain any further. He was just looking for me, and he seemed satisfied with that answer. "See? We're doing good already." He nudged my shoulder and smiled up at me. I rested my head on his shoulder.

He had destroyed what I believed then was the greatest thing that ever happened to me in just a few short words four years ago. He must have hated me still for what he believed to be my betrayal. I couldn't just bring him into my life, even if he wanted to be a part of it. I didn't want to be hurt anymore. And I didn't want to hurt him. We'd almost healed each other once, and the pain of being *almost* healed is worse than the pain of being broken to begin with. And Georgia needed a mom who wasn't an emotional mess. She also didn't need someone in her life who would eventually resent her very being. That girl deserved the world, and I fully intended to give it to her. "What are we doing, Jake?"

He kissed my collarbone and blew out a long held breath onto my skin.

"Pass."

I SLEPT IN the next morning, well as much as the mother of a three-year-old who thought five a.m. was a perfectly acceptable time to jump on my bed could sleep in. Even after the confrontation with Owen, my time with Jake had lifted some of the thickness that had hung around since he'd left. Just his presence seemed to make things lighter. It was funny to think that someone so emotionally heavy on my heart could actually make things lighter.

Georgia must have slept in, too, because it was already seven-thirty, and she hadn't come to my room to ask for her usual Saturday morning pancakes. When I went to wake up the sleepy head, she wasn't in her bed. I started to panic but when I got to the kitchen there was a fresh pot of coffee on the counter and a sticky note on the pot written in adult handwriting in crayon: *We're out back*. With a smiley face drawn under it.

Tess had a key to the house. Maybe, she came over before her shift.

I'd called Bethany the night before to let her know that if she wanted a shot at knowing Georgia she'd better keep Owen on a leash. He hadn't bothered me in years, and I expected her to help keep it that way.

I left out the part about putting a gun to his head.

She told me she would handle it. That's all I needed to know.

I'd poured my coffee and almost choked on the first sip when I saw what was happening outside my window. Jake was sitting on the seawall with my daughter, laughing and helping her bait her hook on a little pink fishing pole. He was still wearing in his signature black, but was dressed down in a wife-beater and black board shorts that stopped right below his knees. There was a tattoo I had never seen before peeking out from the underside of his bicep. He was too far away for me to make out the design. His blonde hair was pulled back in a small bun at the nape of his neck. He was even wearing black flip flops instead of his usual boots.

I was going to need a lot more coffee.

Jake spotted me first. Then, Georgia followed his gaze. "Mama, Mama!" She put her little pink pole on the ground and ran to me. Jake stood and walked behind her. "Da—I mean Jake, made me pancakes and showed me how to catch blue crab off the seawall. He's taking us fishing today!" She jumped in the air and clapped. If I hadn't known any better, I would have sworn she was hopped up on caffeine.

Jake approached us cautiously. "Georgia, what did I tell you has to happen first?" he asked her.

She looked down at her feet. "Mama has to say yes."

"That's right: Mama has to say yes." He winked at me then dropped his gaze to where my tank top clung to my breasts. I wasn't wearing a bra. He looked again to the tattoos down my arm, and his smile turned into a smirk. "So Mama?" he asked. "What'll it be? You down for some fishing?"

I knew what he was doing. I couldn't say no to Georgia, especially when he'd already gotten her hopes up. "I don't know," I teased Georgia as she looked up at me, a hopeful glimmer in her eyes. "I suppose we can go." She jumped and squealed. "But first, I need to know something." She held her breath. "Are there any pancakes left?"

"Mama, we made you some!" she exclaimed. She grabbed my hand and dragged me back into the house. How had I slept through the noise of them making pancakes in a kitchen that shared a wall with my bedroom?

After she showed me where the plate that they had made for me was, she ran back outside with Jake. I didn't know if I was ready to spend time with him and my daughter together, and I didn't know what kind of game he was playing. But, I hated to see the look of disappointment on my little girl's face, so I went along with it.

And the pancakes were so damn good.

BY THE TIME I'd finished eating and had put a swimsuit on under my shorts and tank top, Georgia and Jake were waiting for me in a blue boat tied to the seawall. "Hurry, Mama! Jake is gonna take us to catch big fishies."

I had drunk two cups of coffee by then and was fully awake. I saw now that my daughter was decked out head-to-toe in pink fishing gear. She was wearing a pink visor that said "Fisher Girl." Her shirt looked like a miniature version of the collared shirts worn by fishing guides. And though I'd braided her hair the night before, it was now in a bun at the base of her neck...in the same style as Jake's hair.

I gave him the evil eye and he just shrugged. "I went to pick up some stuff and they had the cutest shit for little girls." He quickly realized his error. "I mean stuff."

"Mama says *shit* all the time," Georgia said.

"Thanks, baby." My three year old had just thrown me under the bus, and Jake couldn't have looked more amused by it. "I like your bun," I told her as Jake offered me his hand and helped me into the boat.

"Daddy did it for me."

My stomach dropped.

Jake stepped up to her and whispered in her ear. She smiled even brighter and corrected herself. "I mean, Jake did it for me."

"Oh, did he?" I laughed. "I think you missed your calling as a hair dresser, Jake."

"Oh, I have many *many* talents, Bee." He winked at me, and I blushed like a twelve year old girl.

The rest of the day played like a scene in a movie. Jake took us to a few fishing holes were he baited Georgia's hook and then only pretended to bait ours so she caught all the fish. She'd caught three snapper, two trout, a Spanish mackerel, and a very impressive red fish.

Jake brought sandwiches for lunch and was a very attentive teacher. He taught her how to keep the tip of the rod up to reel the fish in and stood behind her with his arms around her when she had a bite so the fighting fish wouldn't drag her little body into the water. Her excitement at each catch was clearly visible. After Jake unhooked each fish, he would ask her what its name should be before throwing it back.

By the end of the day, she had caught at least three Eltons.

When we finally made it back into the house, the sun was already setting and Georgia was sleeping on my lap, her grip still tight around her pink pole. She had missed her afternoon nap, but it was worth it. She would be talking about this day for a long time.

She didn't even wake up when I cleaned her up, changed her into her pajamas and put her to bed.

By the time I got back outside, Jake was propped up in a patio chair with a cigarette in his mouth and a beer in his hand. "Hey," I said, taking a seat.

"Hey," he said back. He looked content, relaxed even.

"How did you get in this morning?" I asked him. It had been bugging me all day.

"If I tell you, that counts as a secret," he said.

"Okay, fine. It's a secret," I agreed.

"I rang the doorbell. Georgia answered and let me in. You were still sleeping, so we made breakfast." He laughed. It was so much simpler than I thought.

Jake reached out a hand to me, and I took it instinctively. Then, he pulled me from my chair and into his lap; he wrapped his arms around me. My head fell onto his chest. "Can we do all our secrets right now, Bee?" He smoothed my hair. "Let's just get everything out there all at once. We won't even think about the answers. We'll just say them."

"I don't know if that's the best idea." Actually, it was a horrible fucking idea.

"You go first," he offered. "Ask whatever, and I'll answer." Okay, that intrigued me. So, I started.

"Why are you here?"

"Pass, until you answer your questions."

"This isn't starting out well."

"Just ask," he pushed.

"What have you been doing since you left?"

"Same as I did before, except I got some bigger contracts, higher profile stuff. I consider myself officially retired now, though."

"What is your new tattoo?"

He shifted and pulled his shirt to the side revealing an intricate design on the inside of his bicep. "It's not really new," he said. The design was the same as my necklace, except there were no initials in the design.

"It's beautiful." I traced the design with my fingers. "Does it mean anything?"

"Pass."

"We aren't going to get very far this way." I laughed.

"No, I guess not," he admitted. "Ask me one more. Promise I'll answer this one."

So I asked him the question that had been in my mind every day since he'd left.

"Did you ever think of me while you were gone?"

Jake took a deep drag of his cigarette. "Every second of every goddamned day, Bee." He blew the smoke out into the night.

Jake lifted my chin with his fingers and pressed his soft lips to mine. My entire being reacted to him. Tingles and fire and the sweetest burning. His lips were warm and reassuring. Lips I could lose—and have lost—myself in.

I couldn't do it again.

I pulled back.

"What's wrong?" he asked.

"I can't do this."

"Why not?"

"Because I have Georgia to think of." I stood up. "I don't know what you want Jake. I don't know why you're here, I don't want you to get to know Georgia and make her love you and then leave because I know what that feels like and I'd rather spare her that torture."

"I don't want to leave, Bee," he said quietly.

"Maybe not now. But you might want to eventually, and I don't want to put her through that."

Jake stood and grabbed my wrist. "I don't want to put either of you through anything."

I was tired of beating around the bush. I was tired of the secrets.

"But what happens when you get tired of looking at those beautiful green eyes," I asked him. "What happens when you start to resent her because you wish they were blue instead?"

"Abby, I fucking love you. What don't you understand about that?"

The word *love* caught me with my mouth open, and I couldn't close it.

"You love me?"

"Yes, I fucking love you. I've never stopped loving you. But it's not *just* you. It's her, too. I love you both. The second I saw her run to you in the church, I knew she was my daughter."

"But she's not your daughter."

Jake grunted. "You're not understanding me here. I know I didn't contribute to her physically." He paced around the deck. "That's okay with me."

"You could change your mind though."

"The night I came here and she called me her daddy was the best night of my life, no matter how it ended. When she crawled up into my lap, when she wouldn't let go of my hand... it was love at first sight."

Suddenly, I understood. The night she crawled onto his lap, the reason why they couldn't let go of each other. It was love at first sight. That was why he'd gotten so mad when I told him he wasn't her father.

"So, you really think you can just forget everything that happened between us and start over from scratch?" I asked.

"No, I don't want to start over from scratch. I want to start from *now*."

"How can you want that, after what happened the day you left, after what you said to me?"

"You're asking how I can forget that you fucked that son of a bitch."

I cringed. But I still couldn't tell him the truth. "Yes."

"I don't care." Jake held my face and looked right into my eyes. "I don't fucking care. I should have stayed. We should have talked about it. I left you to work after the greatest night of my life with no return date. It wasn't fair, and neither were my accusations. You refusing to talk about what happened, and then you with him on the beach… it made me realize there might be more to the story. But, I don't have to know it all right now. Does it make me sick to my stomach to think about him touching you? Yes. But the real question is, can we move forward from here? That answer is yes, too. For me, anyway. For four years, all I thought about was coming back to you, but my stupid pride kept me from doing it. I needed the excuse of my father dying before even attempting it. I was such a fucking coward. And you were here the whole time, raising Georgia on your own. Being so brave."

"It hurt so much when you left, Jake. If there's a chance that you'll do that again, well…I can't have my baby hurt like that, too. I won't do that to her." The tears started to fall again. I was going to run out of them soon.

"She won't hurt, Bee. She'll be ours. We'll be a family. I promise I won't resent her. It's not even possible. I love her so much."

"But, you could resent me."

He eyed me skeptically. "Bee, it's hard to explain the way I feel. I feel connected, to you and to Georgia, in a way that doesn't make any of that shit matter anymore. Was I hurt? You better fucking believe it. Do I still have an itchy trigger finger around that son of a bitch? Yes, and that will probably never go away. But, I know I can be good here, with you and her, and that we can find happiness…at least, as much as fucks-ups like us are capable of."

Could I really believe him this time?

"I was alone, Jake. I was pregnant. I had no one, and your father rescued me from living in the fucking gutter. Because you left. What's to keep you from doing that again?"

He looked angry and hurt as he approached me. He tilted my chin to meet his gaze. He pecked me on the lips and ripped off his shirt. On the left side of his chest, just below his collarbone, was another new tattoo. It simply read *Bee,* the letters wrapped in vines. He pressed my hand against the other tattoo with the same design as my necklace. "And what the fuck do you think this stands for?"

"I don't know," I answered truthfully.

He shook his head. "It stands for *you*." He pressed his forehead to mine.

Fear and love and regret ran through me, all at the same time.

"I'm just so scared." I loved him so much I couldn't breathe. I didn't know where we went from there. "What if it all goes away?"

"You haven't taken my necklace off in four years. Not only have I tattooed your name on my body, but I've *killed* for you—gladly—and I would do it again, even if you told me right now that you never wanted to see me again. Your bitch of a mother is on my list, too, I've got connections at Georgia Penn, could have her bleeding out by next week if that's what you want." He took a deep breath. "But, you know what made everything so fucking clear to me? The second I saw Georgia—" He wiped his eyes. "—I knew I would kill for her, too. I don't care who fucking made her. She's *my* goddamned daughter!" He was shouting now. "I thought I knew what love at first sight was, because I fell in love with you the moment I saw your face the night we met. But the way I felt when you held Georgia in your arms and she spoke about her Grandpa Frank was... it was so much more than that. It was everything."

The strength I'd built up over the past four years fell away. "I'm still scared."

He held me to his chest. "Me, too," he admitted. "But, I promise to work hard every damned day to make sure our fears don't come true." He kissed the top of my head. I took a deep breath and shook off all the doubts I'd been drowning in for four years. "That little girl broke my heart when she called me Daddy. And I wouldn't have had it any other way."

My chest swelled. I believed him when he said he loved me and my daughter, because I knew what love looked like. I didn't know if I should allow myself to hope that Georgia could really have a father after all. I wasn't convinced that love would be enough.

I wondered how two people so beaten down by the dark reality of their lives could raise another living soul and not fuck it up entirely.

How could *broken* plus *broken* ever equal *whole?*

Chapter Twenty-Seven

S ORTING THROUGH WHAT I thought was the last of the boxes was not my idea of a good time, but it had to be done. I could have smacked Jake when he so thoughtfully reminded me there were still a few boxes over at the apartment. He must have known that I was about to toss the remainder of them into the canal, so he volunteered to go get them for me instead.

We were taking things slow, but I would be lying if I said that Georgia was anything other than completely head over heels in love with him. We'd been functioning like a little family for a week. It was what I'd been dreaming of since Georgia was born, though I never really thought I could have it. I still owed Jake the truth about Owen. It was something I never wanted to relive, even during my darkest days. It was certainly the last thing I wanted to do during the happy ones.

The front door opened and the screen door slammed shut. "That was quick. Just bring them in here, and stack it in the corner. I'll sort it all out tomorrow. I've done so much today, my eyes are starting to cross." I folded the cardboard from the now empty box I'd been working on. When did I get so much stuff? Jake hadn't come into the living room yet, and he didn't answer me. "Jake?" I called out. He didn't answer. "Babe?"

Instead of his welcome voice answering, a much more menacing one called back. "You've never called me babe before. I like the way it sounds." Owen appeared in the room, shotgun in hand that he'd aimed at my chest. When I made a move to run, he cocked it. "Don't fucking move."

My mind was racing.

My first thoughts went to Georgia, napping in her bedroom. *Please don't wake up… please.*

I had to focus on how to get him out of the house and away from my sleeping child.

"Okay Owen. Let's just go outside, and we can talk about whatever you want," I said. I was willing to go anywhere he wanted, as long as it meant getting him away from my baby.

"Not so fast, Miss Abby." He glanced around the room. "It's been a while since I've been in here. Matter of fact, last time I was here I was having a lovely conversation about you, with your Nan."

When had he ever been in this house with Nan?

"What the fuck did you do to her?"

"Nothing. I just talked to her." His face was troubled, like he couldn't understand why I'd be concerned. "I came to see you that day, but you weren't here. Your Nan was kind enough to make me some tea. She was so nice to me. She just talked and talked. And somewhere in the middle, she let it slip that the house was in foreclosure. She knew she wouldn't have anywhere for you two to live but didn't want to rain on your parade, what with graduation coming up so soon, so she kept it from you. She wasn't going to be able to take care of you. I couldn't let that happen." He smiled, as if he thought I'd be happy to hear all of this. "I watched you every day after your Nan died, looking out for you, protecting you. I even let you stay in that junkyard so you could get a taste of how it felt to sleep among the trash before I came to your rescue. It killed me to do this, but I called social services. I needed you to see how desperate things would be for you without help. From me."

Owen took a step toward me, his twisted concern turning to anger. "Then, Jake *fucking* Dunn swooped into town and played the hero. And what did you do, Abby? You jumped right into his apartment and into *his fucking bed.*"

Owen pressed the barrel of the gun against my chest forcing me to step back with each jab until I was pressed against the wall.

"It should have been *me* – not him...not fucking Junkyard Jake. We had one night...one amazing night on the beach together." I almost threw up when he said that. My stomach twisted. "I've done what I was supposed to since then, what you told my mother you wanted. I've stayed away –no, I've been *kept away*—from you all these years against my fucking will. What happens next? That fucking white trash junkyard dog blows back into town *again*, right back into your life after years of not giving a shit about you. Now, he's going to *raise my fucking daughter?* I don't fucking think so, Abby."

My head was spinning. "Why, Owen? What did I ever do to you to make you hate me so much?"

"*Hate* you?" Owen laughed. It sounded surprised and confused and darkly delighted. "I don't *hate* you, Abby. Don't you get it yet? I fucking *love* you!" I felt the growl of his voice vibrate though the shotgun barrel pushing into my chest. "*I* fucking love you. *Me.* Not him."

He was so sick, so deranged.

Please stay asleep, Georgia. Please just stay asleep, baby. I sent my silent plea down the hall to where she slept.

Owen took a breath, gaining some composure. His voice evened out. "After all the trouble I went through to get you, you fucking owe me."

"What trouble did you ever go to for me, Owen?" I spoke quietly, more in hopes of keeping Georgia from coming out of her room than anything. "What did you ever do for me that was truly for *me*?"

"Everything. I did everything." He leaned in closer, and I saw in more detail the black circles under his eyes, how unshaven he was. He wasn't just drunk this time. A powdery white residue clung to the underside of his nose. Owen sniffed, and his right nostril oozed blood. He wiped it on the back of his hand, smearing it onto his cheek. He didn't flinch when he saw the red streaks of blood. His pupils were dilated, and his head restlessly shook and turned with each word. "I did *everything*, starting with your Nan."

Nan...

"Meth labs explode all the time, you know. It wasn't even that hard to get your Nan to say yes to making a last minute trip to that trailer in the woods. All I had to do was tell her the people living in there were poor and starving and in desperate need of her help. She headed right over with a basket full of shit. I watched her go. She was so determined, like she really was on her way to a rescue." He laughed. "It was fucking pathetic. She was so goddamned gullible."

My heart froze to hear him speak so coldly about her.

"It wasn't even hard to make the damn trailer explode. Those meth kitchens usually wind up doing it on their own anyway. They're like ticking time bombs. The tricky part was getting the detonator to cooperate, getting it to explode just as she knocked on the door." He shifted his weight from one foot to the other. "When that fucker went up, you couldn't tell body parts from trailer parts."

"You killed my grandmother because... because you wanted

me to fucking *live* with you?"

"You make it sound so simple. No, I didn't just want you to live with me. I wanted to be your hero. I wanted you to see how much I loved you, so you would love me back."

It was too much to process, especially with Georgia sleeping only feet away from a crazed Owen with a loaded shotgun. I steadied my gaze and numbed myself. Georgia was my only priority. I had to get through this for her.

"Nobody has ever wanted that with me before. To be my hero." I hoped I wouldn't set him off, or raise his suspicion. "I'll go with you now. Let's go. It's not too late." I could hear my voice trembling as I spoke.

"Patience, baby," he cooed. "We gotta wait for Jake to get back first. That bitch has a one way ticket to hell, and his flight leaves today." Owen licked his lips. "I want to watch your face when I shoot his heart out of his chest."

The front door opened and the screen door smacked closed. Owen put an arm around my neck and a dirty hand over my mouth. The burning sensation that used to overwhelm me came back in full force, and the pain of it clouded my vision. Owen dragged me a few steps sideways towards the living room, standing with his back against the wall.

I realized then that I didn't really care what happened to me. I had to protect my family. I was unimportant compared to the people I loved, the people who loved me. I would die for them. My purpose had been fulfilled—I'd had my Georgia. She was the only positive contribution I'd made to the hate-filled world I occupied.

My only hope was that she wouldn't have to suffer in life the way I had.

Owen made a rolling turn off the wall to face the living

room, and I took my opportunity. I broke from his hold and jumped on his back. I tried to wrap my arms around his neck, but I was no match for Owen's size and strength. He easily bucked me off his back. I crashed to the hard wood floor and landed on my tailbone. I heard the crunch and felt a sharp pain run up my spine.

Owen didn't take his eyes off of me as he shot blindly into the living room. The blast from the gun shook the walls. It felt more like an explosion than a shotgun firing. I covered my ears to block out the high-pitched ringing that overtook me. I couldn't hear anything.

"Jake!" I cried out.

When I opened my eyes again, I saw Owen staring into the living room. He let the shotgun drop to his side. It slipped from his hands onto the floor. His eyes were wide, his hands shaking.

"*Jake!*" I cried again. I used every bit of adrenaline I had to rush past Owen and into the living room. He didn't try to stop me. "Jake?"

I still couldn't hear. I didn't know if he'd responded.

And then, I saw.

Of all the things I had been through in my life—the starvation, the beatings, abuse after abuse, losing everyone who has ever meant anything to me in one way or another—none of these things could have prepared me for the devastating sight of my daughter crumpled on the floor against the front door, with her yellow Curious George t-shirt turning a deep, wet red.

I ran to her and slipped her limp body into my arms, propping her up on my knees. I wiped the hair from her face. "*Georgia!*" I screamed trying to wake her up. Her eyes were closed. There was so much blood. I felt her neck for a heart beat, but couldn't feel anything beyond my own.

"Mama," she said. It was weak. She was alive but barely. Help. She needed help. I couldn't lose her.

I couldn't let my Georgia die.

The front door opened again, and this time Jake stepped into the living room, a yellow envelope in his hands. "Bee—where the fuck are you? We need to fucking talk—now!"

He'd barely finished his sentence when his gazed dropped to where I held Georgia on the floor. He dropped the envelope, scattering black and white photos all over on the floor. In one stride, he was kneeling next to us with Georgia was in his arms.

"Owen," I said, looking to the place where Owen had stood just seconds earlier. The shotgun on the floor was the only evidence he'd ever been here.

I pulled open the door and we rushed from the house. Before we got to the truck, Bethany tore into the yard in a bright white Mercedes SUV and jumped out of the driver's side, running toward us. She had the start of a black eye, and blood was dripping from the corner of her lip. Her mouth fell open when she saw Georgia in Jake's arms. "I... I came to warn you... I tried to stop him..."

"Open the fucking door!" Jake yelled.

Bethany swung open the passenger side, and I jumped up into her car. Jake laid Georgia over my lap carefully, so carefully. He jumped behind the wheel as Bethany fell into the back seat.

Instead of using the main roads, Jake drove through a strawberry field and the dairy queen parking lot before turning onto the dirt road that led to the back of the hospital.

"Jake, I don't think she's breathing!" I shouted. I couldn't feel air coming through her nose, and I couldn't see her chest rising.

I wished the hospital were closer.

Jake accelerated Bethany's car to speeds his old truck could've never come close to. He reached out and grabbed Georgia's hand. "We're almost there baby, hold on, Gee."

She wasn't responding anymore.

"Dear God... what has he done?" Bethany cried from the back seat.

Jake managed to turn the thirty minute ride to the hospital into a little over ten minutes. They were still the longest ten minutes of my life.

The SUV was barely in park in front of the hospital when Jake hopped out and ran around to my side opening my door, removing Georgia from my lap. "Daddy's got you, baby girl. Daddy's got you. You're gonna be okay, Gee."

We ran through the sliding doors to an empty waiting room and an even emptier reception area. Jake burst through a door marked *Hospital Staff Only* and I followed quickly. We ran until we saw a group of nurses sitting around a vending machine. "*We need help!*" he roared. "*Get a fucking doctor now!*"

The nurses sprang to life when they laid eyes on my lifeless daughter. One wheeled out a gurney while another paged a doctor. He arrived seconds later and helped us lay her on the gurney. "She was shot. That bastard shot her," I told them. Somehow I didn't think it would be as obvious to them as it was to me.

They placed a mask over her face with a blue ball pump attached to it. Then they were running, the nurses wheeling her down the hallway and squeezing the pump while the doctor shouted more instructions. They disappeared behind a set of double doors.

When we tried to follow them through, another nurse stopped us. "Let them help her," she said, halting us with her hand.

"Get out of my fucking way!" Jake yelled. The nurse held her position, even under Jake's intimidation.

"They can't help her with you hovering over her, sir," she said calmly. "Please, have a seat in the waiting room. The second we know something, I will come tell you myself. I promise." It was a fight we couldn't win. I needed to be in there. I needed to tell her it was all going to be okay. What if it wasn't? What if the last thing my baby girl saw was the doctor and nurses working over her? What if her last feeling in life was fear?

We relented, but only because we didn't have any other options. The nurse led us to a small room with a worn-out pink love seat with frayed edges and a faded white wicker coffee table. Instead of magazines, there were bibles scattered on the table, in three different versions. A beige phone hung on the wall with a long tangled cord dangling beneath, and a rotary dial that had no numbers.

Bethany met us in the waiting room and started dialing on her phone, "I'm going to call Cole. He needs to find Owen and lock him up before he does anything else."

Jake swept the bibles onto the floor and shook the table. "He needs to do more than fucking lock him up. He needs to put the motherfucker *down*!" Bethany flinched, nodding and running toward the entrance as she barked orders into her phone.

I sat on the couch and held my head in my hands. I couldn't lose my baby. She was my reason for being. I loved her more than I thought was possible for anyone to love, not just myself.

"What the fuck happened?" Jake asked, pacing the room.

"It's my fault," I said. "I should have protected her."

"It's not your fault he's fucking insane."

"If I would have just told you the truth, if you would have

known…"

"What truth?"

"The truth about Georgia," I said. "The truth about Owen."

"The pictures," he said.

Then, I remembered the black and white photos he'd dropped earlier. They were the pictures I'd taken after Owen raped me. The pictures I had taken for Jake, to fuel his hatred of Owen.

It was fitting for Jake to be the one who found them. I should have just been brave enough to show him all those years ago. We wouldn't have been waiting for news if my daughter was dead or alive if I could have just sucked up my fucking self-pitying bullshit and told him everything.

"Yes." There was no more denying. No more reasons to keep it to myself.

"When?"

"The night you left."

Jake sucked in his breath.

"I went to lock the storage unit for Reggie. I wanted to walk. Owen showed up near the boat house. He dragged me down to the beach under the bridge."

"Why didn't you tell me?"

"I tried to. I wanted to. I was going to. But when you came back, you were so fucking angry at me. No one had trusted me my entire life, Jake – no one had ever taken me seriously, never believed in me. No one but Nan."

"I didn't trust you either, did I?" Jake pulled me off the couch and into his arms. He sobbed into my hair and spoke between gulps of breath. "I was such an ass. Willie Ray had come up to talk to me when I was filling the bike at the station. I bought you flowers. He asked who they were for. I was practically giddy to see you again. Never felt that way in my whole life. I told him they were for you. There was no point in denying us. Most of them already knew about us anyway. I wanted everyone to know you were mine." Jake squeezed me tighter. "That's when he told me he saw Owen coming out from under the bridge with his zipper down, his hair a mess. Willie Rae asked him what he was doing. Owen told him he was down there with you."

"He was, just not the way you thought." I tried to be strong as I told him. "I put up a fight. I swear I did. He was so strong, and I was barely conscious...."

"I know you fought him, Bee. I know you did. And I wasn't fucking here for you. It's all my fucking fault."

"No. If you hadn't left, I wouldn't have kept her. I would have known she was Owen's, and I would have gotten rid of her because of you. I was so close to doing it anyway. But since I had nothing and she was already such a survivor, I kept her. I needed her because I didn't have you. It was such a fucking selfish reason, but she was the good that came out of you leaving. As much as it hurt, I wouldn't have had it any other way. I should have told you everything after Frank's funeral, on the very first day you came back." My thoughts were back with Georgia, wondering where they'd taken her and how long it would be before someone let us know how she was. "I just can't believe this is happening. I can't believe I *let* it happen."

"We can't blame ourselves right now. We have to be strong for her, for our little girl." Jake tucked a stray hair behind my ears and kissed my forehead.

We both jumped when the same nurse from earlier came into the waiting room. She had no news for us. She just needed my permission to give Georgia a transfusion and to ask what our religious preferences were.

"Religious preferences? For what?" I asked.

"Just in case ma'am," the nurse answered politely. I sank down on the floor while Jake talked to the nurse. Their conversation was a muted blur.

Bethany had come back in. She'd been taking up a seat in the corner. I could see the horror in her face over what her son did. It was mixed with genuine fear over Georgia's condition. She was tortured, just like us. She stood up anytime she heard the sound of shoes squeaking on the linoleum.

It wasn't until the sun rose high above the windows of the waiting room that the doctor finally came in and addressed us. We all stood at attention. He looked past us as he spoke. "She's awake now but won't be for long. Her little body has been through a lot, and she's going to need a lot of rest."

"But how is she?" I demanded.

"It wasn't a direct hit, just scattered buck shots. Miraculously, none of it hit any major arteries or vital organs. There were a few fragments that narrowly missed her spine, but we got them out. She lost a lot of blood during all of this, so we gave her a transfusion." I couldn't believe we were discussing my little girl in terms like these. "Barring any unforeseen circumstances, and even though it'll take a little time, it looks like she's going to make a full recovery." Jake caught me before my knees gave out, and I almost fell to the floor. "We'll keep her for a few nights in the ICU under observation, just to make sure everything stays as it should."

Full recovery. Georgia was going to be okay. She was going to live. "Can I see her?" I asked eagerly.

"Yes, but only for a few minutes. And just one person, please. Also, I don't want her upset because you are upset so stay calm in front of her. We need her relaxed and comfortable. She's a little loopy from the pain medicine, but you can go in."

I bolted past the doctor and left him explaining something to Jake. I realized I didn't ask what room in the ICU she was in, so I found a nurse I recognized from earlier, and she pointed the way. When I got into the room, there was a white curtain pulled around the bed, on the left was an IV drip and a dozen flashing and beeping machines.

I pulled the curtain back, there in the bed, looking so tiny and frail, was my little girl. She was pale, dark blue circles around her eyes, but she was alive and she was going to be ok. I had to keep reminding myself of that or I was going to break down right in front of her.

I put my hand over hers and felt the place where her IV was connected to her hand.

Her eyes fluttered open. "Hi, Mama." Her voice was week and scratchy, but it was the best sound I'd ever heard.

"Hi, baby girl." I felt the tears coming, but I held them back and showed her nothing but calm confidence.

"What happened?"

"You had a little accident, baby girl, but you're okay now. You'll be home very soon."

"Is Daddy here?"

I suddenly realized how much that word meant, and exactly who it referred to. There was only one man who fit that description. "Yes, baby girl, he's here. You can see him after you get some rest."

"Wanna hear a secret, Mama?" she asked me, her eyes now closed.

"Sure, baby." I lay next to her on the bed, careful not to squish any of the wires or tubes. "Tell me a secret." I held her to my side without moving her. I needed her to feel me there, to know she wasn't alone as she drifted off to sleep.

"Jake lets me call him Daddy when you aren't around." Even with her eyes closed she was smiling.

"Oh, does he?"

"Yeah. He says I can call him Daddy in front of you only when you say it's okay." I leaned down and kissed my sweet girl on her cheek. "Is it okay, Mama?" It came on a shallow breath. She was asleep before I could answer.

I smoothed down her hair and whispered to her, "You get some sleep now." I was finally coming to accept that there were some things in life that were just meant to be. Not all of them are good. But Jake being Georgia's father was meant to be.

Two souls who bonded because of love, and love alone.

My parents didn't choose me. They ended up with me after my mother got pregnant. They'd never wanted children. They reminded me every day what a burden I was to their drugged-out lives. I never felt anything even close to love.

Then, Nan came and showed me that someone could truly care about me and love me for who I was and what I was. She took me in because I was her flesh and blood, but she loved me because she wanted to, not because she had to.

Then, there was Jake and Georgia. They had chosen one another. It hadn't been all that long, but they already knew that they wanted to be a family, and regardless of what my feelings were initially, they knew it was meant to happen.

A family by choice, not chance. A choice to love, and to be loved in return. A choice to take care of and enjoy one another, not to put up with or to suffer through one another.

It was the best kind of family. A family on our own terms.

I whispered to my baby girl—my entire world, the centerpiece of the family we'd all chosen to be part of. "You can call him Daddy."

BETHANY WAS THE only one in the waiting room when I came back out. She was sipping from the tiny straw of an orange juice box.

"Where's Jake?" I asked.

"The nurse with the attitude came back in and asked for blood donations." She showed me a small round Band-Aid on the inside of her arm. "He's in there now. How is she?"

"She's tired. They've got her on a lot of meds, but she's going to be okay." It felt good to say it, and after seeing her, I truly believed it. My legs suddenly felt very heavy and weak. I plopped down next to Bethany.

"I'm so sorry, Abby."

I saw the tears fill her eyes, the quivering of her lip. "Stop, Bethany." I made a move to put my hand over hers. It burned, but I ignored it. I needed to comfort her, and that was far more important than my own pain. "You gave birth to him. You didn't put the gun in his hand, and you didn't tell him to pull the trigger. Just like you didn't make him rape me." It was so odd saying it like that, so bluntly, to the woman who helped carry me back to Jake's apartment after it happened. She was probably as much a victim of her son as I had been. "You made a lot of mistakes, but we all have. I don't blame you—for any of it. So stop apologizing."

Jake interrupted us when he stepped back into the waiting room, escorted by a nurse wearing purple scrubs. His face was pale. He was clutching a juice box in one hand and a cookie in the other. He sat on the couch and drained the juice in one long pull. "Well, that sucked," he said. I almost laughed.

The man who danced with the devil got woozy while giving blood.

The nurse motioned for me. "You're next, honey. What kind of blood you got for me? Your little girl's got that rare O we always be needing, so that's what we are looking for today. But I'll take anything your veins will give me. Lord knows we need it *all*."

How could I refuse a request like that?

I wasn't at all light-headed afterward like they warned me I could be—like Jake turned out to be—but I sat back in my reclining chair and drank my juice as the nurse instructed. The nurse came over to me with a card with four drops of blood on it. "You ain't got that O, darlin'…you're just standard ol' A." She flailed her arms when she spoke and flipped a long black braid over her shoulder. "But your tall, blonde and sexy baby daddy out there got the good stuff, so we tapped into that real good."

"Oh, he's not her biological father."

"Oh? Well, since your baby girl's got the O and you don't, the biological baby daddy got to have it. So when you talk to him you send him on up to Miss Karla so I can put that liquid gold on tap!" Miss Karla loved her job way too much. "This biological daddy of yours got baby blues like him over there?"

"No, he has green eyes like my daughter," I said. "It isn't possible for two blue-eyed parents to have a green-eyed child." It sounded so rehearsed… probably because it was a conversation I'd had in my head a thousand times.

"Oh, sure they can. My friend Marni, her husband Brian, has got emerald-green eyes, and both his parents got eyes as blue as the waters of the Caribbean."

"Then your friend Marni needs to tell her husband to check the eye color of the mailman because his parents are lying to him," I snapped. I think Miss Karla detected our conversation was much more serious than the light banter she initially thought it was.

"I ain't making this shit up, honey. Freeman," she shouted, without turning around. A technician in a lab coat, who had previously been sitting in a corner absorbed in a comic book, swiveled around in his chair. "Freeman studied genetics at some fancy college up north."

"Whats up?" he asked, pushing up the bridge of his thick black framed glasses.

"Can two blue-eyed peoples make a green-eyed baby?"

"This is dumb. I have to go." I stood to leave, but Freeman's answer stopped me in my tracks.

"Yeah, it's pretty rare, but it does happen. I've seen several cases." He turned back around to his comic.

"Mmmhmm... that's what I thought," Karla said, declaring victory over my stupidity.

I thanked her and politely refused her offer to assist me to the waiting room.

"Miss?" Karla called to me.

She just couldn't let it drop. "Yeah?"

Her volume dropped, and suddenly she was discreet. "I know it ain't none of my business, but if you ain't sure about who yo baby daddy is, we can do a test. Just bring that fine-ass man back in here, and I'll do it up right." She winked, and I knew she was trying to help. Then, she grabbed a pamphlet from a dozen different colored papers crowding the wall. "This is about blood types. Yours is easy to figure out. Your girl has O and you have A, so the daddy has to have O. It's that simple."

I thanked her and took the pamphlet, slowly making my way back to the waiting room as I looked at it. I wanted to get back in to see Georgia as soon as she woke up, but nurse Karla's words haunted me.

Was there really a chance that Jake was Georgia's father?

More importantly, did it really matter anymore?

I slid down next to Jake. He had his head back on the cushion, but he put his arm around me and pulled me close. "You did better than I did, Bee." He handed me a cup of coffee from the table. It was exactly was I needed.

I had one question in my head, just one little question, and I could put all of this behind me.

"Bethany?" I asked.

"Yeah, sugar?" She put down her magazine and took off her reading glasses.

Then I asked her the question I almost didn't to know the answer to. There was only a small chance… was it really worth me breaking my heart all over again?

"Do you know Owen's blood type?" I glanced at Jake as he tensed beside me, though Bethany didn't seem to notice.

She thought for a second.

Please be anything other than O, please not O.

"He's either A or AB. I always get them confused. Why?"

"He's not O?"

"Not that I know. There are no O-types in the family at all, actually," she said. "Why are you asking this, Abby?" She turned her attention to the hallway where I'd just come from. "What happened in there?"

Jake was as eager to hear my answer as she was. "Because, Bethany," I smiled and took Jake's hands in mine, "Owen's not Georgia's father, after all." Once I said it, he smiled, too –

genuine happiness on his face.

I just smiled back and gazed into those beautiful teary pools of sapphire blue.

The eyes of my daughter's father.

Chapter Twenty-Eight

G EORGIA WAS SLEEPING peacefully in her room after a six-day stay in the hospital. We had brought her home just a few hours earlier. During the day, I'd watched Jake's eyes darken as the sun faded into the horizon, and I knew he was preparing himself for what he needed to do.

I had no intentions of stopping him.

I sat on the seawall, my legs dangling over the edge, staring into the darkness. The sun had set hours ago. A blanket of stars lit up the sky. Jake sat next to me with his arm around my waist, holding me close. I could live in the strength of his arms.

"She's okay," he whispered. I had a feeling he was reassuring himself as much as he was me.

"We're *all* going to be okay," I said. For the first time in my entire life, I believed it. "I need to move, though. I got a letter in the mail from the property management company. It said something about the investor deciding to use the house for himself personally. I have thirty days. I didn't even know they could do that. I guess I should have read the lease more carefully. You want to take him out?"

"It depends," he said, smiling down at me.

"Oh, I thought this was a 'no questions asked' kind-of request, but I'll bite. What does it depend on?"

"On whether or not you want me to kill myself." He handed me a white envelope with a cashier's check inside for nine-thousand six-hundred dollars. "It's all the rent money you've paid."

It all clicked. "You're the investor. You bought Nan's house." It wasn't a question. "When did you do this?"

"I knew the bank had to sell it at some point so I kept an eye on it. I made my bid before I'd even left town. Figured you'd want to keep it no matter where we ended up going. It took those money fucks almost a year to accept my offer, and almost as long to close the damn thing. When it was finally mine, I had it all fixed up for you. Then, I realized you probably wouldn't have accepted it from me as a gift after what I'd done."

He was right. "Nope. I certainly wouldn't have."

"I didn't even know about Georgia then, or I would've put some cool kid shit in here, too." He kissed me on the nose and continued. "I made sure I had personal approval of the new tenants. I had only two flyers made—one they posted in the window of the office, and the other I was going to have Reggie give to you personally. You were so quick to sign the lease that I never had to go with Plan B."

Even when he was gone, he was protecting me, looking out for me.

"You were all I thought about, Bee, the whole time I was gone – this whole four years. When I finally worked up the courage to call Reggie a few years back to ask him about you, I was scared to death he'd tell me you'd packed up and left town, or shacked up with someone else... or gotten married."

That broke my heart a little. "You thought I was with Owen."

"It crossed my mind. Makes me sick to my fucking stomach that I ever considered it a possibility." He ran his fingers under my jaw and pulled my face to his, pressing his forehead against mine. I loved it when he did that. "But when Reggie told me that you weren't with anyone, that you were still living in the apartment and working at the shop, I made myself believe it was because you still needed me. But you didn't. You had it all sorted out long before I tried to step in and help. Reggie never told me about Georgia though, probably because he didn't know how I would react. The bastard. I owe him a punch in the fucking jaw for that." He laughed.

I didn't know what to say about it all.

Jake continued. "I came to the conclusion that if I couldn't be with you myself, I was going to at least try and give you everything I could to make you happy, even if it was from a distance—even if I wasn't going to be part of it. I'm just sorry it took me so long to do it." He brushed his lips over mine. "Turns out you were okay without me after all."

"I wasn't okay, Jake," I assured him. "I wasn't at all. I *became* okay."

"That's what I was afraid you would say. *Abby okay* is not the same as *everyone else okay*." Jake said. "Look at your arm. Look at my brave fucking girl and her warrior ink." He ran his fingers down the artwork covering my right arm. "I know this is one of your pictures, and this is obviously me." He tapped the angel of death image on the motorcycle. "And this is our quote, but what is this one?" he asked. His fingers landing on the black and gray version of "The Scar" painting.

"It's my favorite painting. The real one is in color, but I had him do it in black and white instead. It's a woman with a scar down the middle of her entire body."

"But he didn't tattoo the scar itself?"

"He didn't need to." I'd had the artist use one of the reddest, most jagged of my scars as the red line down the center of her.

"Wow," Jake said. "It's beautiful and fucking amazing, just like you." His eyes were darkening, but it didn't push the crystal blue out entirely. Both the devil and angel in him were with me that night. "I don't know how I ever survived without you, Bee."

I hadn't thought of it from his side. At least I'd had Georgia. Jake had no one. I could see how the last four years were so difficult for him.

"I turned off my feelings the second I walked away from you on the bridge," I told him. "But when Georgia was born, it was like she just broke through it all. It was hard to do, but I had my baby, and when you have a screaming three month old with colic who won't sleep through the night, it's hard to get caught up in your own bullshit. The things that happened to me in the past just started not to matter with her around. They still hurt, and I didn't avoid them. They just weren't the most important things in my life anymore. She saved me."

"You *both* saved me," Jake said. "As much as I can be saved." His tone became serious. "I need you to do something for me, baby."

"Anything." If he asked me, I would do it. It was that simple.

"I need you to tell me why you took those pictures, the ones of you after…"

"I took them for you," I admitted. "I wanted you to see what he did to me. I wanted you to be mad because I wanted you—" I stopped just short of saying it.

"Say it Bee," he insisted. "I need to hear it."

"I wanted you to kill him." The words didn't hurt, and I wasn't embarrassed. It was actually liberating saying aloud that I wanted Owen to die. "There's something else, too, besides what he did to me and Georgia."

His eyes were fully dark now. "What is it?"

"He killed Nan."

"I need to see them, the pictures, now, and I need you to show them to me."

"Why?"

"Because, baby, I am going to leave here tonight, and I'm going to track him down wherever he is, and I'm going to take him out of this world. I'm going bury the pieces of him where no one will ever find them."

I hadn't looked at them since I developed them that night at the high school darkroom. I didn't know if I could see that part of my life again. "What difference will the pictures make? You know what happened."

"I need to see exactly what he did to you, because the more I know, the more detailed your description of your pain... the more satisfying it will be for me when I kill him, and the more I'll enjoy it."

"You want to enjoy it?" I knew right away that I was judging him. Who was I to judge anyone? Beneath that was a curiosity within me about what he felt when he did something like this. Jake had so many things at war inside him. I wanted to know as much as I could about what made him tick.

"Yes, I want to enjoy it. As much as possible. I know that sounds fucked up. But in order to move forward, to enjoy what we have with our family and the rest of our lives together, I need to close this chapter first. But I can't just kill him, Bee. I need you to understand..." He tightened his fists into balls. "I need to feel him die under my hands. I need to feel it so badly."

He pressed his lips into my neck, and a rush of heat shot right to my core.

Then, he whispered into my ear, "When this is all over, what we have will be complete. The three of us under one roof, forever, as it should be, with no trace left of the fucker who tried to ruin everything for us." His beautiful promises mixed with his warm breath on my ear made me whimper. "Not to mention, we have a lot of time to make up for, and I plan on spending a lot of that time with my head between your thighs." He cupped his hand over my jeans between my legs and squeezed. I jumped at the sensation. "I've never gotten to taste that sweet pussy of yours, baby, and I think four fucking years is long enough to wait."

I groaned.

"How about we start now?" I asked, pressing my chest to his. He shook his head and sighed, placing his hands on my shoulders and distancing himself from me.

"The second I get back Bee... the very second. I promise." Jake leaned in and softly kissed my lips before deepening the kiss and opening his mouth to me. His tongue danced across my lips, and then inside my mouth and over my tongue. It had been so long. I didn't know if I was going to be able to wait much longer without bursting apart. He pulled away again as if he were reading my mind. He closed his eyes. "I love you, Bee."

"I love you, too, Jake," I said. "So much." I'd never meant it more.

We spent the next hour inside, sitting on the living room floor. Jake sat silently while I told him the details of the night Owen raped me. I didn't leave any detail out, as he'd requested. I used the pictures to explain each injury as it happened. As I spoke, his mood darkened into a much more sinister version of himself. My sapphire-eyed Jake shared his body with a monster. I could feel him moving aside as the beast within him firmly took control.

By the time I'd finished telling him, I was shaking like it had just happened yesterday. I remembered the feeling when I woke up in unending pain, wishing I was dead. And yet somehow, I had made it through, and my little miracle Georgia had survived as well.

Jake put his hands on my shoulders and pulled me to him. He kissed me with so much raw anger and passion I didn't know if I was going to be able to survive the overwhelming feelings building inside of me.

Jake may have had a monster living inside him. But nothing about either of us had ever been just one way. Nothing was black or white, light or dark.

Coral Pines was a place that looked like heaven on the outside and felt like hell on the inside. Owen, the golden boy of our town, turned out to be the biggest monster of them all. And Jake, who had become accustomed to living within the dark shadows of his tortured soul, turned out to be one of the brightest lights in my life.

I had lived my life in both the dark and the light. Having my new family meant I had to walk a blurry line between the two. I was never going to be a normal person with normal thoughts and feelings.

I'd never known what "normal" meant, anyway.

Maybe what set Jake and I apart from other people was our acceptance of our feelings and emotions—the dark as well as the light. All I knew is that there was no darkness in the world that could compare with the love we had for our daughter. Jake was proof that even the blackest hearts were capable of love. He was light and darkness, all at the same time.

Jake the angel, who comforted me in the hospital.

Jake the killer, who stood to leave, tucking his gun into the back of his jeans and checking for the additional clip in his boot.

"Tell me again you're okay with this, that you won't look at me differently afterwards." His tone carried worry.

"I knew Owen's death would be coming from the very night he raped me, and I wanted it to be you who killed him." I didn't hesitate to tell him. "I still do." I held up the last of the pictures to him. It was the photo I had taken last, kneeling in the mirror with my legs spread open for the camera. The lens caught the bruises and dried blood caked in every nook of my body, over every inch of my already marred skin.

Jake's nostrils flared and his eyes lost their light. The killer in him was being fed. I turned over the picture. In my handwriting was a note I'd written years ago.

Send him to hell, Jake.

Jake took the picture from me and read and reread the note on the back before folding it and tucking it into his leather jacket. He picked me up off the floor and gave me one last furious kiss before putting me down and stalking to the front door in quick, determined strides. "Thank you," he whispered.

"Make sure you come back to us," I reminded him. I hoped I hadn't needed to.

"Leaving you was the worst mistake of my life, Bee. I won't make it again." Then, he was gone, disappearing into the blackness of the night.

The roar of his bike announced his leaving, but in minutes it was silent again, only the echoes remained.

"Make him suffer, baby," I whispered to no one.

I once wondered if two broken souls could heal one another.

I hoped the answer was *yes*.

We may not have been perfect, or even acceptable by anyone else's standards. But together, we were perfect.

Together, we were just us.

Battered and broken. Dark and difficult. Impulsive and scared.

I'd accepted Jake for being all of those things, yet for so long, I couldn't accept them within myself. I finally realized that it's possible to love within a space that sometimes holds nothing but emptiness... or nothing but darkness.

After all, we all have darkness within us.

Some of us more than others.

Epilogue

Jake

TWO NIGHTS PASSED before I was able to make it home to Georgia and Bee, to my family. My clothes and skin were soaked with blood, mud, filth, and the other remnants of the dark places I had been. Bee threw herself into my arms without hesitation the second she saw me, despite my disheveled condition.

I'd pulled Bee into her bedroom that night, and she didn't even let me shower before she asked me to describe to her what I had done to Owen in detail. Then, we had ourselves a long overdue, blood-covered, lust-fueled fuck-fest that lasted all night. For a woman who had once been afraid of my touch, she now devoured every moment of twisted carnal bliss between us.

Making love wasn't our thing. We already had *love*. We made that every day. It was in every look, every touch, every understanding word.

Our sex? That was about owning one another. Finally being able to feel after years of pushing that shit aside in order to live and survive was an amazing fucking feeling. I wanted to live inside Bee, and I almost believe I do. That girl had gotten under my skin and inside my black soul the very first night I'd ever laid eyes on her.

I would walk around wearing her on my dick if I could.

I never thought I would be calling the house that used to hold so many ghosts, my parent's old house, my home again. *Our home.* Truth is I could call a hollowed out tree home as long as Bee and Georgia were there with me.

My wife, my daughter, my entire life.

The reasons for my existence.

Yeah, we got married. We didn't make too big a deal out of it. It was just something we felt we needed to do. Not to mention that I really wanted to. My girls were always meant to share my last name. It became more important to me than I thought it would be. Our wedding was just the three of us and a justice of the peace. We had the ceremony in the orange grove clearing during sunset, where more than my secrets were laid to rest.

It was perfect, our kind of perfect.

I became a better person because of them. The monster in me had been tamed, tucked away for the time being. He was still there deep inside, in a sort of semi-permanent hibernation. It was a comfort to know I could call on him if I ever needed to. Because if my family were ever to be threatened or harmed again, he *will* be fucking called on.

Truth of it was, I needed them more than they needed me. I've never fooled myself into believing that I was even remotely good enough for either of them. Instead, I made a promise to myself that I would give them the life they deserved, and be the man they needed me to be, even if being that man took more work on my part than I imagined others needed.

I no longer traded lives for money. I put that behind me and focused on helping Reggie run the shop. We got ourselves another receptionist so Bee could focus on her photography.

I hadn't killed since the night I was given permission by my woman to end the man who killed her grandmother, raped her, and shot my daughter.

If it had been possible, I would have killed that fucker three times over.

A sense of elation washes over me mixed with pure heated rage when I think of that sick fuck laying his hands on Abby the very night she let me into her heart and into her bed or about my poor frail Georgia in the hospital clinging to life, even when I thought of a defenseless and harmless old woman, walking to her own death while thinking she was doing nothing more than helping people.

Abby and I stopped talking about Owen entirely after that. The people of Coral Pines assume he was drunk one night, fell of the seawall and drowned, like so many of the town's alcoholics before him. I'm sure they thought his body had been made a good meal of by an alligator or wild boar in the mangroves somewhere.

No doubt, some of the town folk had their suspicions about me. I'm sure they thought I could be responsible in some way. After all, Owen had always hated me, and we'd publicly brawled on occasion. They knew how little we cared for each other. But, the sad fact was that not many people gave a shit about where Owen might have gone.

I had his very own mother on my side.

Bethany knew I killed Owen. How? I told her. I was no fucking coward. I told her while we were still in the hospital what I was going to do the second I knew my girl was okay. She knew she couldn't stop me and said she wasn't even going to try. She knew as well as I did that Owen was like a rabid dog and had to be put down.

What I hadn't expected was for her to ask me to kill her as

well. She practically begged me.

It was sad, really.

She told me she couldn't live with what she'd done to our family, and she didn't know if she could survive the death of her only son. She still loved him, no matter how broken he was.

Story of my life.

Bethany had called herself a "human wrecking ball". Fitting, maybe, but not punishable by death. Honestly, I had considered it. But, I wasn't a fan of killing women, and Georgia and Abby seemed to actually like the bitch.

So, I made her a deal.

Instead of killing her, I promised her that even though I was Georgia's biological father and not Owen, she could still be part of our lives and our family if that was what she wanted. She just needed to heal.

We knew a thing or two about healing in our house.

It wasn't easy in the first few weeks after Owen "disappeared". Bethany came to see Georgia, but couldn't look me in the eye. As time passed, she became more accepting of our new—and unusual—family dynamic and became a regular at our house.

As a consolation of sorts for killing her son and refusing to do her in, too, when she mentioned filing the divorce papers, I offered to take out her husband for her instead. Abby kicked me under the dinner table.

Bethany opted for the divorce.

I killed her son, and she comes over every Sunday for family dinner.

My daughter calls her Grammy.

The world is a twisted place, for sure.

It may have appeared that I was a changed man on the outside, but I couldn't help but smile when I thought of the night I sank Owen's body into his deep dark grave at the bottom of the swamp. A laugh would sometimes involuntarily escape my lips when I glanced above the mantle and saw my knife collection on display, hanging from on the little hooks Bee bought for me at the flea market.

The knife in the center, the one with the red handle and serrated edge, was the one I used to slit Owens throat.

I'm not sure whether I viewed it as my prize possession or an inside joke.

Maybe, it was both.

Slitting someone's throat may have sounded like the pussy way to kill someone, and I would have agreed with that... if it was done from behind like most pussies would do it.

That's why I looked that motherfucker dead in the eye as I told him he was going to die. That's why I pushed him up against the wall of the boat-house and covered his mouth with my left hand and used my forearm to hold him still while I slowly carved out his throat with the knife in my right.

I stared right into the depths of that scared motherfucker's non existent soul and ignored his pathetic gurgling pleas while I watched the life flow out of him with the blood that poured from his neck, sending him into the depths of hell where he belonged.

Someone might as well have wrapped up that day and given it to me on Christmas morning. A revenge kill is the best kind of kill.

But a revenge kill for your family, *with* your woman's permission?

That's borderline erotic.

Now, I'm just a simple family man, receiving love I know I

don't deserve, and sleeping like a baby after a fifth of Jack Daniels.

I'm not stupid. I have no doubt that when I meet my end, I will descend into the hell that's been saving me a spot in its torturous embrace since the day I was born.

I also know that when I get there, I'm going to spend my time finding Owen and killing him over and over again.

T.M. Frazier's Other Works

KING

TYRANT

LAWLESS (December 2015)

SOULLESS (February 2016)

The Dark Light of Day Playlist on Spotify

open.spotify.com/user/22expbtkukermg26omw6fztri/playlist/52dlypsUdTb8ycjX5mEdqL

CPSIA information can be obtained
at www.ICGtesting.com
Printed in the USA
BVOW08s1202161116

468046BV00002B/64/P